MW01171048

LEGEND

A SCI-FI ALIEN ACADEMY ROMANCE

WARRIORS OF THE DREXIAN ACADEMY
BOOK THREE

TANA STONE

BROADMOOR BOOKS

CHAPTER
ONE

Fiona

My infuriated huffs echoed in the stark corridor, each breath punctuating my anger and each step a defiant drumbeat against the stone floor as my fingers curled into fists at my sides, the nails digging into my palms. I navigated the labyrinth of the Academy, the interconnected passageways and buildings now familiar to me, even though they'd been intimidating when I'd first arrived.

A lot had changed since I'd first stepped through the stone archway of the ancient, alien school, but one thing hadn't. I still had no intention of taking crap from any of the cocky Drexians who thought they were better than me just because I was a human. Worse even for the old-school aliens used to an all-male military school? A *female* human.

Unlike the first day I walked through the door of the Drexian Academy, no cadets rushed through the corridors with their footfall echoing off curved ceilings and their voices bouncing off polished, black rock. The cadets had completed the year at the alien training school, which meant most had left for a break, leaving the buildings empty and silent. Silent except for my pounding steps, as I stormed across open air bridges between towers and up the wide, curving stairs of the main hall.

Every corner I rounded brought me closer to Vyk's office, and with each step, my resolve hardened. The security chief was the worst when it came to arrogant Drexians who disdained humans, but I didn't care about what he thought of me now. My rage fueled me, lending an edge to my stride and a clench to my jaw.

As I reached the door to Vyk's office, I didn't hesitate. No polite knock, no waiting to be granted entry. I slammed my palm against the iron door, somewhat surprised when it slid aside with a hiss, and I strode inside with fury eager to be released.

I took a beat to take in the Drexian's domain, noting that it was exactly what I would expect from a former Inferno Force commander who was notorious for his interrogation techniques. Weapons hung on the stone walls, some of them battered and worn, and there was no rug on the black floor or welcoming fire burning. Vyk sat behind his stark desk, all imposing muscle and battle-hardened presence, his silver scruff catching the flickering light as he looked up. His eyes were icy and his expression unreadable, yet even he couldn't fully mask the spark of curiosity as he registered my presence.

When I reached his desk, I braced my hands on the surface and heaved in a breath before unleashing my storm of complaints.

The air between us thrummed with tension, the fact that we were both members of the Academy staff doing nothing to soften the edges of our standoff. This collision of worlds, human and Drexian, old ways and new, male and female, had been a long time in the making. And it wouldn't be pretty.

I narrowed my eyes at him. "Do you want to tell me why there are still beasts in the dungeons?"

He leaned back, his cold gaze never leaving mine. "I did not know I owed a...Strategy instructor any explanations on how I protect this school."

The deep rumble of his voice was so calm that it enraged me even more. I could almost hear the unspoken words beneath the velvet purr. *Human. Female.* He didn't think he owed someone like me anything.

"Don't you mean you don't owe a *human* any explanations?" I shot back.

"Your species is irrelevant. I do not allow any instructors to dictate the security protocols for the Academy."

"Security protocols? Is that what you call keeping alien monsters in the same building where cadets learn? Is that what you called what happened in the trials—" I cut myself off, realizing I was losing composure. Dredging up his part in the deadly maze would not endear me to him, although I wasn't sure I cared. I straightened up, took a measured breath, and fixed him with a piercing gaze. "Your job is to protect the cadets and this school. Not expose them to more danger."

He flicked his gaze away for a beat. "The Drexian Academy has never been about coddling cadets. Our warriors must be the toughest to survive and defeat our enemies. If humans wish to be true allies, they must meet the same standards and survive the same dangers."

I gritted my teeth, despising the truth in his words. Human cadets had proven themselves to be just as capable during the trials, so why had the discovery of beasts remaining in the dungeons set me off like it had? Why had it ignited my fury and propelled me to confront the Drexian I knew was responsible? "Haven't we already met the same standards? No humans have died or washed out of your brutal school yet."

He inclined his head a touch as if studying my face. "That is true."

"Does that bother you? Do you hate the fact that you haven't been able to prove that we're weaker than Drexians?"

He stood and pressed his own palms to the desk, his impressive height making him tower over me. "Do not pretend to know my mind."

I flinched at this. Before I'd entered his office, I would have sworn that he despised humans, and most of all, that he despised me. But as his eyes burned into me, there was more than anger flashing behind them. I didn't step back, even though I couldn't explain the pulse of desire that hummed between us.

There should be nothing but mutual disdain and a healthy amount of suspicion. Vyk had proved that he didn't believe humans were worthy of teaching at the school or attending it, which meant the last female he would ever desire would be me, a Strategy instructor, who was both a woman and from Earth.

My heart hammered against my chest, fueled by a mixture of arousal and fear. Why did the Drexian have to be a big, gruff, silver fox packed with muscle? And why did the thought of him coming even an inch closer both excite and terrify me?

Vyk's office suddenly felt smaller, as if the tension between us filled every crevice, yet he remained motionless as he held my gaze.

"I don't claim to know you at all." The warble in my voice betrayed me. "But the beast in the dungeon is proof that you haven't changed."

A vein in his temple pulsed—a crack in his otherwise impenetrable façade. "I regret what happened in the trials, but I do not owe you an apology. I have made amends to the admiral. If he still believes—"

I couldn't stifle the mirthless laugh that erupted from my lips. "It isn't me who deserves an apology. It's the cadets who died trying to prove themselves in a sabotaged maze. *Drexian* cadets."

He drew in a ragged breath, his jaw so tight I could hear the teeth grind as he squared his shoulders. "Are all females like you?"

The change of subject caught me off guard. "What?"

"You came in here uninvited and challenged a Drexian twice your size who could snap you in half." His voice dropped to a deadly hum. "Aren't you afraid?"

My heart skipped a beat as a trickle of fear slid down my spine. Now that he put it like that, maybe he hadn't been the best Drexian to insult. But I refused to let anyone frighten me. I hadn't gotten to where I was in the military by letting bigger guys scare me. Almost every guy was bigger than me, but not many were as smart or as clever. Not that storming into Vyk's office had been my smartest move.

I slowly curled my hands until they were two fists on his desk. "Do I look like I'm afraid?"

"You do not." His gaze wandered to my lips, and he drew in a quick breath before his eyes returned to mine, and he stiffened. "But maybe you should fear me."

Something in his expression made me want to push his limits, even though my instincts told me I shouldn't. I leaned my face forward so that I could feel the warmth of his breath. "Would you like that?"

In the electric space between us, neither one of us moved. Neither breathed. Then Vyk growled and jerked back, putting distance between us. "I will have the beast removed, Captain."

I was so shocked by his reversal that I could only gape at him.

"Is there anything else?" He dropped back into his chair, his gaze locking onto his tablet as he made a point of not looking at me.

I shook my head as I backed away, too startled by what had transpired to utter another word as I left his office. I should have felt victorious that I'd won. He'd agreed to remove the monster just like I'd demanded.

Then why did I feel like I'd merely awoken the real beast?

CHAPTER
TWO

Vyk

I should not have been thinking about it. I should not have been thinking about *her*.

The corridor was deserted with only the rhythmic slapping of my boot leather against the floor as I stalked through the academy. But it was the pounding of my heart that was distracting me. Fiona had left my office long ago, yet I could think of nothing else.

Infuriating female.

As much as I wanted to sneer at the human for daring to tell me what to do, I could not help but admire her courage. She had risked my wrath by giving me an order that was not hers to give, and she had shown no fear. Then she had challenged me when I'd told her she should fear me.

"Would you like that?"

Her breathy question echoed in my head and sent heat rushing to my cock. I groaned and shifted my gait so I would not injure myself or arrive at the Academy Master's office with a noticeable lump tenting my dark, uniform pants.

I was used to being despised by others—the enemy combatants I interrogated, the Inferno Force recruits I initiated through toughness, the cadets at the academy who feared my punishments. It did not bother me because I was generous with my disdain. You did not become notorious and feared by being kind or having legions of friends, and it had taken me most of my career to engender the level of fearful respect that I now commanded. Fearful respect that Fiona clearly did not feel.

How was it possible that a human—a female human—was willing to stand up to me when most Drexians would not dare?

She had courage. I would give her that. I had already learned that humans were stronger and braver than I'd ever imagined, as much as I hated to admit it. They had proven that in the trials, but there was a part of me that still rejected the idea of the smaller species training alongside Drexians. We were allies with the Earthlings, but it was as much because our people needed mates as anything. Until recently, human females were mates for Drexians. Pretty, biddable mates.

The thought of Fiona being anyone's mate made a growl tease the back of my throat and my cock twitch. Then a gruff laugh escaped my lips and echoed off the vaulted ceiling. Fiona might be beautiful, but she could never be called biddable. Any male who tried to tame her would as soon lose an arm as win a kiss.

I thought back to the first time I had seen her across the crowded main hall when cadets were bustling between classes. Her golden wavy hair had caught my gaze because it was so different from the dark hair of Drexians. She was so different from Drexians in so many ways, which was probably why she'd provoked such strong feelings of resistance in me.

She meant change. A change in the way things had been done for millennia. A change in ancient traditions. A change that would alter the future of my people.

She had been right about me. I had despised the idea of humans at the Academy—my Academy. When I had attended as a cadet, the buildings had already been weathered and the stone well-worn, but there had been only Drexians and only males. It had been a rigorous and often dangerous training ground for those of us willing to venture into the universe as warriors. Like I had told Fiona, it was not for the weak.

"Not that she is weak," I muttered to myself, my words vanishing into the ominous silence clinging to the stone walls and lurking behind the flickering light from the sconces.

No, Fiona had proven that she was strong enough to stand up to me. Not even many cadets could claim that. My mind wandered traitorously to thoughts of what else she might be strong enough to withstand, of what challenge I would like to issue.

"Commander?"

I jerked to a standstill, blinking at the admiral's adjunct as he stepped from Zoran's office. Had I reached the Academy Master's domain so quickly?

"Tivek." I gave the Drexian a nod of my head. "Admiral Zoran summoned me."

He returned the gesture as he moved aside to let me pass. "He is waiting for you."

I squared my shoulders and walked into the long office flanked by black stone walls, with a single, tall slat of a window that overlooked the Restless Sea. The admiral sat at the desk in front of the window with his head down. Like me, he boasted silver in his hair, but unlike mine, his was only shot through the temples.

"Commander Vyk." He glanced up as I strode forward. "Thank you for coming. I wished to discuss the security measures that have been put into place since the Kronock attack. I know you inherited a school riddled with security issues, but it seems that the added measures have been successful."

I stood across from him and grasped my hands behind my back, well-aware that my predecessor had been a mole responsible for allowing the enemy access to our security codes. I had been brought on to enforce stricter security measures, but my original task had also included a directive from the Drexian High Command that I regretted. A directive to ensure that the humans at the academy failed.

"They have been, although I cannot take credit for much of it. You did an impressive job of rebuilding the school's defenses before I arrived."

Zoran shrugged one shoulder. "It was what had to be done."

I nodded, understanding Drexian duty as well as anyone, and understanding that Zoran had also been Inferno Force. It was a brotherhood we shared, which was why I suspected he had insisted I remain in my position after the scandal of the trials. He had given me another chance. It was a chance I would not squander.

The admiral touched the flat panel of his desk and a holographic image appeared and hovered between us. He gestured to the scrolling text and rotating schematics of the academy. "Update me."

I cleared my throat. "The shields have been fortified, there are patrols flown on a rotating schedule, and new sensors have been installed in the perimeter defenses around the school."

He nodded. "Any indication that the Kronock will try again?"

I bit back a protective snarl. "No, but if they did, they would regret it. Our fortifications are secure, and our defensive weapons are the most advanced in the fleet. I have updated and modified them myself."

Zoran grinned. "I knew I would not regret bringing on an Iron as my security chief."

I flushed from the compliment, always proud to have come from the Academy's School of Engineering, and I decided to take the opening. "We have not spoken directly about the trials, aside from when I was questioned with you present. I want to be sure I still have your confidence, Admiral."

His smile slipped, and his expression turned solemn. "I am satisfied that you made all attempts to stop the trials when you discovered the true intent and the extent of the sabotage. I believe that you would have stopped them, if the High Commanders had not imprisoned you."

My throat was tight as I gave him a curt nod, remembering the frustration of being thrown in the academy's dungeons before I could stop the trials. "I could have stopped things sooner."

"You could have." He held my gaze. "We all make mistakes, even battle-hardened Inferno Force warriors. It is how we face them that defines us. You have done nothing but work to repair the damage and restore faith in our school's traditions. I hope you have also realized the error of your belief regarding humans."

My mouth went dry as my mind instantly went to Fiona. I had gone from being irritated by her presence to being haunted by thoughts of her. Then I remembered that Admiral Zoran's wife was human. "My beliefs are wholly changed, Admiral."

He held my gaze for a few more beats, the silence hanging heavy between us before he tapped his fingers on the desk and the holographic image vanished. "Then you have my complete trust to protect every cadet and every instructor at the academy."

I puffed out my chest and lifted my chin. "I will defend them with my life."

"I have no doubt." Zoran thumped a fist across his chest in salute, which I recognized as an extreme sign of respect, since he outranked me.

I returned the salute before pivoting and striding from the room, allowing myself an exhale only when I was on the other side of the sliding door.

"You were summoned by the Admiral, as well?"

I turned to the sound of a familiar voice. Lieutenant Volten. The Drexian I'd enlisted to help me save the cadets in the maze before I had been thrown into the dungeons. We had never spoken about the night before the trials when I had confided in him, but there remained a bond between us.

"Lieutenant." I tipped my head to the young flight instructor then noticed that his friend, Lieutenant Kann, a Blade instructor, was with him. I inclined my head to him as well. "Lieutenant."

Kann stiffened slightly, even though he saluted me just as Volten did. It was not lost on me that many of the staff still eyed me with suspicion, even if Zoran trusted me.

"I was just leaving." I stepped to one side so they could enter the Admiral's office.

Volten cut a questioning look at Kann before he spoke. "Since the term is over and most of the cadets have gone, we were talking about getting a game of cards together with some of the staff. Can we count on you?"

I stared at him. He was inviting me to join them in a card game? From the way the Battle instructor's eyes popped wide, Kann seemed just as startled. "A game?"

"Nothing serious, but we thought it could be a way for our staff to get to know each other better."

Kann managed a lopsided grin. "The female instructors will be joining us, so it will not be what Volten's mate calls a 'sausage party.'"

I did not know what that meant, but it did not matter. He had said the females would be there. More than one, which meant not only Volten's mate, Ariana. It meant Fiona. As much as I knew that I should stay far away from the woman who despised me, I could not help but subject myself to the sweet torment of being around her and feeling how deeply she disdained my presence. "I would be pleased to join your game."

"You would?" Volten seemed surprised before his grin widened. "I mean, good. We look forward to seeing you."

I did not care that Volten and Kann exchanged a bewildered look before I left them. I did not care that a card game was a trivial use of my time. I did not care that it would mean opening myself up to the judgment of staff members who had not forgiven so quickly. I only cared that I would get a chance to be around Fiona, and maybe I could show her that I was not as hard and unyielding as she believed.

Then I touched the scar on my cheek that was covered in silver scruff, a reminder that Drexians needed to be tough, that we had to be hard to survive. I thought about all I had done and all I had been forced to do to keep other Drexians and other planets safe. My stomach sank. "Which is why no human would ever want a monster like me—not then and not now."

CHAPTER
THREE

Fiona

The Stacks loomed around us, dusty and quiet, shelves upon shelves crammed with leather bound books that had been tucked away for centuries. The wooden table in front of me was covered with yellowed papers, unrolled parchments, and glowing tablets.

In the dim light from wrought-iron chandeliers that dangled from the vaulted ceiling, Ariana's face was etched with worry lines I'd come to know all too well since she'd learned that her sister was being held as a prisoner of the Kronock.

"Thanks for staying, Fi," Ariana's voice echoed softly off the stone floors. "I couldn't do this without you."

"Wouldn't dream of being anywhere else. We're going to find her."

Ariana nodded, but her top teeth worked the corner of her bottom lip. "You're sure you wouldn't have rather gone back to Earth between terms?"

I scoffed at this. "And miss the chance to walk around without hundreds of massive Drexians stomping around like they own the place?"

"They do own the place." Ariana allowed herself a small smile.

I shrugged. "Point taken, but I still like the academy better when there's less testosterone. Besides, even with jump technology, it takes a while to get all the way back to Earth."

My friend grimaced. "And a lot of jumps."

I didn't hate jumping through space as much as Ariana did, which was unusual, since she was the daredevil pilot, and I was supposed to be the rational strategist. But I'd learned that my pilot friend did not like space travel she couldn't control, or heights, which was another unusual fact about the woman.

"We aren't the only ones who stayed," I reminded her. "Only a few human cadets went home."

"And not all the Drexian instructors left." My hostile meeting with Commander Vyk was an all-too-potent reminder that he had remained.

Footsteps broke the quiet, and Jess strode into view, her brown hair in a high ponytail and her posture relaxed, a stark contrast to the tension knotting my shoulders. She flashed us an apologetic grin. "Sorry I'm late." Then she swept her gaze around the table that was empty except for me and Ariana. "Am I late?"

"Not really. Since we're between terms, it feels like everyone has switched to vacation time."

16

Jess wrinkled her nose. "I don't think I've ever been on vacation time, but you're right that the school feels different now that there aren't classes and schedules."

The way she said it made me laugh. "I take it you're not a fan?"

Her cheeks colored slightly. "I don't mind having more free time, but the place feels almost eerie. I'm starting to believe the stories that it's haunted."

I knew that Jess had chosen to stay at the academy between terms not because she disliked jumping through space to return to Earth, but because her boyfriend Torq was staying. He was no longer welcome in his clan since he'd chosen a human, since he'd chosen Jess. I also got the feeling she didn't have much to return to on Earth.

"Who says it's haunted?" Ariana straightened and then glanced nervously around the ancient library that was shrouded in shadow.

"Every old building everywhere is said to be haunted." I shook my head, dismissing the idea out of hand. "Maybe we should take the academy being deserted as an opportunity to stage a coup."

Jess barked out a laugh. "If I was going to stage a coup, I would want to take over a place that needed considerably fewer repairs and less cleaning."

The old, alien school had endured an attack by the Kronock before we'd arrived, and although most of the damage had been repaired, there was no denying that the place was worn and weathered from hundreds of years of cadets passing through its stone halls.

"Where is Torq?" Ariana narrowed her gaze at Jess. "I thought he would be with you."

"He's coming from a session in the holo-chamber with your guy."

Ariana bobbed her head slowly, as if just remembering where Volten was, as well. "I'll never understand why they think it's fun to pretend to be attacked by various alien monsters."

"Like I said, too much testosterone." I cut a glance to the table with our research. "They can catch up when they get here."

Jess took a seat and pulled out her tablet, tapping her fingers on the surface. "We've managed to narrow down the long list of places they could be holding Sasha to a few sites. Vyk's intel on Kronock territory has been invaluable."

Ariana breathed a sigh of relief, and I couldn't help but groan inwardly at Vyk's name. "Speaking of Vyk," I was unable to suppress the shudder that ran through me, "he may not be so eager to share more if I'm around."

Both Ariana and Jess turned to me.

Heat flushed my cheeks. "I might have barged into his office and demanded he get rid of the last monsters in the dungeons." My hands balled into fists at the memory of our heated exchange. "I might have lost my temper...and raised my voice."

"Good." Jess's voice carried unexpected steel. "After what I saw down there, someone needed to say it."

"Your request wasn't unreasonable, Fiona." Ariana's hand found mine in a comforting squeeze. "Not after the trials."

"Maybe, but diplomacy isn't exactly my strong suit, and I shouldn't have lost my temper at a Drexian we need for this mission."

"Vyk terrifies me," Jess whispered, as if he might be lurking nearby to overhear her, "even if he did help save me last term."

"He's pretty intimidating," I admitted.

"But I thought he was your type." Ariana nudged me, laughter dancing in her eyes. "Hot silver fox?"

"Please." I rolled my eyes. "Vyk might be easy on the eyes, but his disdain for humans is a colossal turn-off. He wants us gone from this academy—how could I possibly see past that?"

"True," Ariana frowned "No woman wants to be with someone who thinks she's beneath him."

"Exactly," I agreed, feeling the heat rise to my cheeks once more at the thought of being romantically linked to a Drexian who saw women, especially human ones, as inferior. "I could never be with someone like Vyk—" My sentence cut short as movement caught my eye, and a figure emerged from behind a monolithic bookshelf.

Vyk.

The man was a fortress of muscle and scars, his presence commanding the air itself. Gray streaked his dark hair, silver scruff framing his tense jaw. Fuck fuck fuck.

"Commander Vyk." My voice cracked as the tension around us snapped. His expression, unreadable as ever, gave nothing away.

I exchanged a quick glance with Ariana, who had stiffened. Jess shifted uncomfortably beside me, her earlier smiles dissolving under Vyk's steely gaze.

"Apologies," Vyk rumbled, his voice deep enough to resonate against the Stacks' old stone. "I did not mean to intrude."

Sure, like a Drexian battle commander ever 'intrudes' unintentionally. But I wasn't about to call him out on it—not when the possibility hung heavy in the air that he'd heard every word of my outburst against him.

"Um, we were just discussing the plan to find Sasha," I managed, forcing my tone to steady.

"Indeed," he replied. His gaze briefly locked with mine—a flash of something there, something unreadable, yet intense.

Why did this gruff warrior make me feel like a misbehaving child, and why did a deep dark part of me want him to punish me?

CHAPTER
FOUR

Vyk

I hovered at the edge of the meeting around the table, my arms crossed tightly as I listened to their voices blend into a buzz of strategy and concern. Fiona's words sliced through the hum, sharp and clear, displaying intelligence and shrewdness. My previous declarations about human females had been brash and arrogant, but now they tasted like ash in my mouth, especially since Fiona was proving them to be so wrong.

As much as I wished to focus on the meeting and the mission being planned, I could not snatch my mind from what I'd overheard. I could not force Fiona's words from my brain. Despite my thick skin, honed from battles and barbed commands, her opinion mattered. It mattered more than it should.

"Sending scouts into Kronock territory is risky." Lieutenant Volten tapped his finger against a data pad.

Kann's eyes flickered with the kind of excitement that only imminent danger could spark in an Inferno Force warrior and Blade. "Highly risky."

"Is there really any other choice?" Ariana's voice cracked. "Sasha is out there."

Volten put a hand on her back. "It's a risk many Drexians would gladly accept."

I cleared my throat, standing taller, every inch the commander I was expected to be. "Inferno Force warriors would think nothing of the risk. They're adept at reconnaissance and survival in hostile conditions."

Fiona barely glanced at me, her gaze skimming away so quickly it might have been my imagination that it lingered at all. Though the others nodded in agreement, it was her silent dismissal that chafed.

"The commander is right." Kann folded his arms over his chest. "This is a task for Inferno Force."

I inclined my head to the Blade instructor in recognition that we still shared a bond by having served in the elite fighting unit. "I will reach out to my contacts."

There was more talk of what would happen after Inferno Force carried out the reconnaissance, but then the gathering was dispersed and followed by the scrape of chairs and shuffling of boots.

I waited until almost everyone had drifted away before approaching Fiona. "A moment of your time?"

Her body tensed, but she nodded curtly. Ariana hesitated, protective concern etched across her features.

"Your friend will be fine," I said, the lie sitting heavy on my tongue because the truth was, I wasn't sure if I was fine around her.

"It's not her I'm worried about," Ariana muttered, before casting us a final glance and joining Volten at the end of the row of high bookshelves.

"Commander?" Fiona's voice sliced through the silence and sent an unbidden shiver down my spine. She stood there, arms uncrossed and braced on her hips, the very image of a force not to be reckoned with—a force I admired. "Why the need for a private talk? I said everything I needed to say to you earlier."

I locked eyes with her in the dim, golden light. I could almost see the memories playing behind her eyes—the trials, the chaos I had been part of, all the reasons she had to distrust me. What I wanted was for her to see past the battle-hardened exterior, to give me a chance I wasn't sure how to request. "We must work together. On this team. As members of the academy staff."

Her stance softening ever so slightly, as she tilted her head as if testing the concept. Then she nodded once, sharply. "Agreed."

I nodded back, the warrior in me recognizing the tentative ceasefire. I locked my gaze with hers, hoping she'd understand the unspoken need to be given another chance.

Her scowl deepened. "You might have agreed to clear out the last creatures from the dungeons, but it doesn't erase your past words...or actions. I know how you feel about humans, Commander."

"Perhaps that was true once." My denial came swiftly. "I'm not the same person who stood against the integration of our kind with humans. The past term, the trials, this mission...they have changed me."

Her eyes narrowed slightly, searching mine as if they could unveil a lie hidden beneath the words. "Prove it."

"Tell me how." The words were out before I could fully grasp the gravity of what I was offering.

Fiona took a measured breath, as if considering the weight of her next words. "I heard you'll be at the staff card game."

"I will be."

She tilted her head, appraising me with a mix of curiosity and defiance. "So play against me," she suggested, a daring edge clinging to her voice. "When I beat you, you'll acknowledge that I'm just as smart as any Drexian."

The gauntlet thrown down, I couldn't suppress the smirk that tugged at the corner of my mouth. "I accept your challenge," I said without hesitation. Cards had been a pastime aboard every Inferno Force ship—a way to keep a warrior's mind sharp and battle-ready. Not only that, I had honed my skills in many alien outposts and cantinas during missions.

"Let's make it interesting, then," I proposed, already savoring the anticipation of the challenge. "We play Drexian cards. We are at the Drexian Academy, after all."

For a moment, she hesitated. Uncertainty flickered in her eyes before resolve swiftly replaced it, her gaze igniting with the kind of fire that could only come from someone who refused to back down. That fierce spirit drew me to her like a *carvoth* to a flame.

"Deal, Commander, but you'd better bring your A-game. And lots of credits—you're going to need them."

The thought of losing to her was an itch at the back of my mind, but it wasn't the credits that concerned me. Could I admit that a human female had what it took to beat me?

She squared her shoulders, preparing to depart. "And Vyk, don't think you can play the good guy by letting me win." Her eyes narrowed with suspicion, as if she could already see me contemplating a strategic loss to win her favor.

"Trust me, I wouldn't dream of it," I replied, but she was already turning away.

"Good," she called over her shoulder. "Where would be the fun in that?"

I didn't even try to pull my gaze from her shapely ass, thinking of things that would be much more fun than cards. But none of that was within the realm of possibility when the female despised me so completely.

"But not for long." I murmured into the quiet. My pulse quickened with the thrill of the upcoming challenge. The game was a chance to show the female captain that I was more than a hardened Drexian who cared only for battle and blood. But, as I'd promised, I had no intention of letting her win. There was more at stake than mere credits or pride. And I knew what I wanted to claim when I won.

CHAPTER
FIVE

Ariana

"We have to wait for her." I put a hand on Volten's arm once we stepped outside the doors to the Stacks. Jess had already walked ahead, but Volten had waited with me, along with his friends. "Fiona is right behind me."

Volt, Kann, and Torq glanced around, as if they'd just realized that Fiona wasn't with us.

"I'm sure she won't be long," I added, hoping the Drexians wouldn't ask too many questions about why Fiona had lingered and who had lingered with her.

"While you wait, I am going to take a little trip to the kitchens." Kann rubbed his hands together and nudged Volten in the side. "Care to join me?"

Volt cut a momentary glance at me before shaking his head. "Go without me."

I gave him a gentle shove. "Go. I know how much you two eating machines love stealing bread from the cooks after hours. I'm fine waiting for Fi by myself."

Volt eyed me as if trying to determine if I meant the words I said. "You do not mind?"

I shook my head. After the tense meeting discussing my sister's fate, I wouldn't mind a few moments alone. I adored Volten, but like all Drexians, he took up a lot of space and made a lot of noise. I would not say no to some alone time. "I don't mind, as long as you bring me some."

He grinned, brushing my side-swept bangs from my eyes, before running one finger along my jawbone and tipping my chin up. "My quarters again?"

My cheeks warmed as I felt the eyes of the other Drexians on me. I was glad that Volten did not feel the need to be shy about his affection for me, but it was hard to be discreet when everyone in the academy knew you were shacking up. That didn't mean I wanted to start sleeping alone. Not when sleeping in Volten's strong arms was one of the few things that was keeping me sane. "I'll meet you there later."

He growl-hummed as he kissed me, and frissons of desire sizzled my lips and made heat churn in my core as I pressed a hand to his chest to push him away and ground myself.

"I wish I had a female to warm my bed," Kann said, making no secret of staring at us.

Volten gave me a slow wink as he pivoted to his friend. "That would mean settling on only one female."

Kann grinned wickedly. "Would it?"

Torq shook his head. "If you wish to warm your bed with one of the human females at the academy. I might not know much about them yet, but I do not think they like to share."

"Some do," I told them, enjoying watching their mouths fall open. "But none of the women that I know here would be into that."

"Too bad." Kann shot Volten a pointed look. "I could go to one of the nearby outpost bars, but I seem to have lost my wingman."

Volten shook his head hard. "I was not a good wingman even before I lost all interest in chasing alien females."

Kann slapped him on the back. "What do you mean? You were great. All the females wanted me because you were so bad at charming them."

Everyone laughed, including Volten, who bent down and whispered into my ear, "At least I was charming enough to seduce you."

His breath tickled my ear and sent a shiver of pleasure down my back. "I thought I was the one who seduced you?"

"Speaking of human females at the academy," Torq said as he turned to Kann. "I thought I saw you with one of the cadets the other day."

Kann cocked his head. "Do you mean the Iron who was working on the holo-chamber?"

"Britta?" She had told me that she'd been helping to update some of the holo-chambers in the School of Battle.

"It looked like you were working closely with her." Torq eyed Kann with his arms crossed.

Kann shook his head. "I assure you, Britta and I are only friendly colleagues."

"Actually, you are her instructor," Volt reminded him. "She is only a cadet."

Kann blinked rapidly as if just remembering that fact. "Whatever she is, we are not involved. We agreed to be friends and nothing else."

Volten's brows jerked up. "Was that something she decided, because that doesn't sound like a decision you would—"

"Yes," Kann cut him off. "I might have suggested a friendly drink, but she insisted on remaining friends, which we have." He tapped one finger on his chin. "She might actually be my first ever female friend."

Volten put an arm around his friend's shoulders. "I am proud of you, Kann. This is a big step for you."

Kann jammed an elbow into his gut. "Very funny. Now are we going to raid the kitchens or not?"

Volten blew me a kiss as the three Drexians backed away, laughing and shoving each other like they were children. I spun back toward the looming doors to the Stacks, grateful to have a moment alone, even though another part of me wondered how much longer I should wait for Fiona before going in after her with metaphorical guns blazing.

CHAPTER
SIX

Fiona

"What was that about?" Ariana was waiting for me when I emerged from the heavy doors guarding the entrance to the Stacks.

I blew out a breath, releasing some of the tension that I'd been holding when I'd been around Vyk. Then I noticed that Ariana's mate wasn't with her. "Where's Volten?"

"He and the other guys wanted to sneak down to the kitchens for a snack."

I allowed myself a grin. That didn't sound too bad, although my stomach was still in a knot from talking with Vyk. "He wants us to play nice."

A look of outrage flicked across my friend's face. "*He* wants to play nice? After everything he's done?" She huffed out a breath. "Typical guy. As soon as they get called out for being a dick, they want to be forgiven."

"Exactly. Does he actually feel regret, or does he just regret getting caught and having all of us hate him?"

Ariana eyed me as we walked down the empty corridor. "I hope you didn't forgive him so easily."

I slid my gaze to her and tilted my head. "Does that seem like my style?" I shook my head. "I challenged him to a card game."

Her eyes flared. "You did? Does he have any idea how good you are?"

I twitched one shoulder up. "Who knows? I doubt it. I don't get the feeling he's spent much time learning about the talents of the humans who joined the academy."

Ariana stifled a laugh, sneaking a final look behind us as we rounded the corner. "Good point. I'm sure he has no clue that you wipe the floor with the rest of us when we play."

We approached Jess, who was talking with Britta, whose silver hair was pulled high in a tight bun, and Morgan, who looked like she'd just woken up. All three women pivoted to us.

"Sorry I missed the meeting." Morgan swiped a blond curl from her eyes, revealing a sheet mark on one cheek. "I planned to lie down for five minutes."

Jess elbowed her playfully. "Famous last words. At least you didn't sleep through the night."

Morgan poked out her bottom lip. "It sounds like I missed a lot."

"It sounds like we all missed something." Britta slid her gaze between me and Ariana. "Are you talking about how Fiona beats our asses in cards?"

"I don't beat you that badly." I swung my gaze from woman to woman but they all stared at me. "Okay, I might win most games..."

"Try *all*," Jess said, with a pointed look.

"It's only because I've practiced more."

Britta eyed her. "And being a famous strategist doesn't hurt."

Ariana threw an arm around my shoulder. "We're just teasing you. Don't feel bad about being good at something. That's why you're going to beat Vyk and shut him up once and for all."

Britta's and Jess's mouths gaped.

"You're going to play against the security chief?" Britta's words were barely a whisper.

Jess blinked at me. "Are you sure about this? That guy does not seem like the type to play games."

I resumed walking toward the female tower, forcing the rest of the women to follow me. "It was my idea. I want to beat him and prove that humans—especially females—aren't weaker or less capable than Drexians."

"You challenged the academy's security chief to a game of cards?" Britta looked at me like I'd lost my mind.

We all went quiet as the Academy Master and his adjunct swept by us with silent nods in our direction.

When the two Drexians had passed, I gave a shrug. "He told me to pick a way so he could prove that he'd changed, and I knew he was going to be at the staff card game."

"So you picked cards?" Jess rubbed a hand across her forehead as we continued through the main hall. "Why didn't you make him clean the latrines or be your personal servant?"

I hesitated. Now that she mentioned it, those did sound like pretty good options.

"She's an Assassin," Ariana said, before I could respond. "Of course, she's going to pick some kind of game or puzzle that she can win."

I wasn't sure if that was a compliment or not, but it was accurate. My mind instinctively went to strategic challenges, not mental tasks, although the idea of Vyk in a ruffled apron did bring me more happiness than it should have.

"It's not like I'm guaranteed to win. We are playing Drexian cards, and you know that's harder than poker or blackjack."

"Drexian cards," all the women murmured at once.

That sent a shiver through me, and for the first time I had some misgivings about the challenge I'd accepted.

"When is this game?" Britta asked.

"It's part of the staff card game that he's joining. I challenged him to play me there."

Morgan inhaled sharply. "So, it's soon."

Jess jogged ahead and waved for us to catch up. "Hurry up, then. We don't have much time."

I exchanged a glance with Ariana. "Time for what?"

"Time for you to get in more practice against us." Jess walked backward a few steps. "I know we aren't the best players to hone your skills against, but we're all you have."

A figure stepped from an intersecting corridor to block our way. "That is not necessarily true."

CHAPTER
SEVEN

Vyk

I waited until Fiona was gone, savoring the hush of the Stacks as thoughts of Fiona's challenge swirled through my mind. I drew in a breath that was heavy with the scent of crumbling books and layers of dust and let it out slowly to steady the breath that had quickened at her provocation.

Had that actually happened? Had the female challenged me to a game of cards?

I fought the urge to laugh, the sound bubbling up in my throat and teasing my lips. I should not find so much pleasure in her mistake. I should not be reveling in the strategist's strategic mistake. She could not have known. She clearly had no idea.

I finally took plodding steps through the labyrinth of looming bookshelves, the rhythmic sound marking my walk to the door. I heaved it open and stepped out, sucking in the cool air of the academy corridors that was not laden with dust and age. The door thudded shut behind me, and the sound echoed off the unyielding rock.

"Commander Vyk,"Admiral Zoran's voice cut through the quiet with the precision of a Drexian blade.

I turned, finding the seasoned officer's piercing gaze fixed on me as he approached. A hint of amusement played at the corner of his mouth, an expression incongruous with the stern set of his jaw. Only when he reached me did I notice his adjunct disappearing down the far end of the corridor.

I forced my own face into a mask of disciplined calm. "Admiral."

"I happened to be walking by some females, and I overheard Captain Douglas mentioning that she would be playing you in cards." The dim lighting of the sconces cast shadows over his face, but it couldn't hide the knowing gleam in his eyes.

"Did you? " I kept my tone neutral, though a flicker of annoyance sparked within me. Of course, word had reached the admiral already. Despite its size and maze of corridors, the academy did not seem to hold secrets as well as it had in the past.

"I did. She seemed unaware of your skill level. She appeared to be ignorant of the way you made extra credits during your time in Inferno Force. I can only assume you did not inform her that you have ruled nearly every card table you've played at over the years."

A muscle twitched in my cheek. It would have been a fair match if not for my past; a past she knew nothing about. "She threw down the gauntlet. I simply picked it up," I replied, the words smooth and even, betraying none of the conflict churning inside me.

"And what happens when she learns of your past?"

It took no imagination to know how she would react. I had already been on the receiving end of her rage. But now, the very notion of playing against her, of winning, of claiming a prize of my choosing—even under false pretense—was a temptation too potent to resist.

My silence must have spoken volumes. Zoran clapped a hand on my shoulder, his touch surprisingly heavy. "Be careful, Vyk. Human females are more dangerous than they appear."

"Your concern is noted, Admiral." I shrugged off his hand with a discreet firmness. The weight of his warning lingered, but I ignored it.

Zoran gave me a curt nod, the lines around his eyes softening for a moment before he turned away.

I waited until he had vanished around the corner, until I was alone again.

"Am I playing with fire?" I murmured to myself, the hush of the corridor amplifying my internal debate.

The urge to be near her, to decipher the enigma of her, clawed at me with relentless tenacity. Perhaps this card game would quench the burning curiosity that consumed my thoughts. Maybe engaging in battle with Fiona would put my desire to rest. If I beat her, maybe my thoughts would be purged of her.

37

Or maybe, she will beat you.

I choked on a laugh at this. I might believe that the females were tougher than I'd originally thought. I might be willing to admit that the humans were clever and shrewd. I might even be willing to concede that Fiona was the most intriguing female I'd ever encountered of any species, but I did not believe that she would beat me. I had played too many games against too many outlaws to fear losing.

No, I would play her as she wished, and I would win. But I would not leave the table empty handed. I never did.

CHAPTER
EIGHT

Fiona

My heart pounded as the figure in shadows stepped into the light. "Tivek?"

The admiral's adjunct was one of the last Drexians I would expect to be lurking in the shadows of the corridors, and definitely the last I would expect to challenge what Jess had said.

"What do you mean, we aren't her best bet for honing her cards skills?" Jess asked before I could.

The tall Drexian had light brown hair cut short, and his dark academy uniform was pristine. He looked every bit the tough warrior, even though I knew he'd never graduated from the academy or served in the Drexian forces. There were rumors that he'd washed out of the academy and been taken under-wing by Admiral Zoran, but I knew no more details than that.

Despite his lack of military service, the alien radiated intelligence and a certain aura of mystery and danger. Maybe it was because no one knew his whole story, or maybe it was because he served the admiral and was privy to so much information, but I had always gotten the idea that Tivek should not be underestimated.

"I mean that none of you are up playing Drexian cards. Not like I did."

I gaped at him for a moment, trying to determine if he meant what I thought he did. "Are you offering to coach me?"

He inclined his head ever so slightly. "I am."

I was struck dumb. Why would someone I only knew in passing want to help me? He didn't even know details about the game or who I would be playing.

After a few more moments of uncomfortable silence and the other women glancing at each other, he shifted from one foot to the other. "I suggest you accept my offer."

"Are you good?" Ariana blurted.

He slid his gaze to her, his lips quirked, and he slid his gaze back to me. "I am very good."

Something about the way he said that made me believe him. I'd heard lots of arrogant boasting at the academy, but never by Tivek. "I accept. When do we start?"

Without answering, he pivoted on one heel and started walking back in the direction from where we'd come. When none of us moved, he stopped, glanced over his shoulder, and released a small sigh. "If you wish to be ready by the staff card game, we start tonight. Are you coming?"

"Yes." I rushed forward, and the rest of the women fell in step with me. I wasn't sure if the invitation was officially for all of us, but I would feel better with my friends around me. I also knew they'd never let me go off to be tutored by the enigmatic Drexian without them.

We proceeded back to the main hall and up the sweeping staircase, which would usually be swarming with cadets. Now, we were the only ones walking up, and we could fan out and take up the entire sizable width.

For a moment, I wondered if he was leading us to the cadet dining room, which would be deserted. But we breezed by the tall doors. We kept walking down a dimly lit hallway with vaulted ceilings until we reached a doorway I recognized.

"The Admiral's office?" Ariana prompted my question.

"The Admiral is not in his office."

Jess drew in a sharp breath. "Are we breaking in?"

Tivek cut her an amused glance. "He has authorized me to use his private space so we will not be interrupted."

"And so Vyk will never know," Morgan added.

Tivek locked eyes on her for a beat, his lips quirking even more. "That would be optimal."

He pressed his hand to a panel and the door slid open, to reveal a long room. Moonlight streamed in from a far, narrow window that was cut into the stone, and the massive black desk glowed in the blue-white light. The office was large enough to hold us all, but it wasn't lost on me that there were only two stiff chairs on this side of the desk.

Tivek strode inside, but instead of continuing to the desk, he stopped in the middle of the room and touched his palm to the right wall. A panel I would have previously sworn did not exist, glided open silently.

"Whoa," Britta whispered, as Tivek stepped through the gap and vanished into the wall.

I hurried after him, any trepidation dwarfed by my curiosity. The admiral had a secret lair.

As I stepped inside, the hidden room embraced me with its warmth and my feet went from tapping on hard stone to sinking into plush carpet. There was a fireplace inset in the wall directly facing us, its dancing flames casting a mesmerizing glow across the dark couches facing each other across a low table.. The scent of woodsmoke, rich and earthy, enveloped us, mingling with the faint aroma of aged paper and exotic spice.

"Are you sure we're allowed to know about this?" I asked, my eyes widening as I took in the side walls, one which contained floor-to-ceiling glass shelves that held glittering bottles of liquor and the other which was lined entirely in bookshelves jammed with leather-bound books, their gilded spines catching the light from the fire.

Tivek chuckled, his laughter a deep, husky sound and not at all what I would have expected from someone so reserved. "I am sure. Now, shall we play?"

A deck of Drexian cards was already on the table, the emblem of the academy in metallic gold on the tops of the cards. Tivek sat on one of the couches and scooped up the deck, his fingers deftly shuffling the cards before dealing them face down on the table.

I took a seat across from him and slid my cards from the table, assessing them as he briefly reviewed the rules. I knew the basics of the game, but I'd taught myself and had only played against humans.

"You may discard first," he offered.

I played a card, which he immediately matched and took. That was fast. As we immersed ourselves in the game, Tivek's mastery became increasingly apparent. His moves were calculated, his decisions swift and precise. The firelight danced across my cards, casting an ethereal glow that seemed to intensify the competition.

"You're really good at this," I said, as he easily won the game.

Tivek shrugged. "I have been playing for much longer."

I eyed him as he reshuffled the cards. "It isn't just practice. You're amazing."

He leaned back, his eyes glinting. "When I was a cadet, I was one of you."

For a moment I was confused, then my jaw dropped. "You were an Assassin? Well, that explains your strategic prowess."

"Who's in the mood for a drink?" Ariana called out. She'd taken up residence at the bar, pulling down bottles and lining up glasses. The clink of glasses and the gentle slosh of liquids added to the sounds of the snapping fire.

"Count me in." I probably shouldn't drink while playing, but it had been a night.

"And us," Jess said, as she and Britta stood at the soaring book-shelves, their fingers tracing the spines of ancient tomes.

"This place is incredible." Morgan stood near the fire watching the game as she warmed her back. "How long has it been here?"

Tivek stole a glance at her before returning his eyes to his cards. "A long time. This is the part of the academy that was the original castle, so it must have been a secret room for an ancient Drexian ruler."

A shiver went down my spine at the thought of the millennia that the walls in the academy had seen pass by. It was enough to make me almost miss another furtive glance by Tivek toward Morgan, his eyes lingering on her for a moment too long. Was it possible that the adjunct had a crush on the cadet? He was older than her, but Morgan was already an officer in the Navy, so she wasn't a teenager.

I narrowed my eyes at my opponent. Or was he doing this to distract me? I quickly banished the thoughts of a blooming romance, focusing instead on the game at hand.

When I played my next card, Tivek stopped me. "You have gone too high too quickly. Unlike everything else in Drexian culture, our card games reward patience."

"Then I should be able to win easily against Vyk. He's all bluster."

Tivek lifted an eyebrow. "Never underestimate him. His dangerous reputation is not only because of his battle skills."

I swallowed hard at this, wondering if I'd made a fatal error in challenging the Drexian to cards. Was I the one who'd been too cocky?

Ariana approached, a dazzling purple cocktail in hand. "A little liquid courage."

I accepted the drink gratefully, the cool glass a welcome contrast to the warmth of the room. As I took a sip, the flavors exploded on my tongue—a perfect balance of sweetness and bite, with a hint of alien flavors I couldn't place. I even welcomed the buzz of the booze on my tongue and the heat as it hit my stomach.

After a few more hands, my skills at the game began to sharpen, thanks to Tivek's expert tutelage. The pressure of my impending match with Commander Vyk still loomed large, but I allowed myself to enjoy being in the moment, being in the secret room, being with my friends.

Besides, now that I really knew how to play, I had no intention of losing.

CHAPTER
NINE

Torq

I leaned back in bed and glanced again at the timepiece on my bedside table. Where was she? More importantly, what had happened to me?

Only a short time ago, the idea of having a girlfriend, much less a human one, would have been unthinkable. I was a high-born Drexian who was expected to marry well and enjoy sampling as many females as possible before then. But then I'd met Jess, and she had changed everything.

I released a long breath as I thought about how I'd gone from instant fascination with her, despite her clearly lower birth and her unusual independence, to a barely controllable desire. My hunger for her had driven me to blackmail her and then to fall for her body and soul. It was hard to remember what I'd been like before she consumed my thoughts, but I knew I'd been insufferable and arrogant. I knew, because Jess had no problem reminding me.

"Infuriating female," I muttered to myself, although I could not suppress the grin that emerged every time I thought about my mate.

In truth, I loved that she challenged me and kept me humble. It had been a first for me, but I had grown to value her opinion. Before her, I had relied on the opinion of my clan, even though I had rarely measured up to their cruelly impossible expectations. Once I had freed myself of them, and their toxic influence, I had been able to fully embrace Jess and her oddly fulfilling concept of "keeping it real."

If I was too cocky, she told me. If I acted like an elitist, she reminded me that we were all equal. If I tried to control her, she was quick to tell me that she was not my property.

That did not mean I agreed with everything. Despite her protests, Jess was still mine. I might not own her, but she was mine. Mine to love. Mine to possess. Mine to protect.

I missed her when she was not with me, and I worried when she was late—like now. Jess had been on her way to meet me in my quarters after the meeting in the Stacks. I had been the one who had agreed to make a quick trip to the kitchens to snatch some warm bread with Volten and Kann, so why was she not here?

I had disrobed and slipped beneath the sheets, or I might have been tempted to storm from my room and search the corridors for her, something she would not like. We were still feeling our way around the parameters of being together as cadets, and hunting her down would be overstepping my boundaries.

I released a low rumble of displeasure as I stole another furtive glance beside me and saw that virtually no time had passed. I would go mad before the night was out, especially if I let myself think of all the things that might happen to her. She'd already been put at risk because of me. Was I being a fool for not making sure she was not in danger now?

It took little to convince myself that finding her was imperative, so I tossed back the sheet and stood. Before I could put on clothes and leave my room, the door slid open, and Jess hurried inside.

She stopped short when she saw me standing completely naked beside the bed. Her jaw dropped, and her cheeks mottled a pale shade of pink. "I..."

"You are late," I rasped, my voice harsher than I'd intended.

She pulled her gaze up even as her chest heaved. "I know. I'm really sorry. I lost track of time."

"On the way from the Stacks to here?" Even though I was supposed to be upset with her, I could not stop my body's natural reaction to her presence. My cock twitched to life, thickening as I tried to retain my rightful indignation.

She gave me a sultry smile as she walked to me. "You know I would rather be here than anywhere else, don't you?"

I cleared my throat as she closed the distance between us and pressed her hands to my chest. How had this woman gone from a shy, unsure creature to a confident seductress? I wanted to believe that my sex tutoring had been the reason, but I knew I could not take all the credit. Jess had always been a wildcat waiting to be released.

My cock ached with need, and I curled my arms around her waist. It did not matter that she had been in my bed last night and the night before that. I could not get enough of her. I would never tire of the feel of her, the taste of her, the sound of her when she shattered in my arms. I was so lost in thoughts of her that I almost forgot the question that I'd been asking myself half the night. "Where were you?"

She hesitated, her breath catching in her throat. She ran her fingers over my bare chest, the sensation sizzling my skin. "Do you really want to talk now?"

I unwound my arms from her waist and closed my hands over hers, stopping them from drifting farther. "Are you hiding something from me?"

"No," her answer burst from her lips. "It's nothing to do with us."

Now my curiosity was piqued. "What is nothing to do with us? What are you not telling me?"

She let loose a tortured sigh as she peered up at me. "Every other woman can distract men with sex, but you aren't going to let this go, are you?"

I smiled at her. "Trust me, *cinnara*. You are distracting me a great deal." I leaned closer so she could feel just how much, and her eyes widened. "If I hadn't been sitting here for a long time worrying, your seduction might have worked."

She bit her bottom lip. "You were worried? Of course, you were. I'm really sorry. I didn't think we'd be with Tivek for so long."

"Tivek?" That was a name I had not expected to hear, and I was not sure I had heard right.

She sighed again. "You have to promise not to breathe a word of what I tell you."

"Does it have anything to do with academy security? Will anyone be in danger if I keep your secret?"

Jess wrinkled her nose. "No and no."

"Then you have my word."

She nodded and her shoulders relaxed. "Tivek was helping Fiona prepare to play against Vyk in the card game. He took us to the admiral's secret study, although it's more like a lair than anything."

I would have never guessed this in a million light years. "I have been there. How did Tivek know about the game?"

Jess bobbed one shoulder. "Who knows? I get the feeling the Drexian knows everything that goes on in the academy."

I often got the same feeling. "You have been in the admiral's private lounge all this time?"

"I got distracted by all the books, then Ariana made us cocktails..." Her words drifted off and she pressed her body closer to mine. "I'm happy to be with you now, though."

"My quarters are not as luxurious as Zoran's lounge, with his collection of books and liquors."

"No." Jess gave me a mischievous grin. "But you have something that his lounge doesn't have."

My pulse spiked as she slipped her hands from beneath mine and dragged her fingers down my chest to the ridges of my stomach. "And what is that?"

"Why don't I show you?"

Jess slid her hands lower as she dropped to her knees. I barely had time to think before she'd curled one hand around the base of my cock and closed her lips around the crown. I tangled my hands in her hair as she sucked my length deeper into her mouth and made my eyes roll back into my head.

Grek me, she had gotten so good that I couldn't imagine giving her any instruction. Not when she took my cock down her throat like she'd been doing it for years. Not anymore. Well, there was one thing I wanted to tell her.

"Don't get too comfortable on your knees, Jess, because soon it will be my turn, and I'm going to have you on your back and screaming my name."

She laughed, the sound reverberating through my cock. Then she dragged her mouth up the length of me and pulled away for a beat. She gave me a hard shove, and I fell backward onto my bed. "You first, Drexian."

Vyk

I DETECTED voices before I even reached the doors to the staff dining room, and I hesitated before walking through them. What was I doing? I'd agreed to join the card game so I could form closer bonds with my colleagues and dispel any lingering mistrust they might harbor against me. But now, I'd turned the card game into a face-off between me and Fiona. She wanted to prove herself to me, and I wanted to do what I always did when it came to Drexian cards. I wanted to win.

Memories of past card games—of smoky backrooms that smelled of stale liquor and sweat, of surly aliens glaring at me across the worn tables, of scooping up credits as my opponents cursed me—made my fingers buzz with anticipation. It might not be fair to accept Fiona's challenge without telling her of my prowess at the card table, but this was not about playing fair. I'd gone from wanting to use the game to show her that I was not the evil commander she believed me to be, to wanting to prove that I respected her enough to play my best.

You want more than that.

I forced the taunting voice from my mind as I entered the dining room. Two of the long tables had been shoved together to make one large square, and I recognized most of the instructors sitting on benches around it.

Kann and Volten sat next to each other on one side, as Kann shuffled a deck of cards. He rapped the glossy cards on the wooden surface before cutting them and placing two equal stacks next to each other.

Across from the two friends sat Fiona and Ariana. My heart squeezed when I saw that the captain wore her wavy, blonde hair loose, so that it fell forward as she leaned her elbows on the table.

She glanced up when I entered, her eyes flaring in challenge. "I thought you might have decided to back out."

I let out a gravelly laugh. "Never."

"Back out of the game?" Kann's brow wrinkled. "Why would the commander back out of a friendly card game?"

"Because it's not a friendly game." Fiona leaned back, her gaze never leaving me. "Commander Vyk has accepted my challenge to a one-on-one match."

Volten and Kann both flicked their gazes between the captain and me, as if waiting for one of us to reveal the joke.

"She is telling the truth," I said, as I strode forward and took a seat perpendicular to all four players. "The captain issued a challenge, and I accepted."

Kann opened his mouth, as if to reveal that I was the last person Fiona should play against, but then he met my severe expression and clamped his lips shut.

"First, we will play as a group," Fiona said, tearing her sharp gaze from me and smiling at everyone. "The last thing I want to do is spoil the fun for everyone."

A pair of Drexian instructors entered, one an Iron and one a Blade, and they greeted everyone before they took seats across from me. Then Volten produced a bottle of Noovian whiskey from under the table and plunked it down next to the cards.

Ariana eyed the bottle and then him. "I hope you don't expect us to pass it around like we're outside a 7-11 at midnight."

"Not sure if that means anything to anyone but me," Fiona told her with a grin, as the rest of us exchanged bewildered glances.

"There are glasses." Kann stood, threw one leg over the bench, and walked to the back of the dining room where the tables usually held platters of food and pitchers of drinks. He stacked several glasses inside each other, making a tower that he could carry back with two hands. Once at the table, he unstacked them one by one and set them around the bottle.

Ariana beamed at him, her expression filled with affection. "Now that's more like it."

For a moment, I wondered why she wasn't sitting next to her mate, but I suspected her choice of seat had a lot to do with supporting her friend when she played me. The pair of female human instructors had appeared to be fast friends from the moment they'd arrived at the academy, and a part of me envied their easy friendship.

My arrival at the academy had not brought me any new friends, even though there were other Drexians who shared my Inferno Force past, others who had also gone through the academy like me, even others who had been Irons. My reputation as a brutal Inferno Force commander had precluded any connections. It had only provoked fear and wariness, which I'd proved to be warranted through my involvement in the scandal of the trials.

But I had never been easily accepted into groups. Not at the academy when I'd been a poor boy from a no-name clan, not in the Irons when I'd had no lineage of proud Irons to boast of, not even in Inferno Force when I'd quickly gotten a reputation for being fiercer than any other warrior. I had been reserved when others had been loud, serious when others had been pulling pranks, and determined to win when others played for fun.

Kann unscrewed the top from the bottle and poured a measure of the whiskey into seven glasses. "Should we start the game with a toast?"

We all picked a glass and lifted it into the air, then clinked them together in the center.

"To playing fair and having fun," Volten said.

Fiona met my eyes and downed her drink in a single gulp. "All's fair in love and war."

I was not familiar with that Earth expression, but I could not have agreed more. I slammed back my shot and let the whiskey scorch my throat.

There was nothing fair about what I was about to do, but I could not stop myself, even if I'd wanted to.

Which I did not.

CHAPTER
TEN

Fiona

Kann leaned back and tossed his cards onto the table. "That's it for me."

I glanced at the cards that were fanned out in my hand and ran one finger across the tops of them as I considered my next move.

Before I could, Ariana put down her cards. "I'm out, too."

Volten, who'd bowed out of the game two rounds earlier, grinned at her. "Too rich for your blood, as well."

I eyed the pile of credits, coins, and even paper dollars from Earth that sat in the middle of the table. Then I glanced at Vyk, who was the only one left in the game with me. "It's not too rich for you?"

He cut his gaze to me for only a beat before sliding a metal bar that represented a hundred credits into the pile to call the bet. "It is not."

My heart trilled in my chest as I allowed myself another peek at my hand, scanning the Drexian emblems that adorned the glossy surfaces. It was good. Not the best I'd ever had, but really good. There wouldn't be many hands that could beat it. I forced myself not to smile. I didn't want to give any indication that I was already counting the money in the pot as mine.

It had better be mine. I had almost everything I'd brought to the game in the pot that had been growing bigger and bigger as the game had progressed. I'd won one game early on, but then Vyk had taken two and the Iron instructor had taken one. Kann and Volten seemed to be in it for fun, making small bets and not risking too much or staying in games too long.

I took a sip from the glass that I'd been nursing the entire night, very aware that Vyk's glass had been refilled. Good, I thought, let him drink while I keep my wits about me.

I slowly lowered my cards to the table, fanning them out so that Vyk could see my hand. It took all my self-control not to reach forward and scoop the pot toward me, but I finally smiled at Vyk and waited for him to show his cards.

"Nice hand, Captain." His voice was a rumble as he stared at the cards splayed on the table.

I tipped my head at him in acknowledgment, my fingers already buzzing with the anticipation of gathering my winnings.

He then lowered his cards to the table and spread them out so everyone could see his hand. My heart sank. His winning hand.

I clenched my teeth together as I forced myself to keep smiling. How had he pulled off one of the few hands that could beat mine?

"Nice hand, Commander," I managed to say without sounding hostile or bitter.

Vyk took another swig of his whiskey before pulling his winnings toward himself as everyone around the table murmured appreciation of the hand he'd played and some of the same surprise I'd felt.

Ariana, who was just there to support me, clearly wasn't enjoying the competition as much as I was. If it wasn't flying, she didn't consider it a thrill. She stood and unwound herself from the bench, stretching her arms overhead and groaning. "I think I'm done for the night."

Volten stood and joined her, on the other side of the table wrapping an arm around her waist. "Good timing, because I am out of credits."

"As am I." Kann poured the last drops of Noovian whiskey into Vyk's glass. "It looks like you deserve this, Commander."

Vyk swirled the liquid in his glass before tossing the entire contents back in a single gulp.

Fucking showoff.

I took a sip of my whiskey, glad I still had all my judgment intact. "I guess this means you're done too?"

Vyk met my gaze and cocked his head. "Why would you say that?"

Now that startled me. Everyone else was standing and gathering their things, m clearly done for the evening. "You want to continue playing?"

"I owe you a match." He said it very succinctly, but the intensity of his words made my pulse flutter.

I could have argued that we'd been playing all night, and we'd never decided that we had to play a solo game, but there was no way I was going to walk away from a challenge. And the way Vyk held my gaze with his own blazing one, it was a challenge.

"Then let's play." I pushed my glass away, as if to let him know that I wasn't going to be easily distracted.

Ariana leaned down and rested a hand on my shoulder. "Are you okay with us cutting out? I can stay if you want me to—"

"I'm good," I told her before she could finish. "I don't think it will take long. One more game, and I'll be back in our tower."

She made a sound that sounded doubtful but patted my shoulder. "Remember, it's just a game."

I almost laughed at that, as I gathered the discarded cards and started to shuffle them. Vyk's eyes did not leave me, and his expression did not soften. This was so much more than a game.

The Iron and Blade who'd sat across from me were already gone by the time Kann picked up the empty bottle of Noovian whiskey and looked from Vyk to me. For a moment, I thought he was going to stay and watch, but Vyk slid a stern gaze his way, and the Blade backed up a few steps.

"I wish you both a good night," he said before hurrying to catch up with Ariana and Volten, who'd left arm in arm.

Neither of us responded as I dealt the cards, put the deck in the middle, and picked up my own cards. I steeled my face so Vyk wouldn't see my reaction as I realized what bad cards I had. I exchanged three while he traded in the same amount.

So, his cards aren't great either. Maybe his luck is finally running out.

That made me feel some better as I looked at my much-improved hand and slid my remaining credits into the pot. Vyk matched my bet, flicked a glance at his cards, then raised the bet.

I stared at him. "You know I can't match that." I looked at the empty table in front of me. "Everything I have is in the pot."

"Not everything."

I met his gaze, the heat of it making my breath catch. "You want an IOU?"

His brow wrinkled, and I wondered if his universal translator implant knew what to do with those initials. "You have not played games where players wagered things other than credits?"

So, he didn't want an IOU.

"I don't have much here at the academy, unless you're into vintage romance novels."

He didn't crack a smile. "I was thinking of something else."

I didn't know what the commander had in mind, or what I could possibly give the Drexian that he would value. All I knew was that my plan to put the security chief in his place was not going according to plan. He was frighteningly good at cards, but there was no way I could back down. Not after everything I'd said. "What do you want?"

"You win, you take everything in the pot." He locked eyes with me, giving me the sensation of being hunted by something much bigger and stronger. Something that would not stop in his pursuit. "I win, you spend one night with me for every point I take."

Outrage flooded me instantly, and I glared at him. "What the fuck kind of bet is that?"

"One you don't have to take." He leaned back as if this was a normal wager, and he hadn't just propositioned me.

Me. He hated me. He'd done nothing but treat me with disdain since I'd arrived, and how he was making a bet to get me into his bed? It made no sense. But I didn't really care, because he wasn't going to win.

"I accept your bet," I said, before I could talk myself out of it. I was moments away from having a huge pile of credits and bragging rights, although I don't think I was going to tell anyone what Vyk had asked me to wager. As if anyone would believe me.

He nodded, his lips twitching at the corners. A tremor of panic teased the base of my spine just before he unfurled his cards and lay them onto the table. Then my stomach dropped.

Fuck me.

CHAPTER
ELEVEN

Vyk

The thrill of my win pumped through my body like adrenaline, the same way it always did when I defeated an opponent. There was the buzz in my fingers as I laid out my cards, the flutter in my chest as I watched them clock my winning hand and realize that their cards hadn't been enough to beat me. Then there was the flush of heat that warmed my cheeks and told me that I was still the best.

But this time, that initial thrill didn't last for more than a heartbeat. I drew in a breath as I savored the win but instead of exhaling and congratulating my opponent—Fiona—on playing a good game, I was watching her push back her chair so fast and hard that it flipped over. The scraping sound was a jolt to my burst of euphoria and jerked me back to reality.

There would be no collegial handshake or displays of polite sportsmanship. The woman was livid. Her eyes flashed as she glared at me, and for the first time I realized that she was not someone to be underestimated. At that moment, I would not have been surprised if she'd leapt across the table and attempted to choke me. My triumph deflated, and my pride withered as she stormed from the room.

Grekking hell, that hadn't gone the way I'd expected. At least, her stomping out had not been what I'd imagined. But what had I imagined? Had I pictured the military officer batting her eyelashes at me and falling into my arms? Had I thought she would calmly accept her defeat? Or had I hoped she would be secretly thrilled to be forced into my bed?

I choked back a gruff laugh. I was delusional if I thought it would go any way but badly. Then why had I made the bet? It hadn't been something I'd planned. I'd intended to win, but I hadn't decided to make such a wager until the words were spilling from my mouth. Or had I? Was this what I'd been subconsciously desiring every time Fiona had glared at me, yelled at me, challenged me? Had I been biding my time until the moment I could entice her into a web she couldn't twist out of, a deal she wouldn't dare break?

I steadied my breath as I gathered my cards from the table and then scooped her cards into the deck. My hands trembled, a result of my spiked adrenaline and my fired arousal. My hands didn't tremble in battle, but this was not the first time Fiona had made my body pulse with nervous energy. It was unsettling to know that the female could trigger a response in me that even the most terrifying alien beasts could not. It meant that she was more of a danger to me than our worst enemy.

"And you just invited her into your bed," I muttered darkly, to no one but myself.

But invited wasn't the right word, was it? I twitched as I thought of Fiona's pupils darkening as she'd understood the wager, and then my own face flamed as I remembered her cheeks paling when it had hit her that she lost the wager and what that meant.

Before I could consider waiving the bet, Fiona swept back into the room with her golden hair bouncing around her shoulders. Her chest heaved as she leveled a finger at me.

"You might have won, but this means nothing."

I was too startled by her reappearance to speak, but her wild expression and her barely contained rage made her look even more beautiful. All thought of telling her to forget about the bet fled my mind. As much as I hated myself for it, as much as I despised being drawn to a human, as much as I wanted to be strong enough to resist her fiery temper and barbed tongue, I wanted her so desperately that I was willing to do anything to get her.

Fiona spun on her heel to leave again, but then continued pivoting and faced off against me again. She braced her hands on her hips and squared her shoulders. "Was this all about humiliating me? You want to force me into your bed to prove that you can? Is that it? Is that your twisted game? Well, you can't force me to like any of it. I don't care how big or hot or ripped you are."

Her words slammed into me like body blows. She was right. I had been so bent on winning and getting her into my orbit by any means that I had forgotten that there was no pleasure in taking something that wasn't freely given. I had no desire to force her to do anything.

"I never said I would force you to do anything."

Her narrowed eyes held on mine. "The bet was I have to spend one night with you for every point you took."

I stood and pushed the bench back. "Spending the night with me does not mean I expect you to spread your legs for me."

Not that I would say no to that, but not if I had to tie her up and muffle her screams. There was no Drexian honor in that. Besides, I was a Drexian warrior who'd had females all across the galaxy more than willing to submit to my desires. I had never needed to force anyone.

But none of them were Fiona. None of them had been females who'd despised me. It was obvious that Fiona would rather slap me than fuck me, and the way things were going, I was heading for the slap sooner rather than later.

"What?" She blinked rapidly as if the words hadn't quite reached her brain. "I thought..."

"The bet is for you to spend the night with me. That is all. What happens during the night is up to you."

She barked out a laugh as she took a step back, still eyeing me like I was a rabid creature about to attack. "Then I can tell you now what will happen. Absolutely fucking nothing."

I gave a lazy shrug, even though the hostility in her voice hurt. I'd wanted the game to be a reason for me to get closer to her. I'd wanted to win so I could show her that I was not so bad. But it seemed I'd done the opposite. Her opinion of me, which already hadn't been good, was now abysmal.

For now, I reminded myself.

Fiona cocked her head to one side. "All right, Commander. You won. You have three nights, but that's all you have." Then her eyes became slits. "And if you tell a soul, I will cut your throat while you sleep."

Then she flounced from the room, leaving me hitching in my breath and unconsciously touching a hand to my throat.

Three nights. I still had three nights to prove to her that I had changed. Three nights where she would not be my captive, but she would be my captive audience. Three nights to be in the same room with her and keep my desires at bay. Three nights to worry she might slit my throat.

I groaned. What had I been thinking?

CHAPTER
TWELVE

Fiona

There was no other sound as I strode through the academy corridors--only the deafening rushing of my blood in my ears. Rage made it pulse hot and fast, and after I stomped down the wide staircase, I paused at the bottom to steady my erratic heartbeat. It wouldn't do me any good if I stroked out before I could prove to Vyk that he hadn't beaten me.

I pressed one palm to the cool, black stone of the carved banister, the solidness of it grounding me and reminding me that I was safe. I wasn't being chased by a predator like my lizard brain was convinced I was.

"Vyk *might* be a predator," I said under my breath, refueling the rage that had been coursing through me since he'd splayed his cards onto the table.

It hadn't only been that he had won. It had been the knowing look on his face when he'd made the bet with me. He knew he was going to win. He'd been sure of it. But how could he be so certain? For a moment, I considered that he'd cheated. But I dismissed that quickly. Despite the fact that the guy irritated me like a bad rash, he'd never struck me as the cheating type. None of the Drexians at the academy had.

They were huge on Drexian honor. Not only that, Vyk had been trying to prove himself as trustworthy ever since the scandal over the trials. He would be a fool to risk that over a card game. Not that I hadn't known plenty of guys who'd been bigger idiots over less. Still, he didn't seem the type, and there had been nothing about the game that had struck me as odd. The cards hadn't been his, there had been no one else in the room during our solo game, and not even the world's best card counter would have had an advantage in a game like ours.

The brutal truth was that he'd beaten me fair and square. He'd been better than me, and he'd won. Not that I should be shocked. I'd been the idiot. I'd played him at his own game, which was a rookie move. But I'd been so determined to beat him without any advantage, so I could prove that he was wrong about humans. In the process, I'd given myself terrible odds.

"Dumb, dumb, dumb." I resumed walking, this time with a more deliberate pace as I crossed the main hall and headed for the female tower.

Now that the fury was leeching from me, exhaustion was washing over me. I wanted nothing more than to crawl into my bed and sleep for a week. Maybe if I slept for long enough, I could forget about the mess I'd gotten myself into. I could forget about the stupid bet I'd made. I could forget that I would have to spend three nights with a Drexian I wanted to beat to within an inch of his life.

I shook my head, imagining how awkward and unpleasant it would be, even if Vyk had promised not to force me to do anything I didn't want to do. I still had to be in the same room with a Drexian who'd made it clear time and time again that he thought humans—especially females— were inferior and had no place at the academy. "Should be fun."

How had I gotten myself into another mess? And how was it possible that I'd found the one warrior in the entire academy who was a combination of hostile, aloof, and gorgeous? How had I attracted another hot, older guy who was the absolute wrong guy for me?

You do have a thing for silver foxes, I reminded myself. Even after multiple doomed affairs with older men who had always been unavailable—and one time so unavailable as to be hiding the fact that he was married—I was still drawn to them like catnip. Was it the superior disdain that I craved? Did I secretly search out older men who had never settled down because they were incapable of commitment? Or was it just my serious daddy issues rearing their ugly head again?

"I should be old enough to be over that," I said, not caring that the words echoed back to me off the vaulted ceiling of the corridor as I made my way through the darkened and quiet school.

But did you ever get over losing your father? Did you ever recover from him leaving one night and never returning? Did you ever stop trying to replace him with someone just as cold, just as distant, just as cheap with affection?

My pace increased as I jogged up a winding staircase and walked across an open bridge, casting a quick glance at the inky surface of the Restless Sea in the distance. Even though I couldn't see the breaking waves in the moonless night, the hint of salt in the air reminded me that the sea was close.

When I reached the other side, I rubbed my arms to warm them from the chill of the air, then I descended some stairs to reach the base of the tower that housed all the women at the academy. I stopped short before starting up the tall tower when I noticed who was sitting on the bottom step blocking my way.

Ariana held out a glass. "Win or lose, I thought you might need a drink. If you won, we could celebrate. If you lost, I could commiserate with you."

My throat tightened. I'd had friends before, but never one like Ariana. Never one who I knew in my gut would have my back no matter what. I grinned at her as my vision blurred and the backs of my eyelids burned. "Thanks." I took the glass and cleared my throat. "I need this."

Ariana stood and studied me. "Is that good or bad?"

I swirled the amber contents in the bottom of my glass and thought about Vyk. I thought about the way he'd looked at me, the way his eyes had burned into mine, the way he'd made me feel seen, the way he'd made my body hum with unwanted desire. I clinked my glass with Ariana's and then tossed back my drink in a single gulp.

It seared my throat on the way down, giving me new resolve. "I lost this battle, but the war has just begun."

CHAPTER
THIRTEEN

Vyk

T he morning light crested the Gilded Peaks, as my feet thudded on the hard-packed earth, and my breath puffed from my mouth and then dissipated into the cold air. I had already made three laps around the walls of the academy and my side screamed at me to stop.

Keep going, I told myself, as I pumped my arms higher. Inferno Force does not stop when it hurts. Inferno Force only stops when they die.

I sucked in another bracing breath, grateful that the cold was keeping me alert, and grateful that I could run outside again. After years of running on holo-treadmills on spaceships, it felt good for my feet to pound on soil again. But I hadn't come for a morning run before the sun had risen because I had missed the sensation of running as the sun rose and breathing in the familiar scents of the woods and streams that surrounded the academy. I had come because I needed to push myself. I needed to remember what it was like to push through pain. I needed to do something to take my mind off the woman I'd entangled myself with, the woman who had haunted every moment of my fitful sleep.

The looming, black stone walls were on my right as I followed them around a tall tower tipped with a ferocious spike. There were two more towers between me and the School of Strategy, which was attached to the outer wall, and then I would round the corner and encounter one more tower until I was at the shipyard. From there, I would pass the School of Flight and start another circuit around the walls.

I snuck another glance at the mountain range, taking a moment to appreciate the light spilling across the ice-capped peaks so they glistened as if they were tipped in liquid silver, as if they were, in fact, gilded. The ancient Drexians had named the mountains well, just as they'd aptly named the sea that tossed waves roughly against the cliffs. The Restless Sea was rarely anything but turbulent.

The mountains gained my awe, but the sea matched my mood. I had been restless and tormented since Fiona had stormed from the card game, and returning to my quarters and climbing into bed had done nothing to quell my racing heart and erratic pulse. I had been through so many battles and had meted out as much death as I'd seen, but rarely had I been so conflicted.

"Over a female," I scoffed, my warm breath dissolving instantly.

But my protest wasn't as forceful, and my words not laced with as much disdain as they should have been. I should have been furious with myself for letting a female get into my head. I should have been focused on my work. But instead, I was running around the academy in the cold in a vain attempt to purge myself of feelings I was sure I'd long since abandoned.

I should not feel anything for the human. I should never feel anything for any human female again. I should have learned my lesson. Being betrayed once should have been enough, but here I was, opening myself up for more pain. And there was no doubt in my mind that Fiona would cause me pain.

She was already a pain in my ass. How could spending more time with her be anything but more pain?

Pain you brought upon yourself. Pain you sought out. Pain you want.

I growled and ran faster, kicking up hard clumps of sod that flew behind me. Why would I want pain? Did I think I deserved it? Did I want to torture myself?

You did betray the first-years, a little voice whispered to me as I raced past one tower and then the next. You are one of the reasons Drexian cadets are dead. Don't you deserve to be punished? Fiona certainly thinks you do.

I gritted my teeth so hard they hurt as I rounded the corner and raced toward the shipyard. The sleek, black hulls of the ships reflected the gold light that was washing over them, and the sight of so many fighters made my chest swell. I thought back to the first time I'd seen the rows of ships lined up on the stone.

I'd been a fresh-faced cadet, with no clue about the academy or what I would have to endure. I had no idea that I would go on to join Inferno Force and spend so much of my life living in shiny, black Drexian ships. I had no idea of the challenges that faced me. If I had, would I have walked through the arched entrance?

"Of course I would have," I said out loud, my deep voice breaking the peaceful silence.

All the sacrifices had been worth it because I believed in the Drexian Empire. I believed in our mission to protect the universe from cruel aliens. I believed in our duty to protect Earth from the Kronock. Above all, I believed in Drexian honor and might.

It was why I'd returned to the academy. I believed I had a duty to give back and train cadets.

A duty you neglected, the small voice whispered like a venomous snake curled around my ear.

"I will not fail again." My feet pounded on the stones of the shipyard as I crossed it, and rounded another tower to hug the wall that abutted the sheer cliffs leading down to the Restless Sea. I could hear the thrashing water as it was hurled onto the rocks, even if I couldn't see it.

I shielded my eyes as the sun hit the water and bounced off, sending blinding gold light off the surface. As bright as it was, I didn't want to look away. I couldn't. It was both cruel and beautiful, like everything I was attracted to, and just like Fiona.

She was as tough as she was striking, and it was her hard edges that pulled me to her, even more than her beauty. It wasn't punishment I wanted when I'd challenged her and made the bet I knew I'd collect. It was the thrill of possessing something both alluring and deadly that I craved.

Not that I possessed Fiona, or probably ever would. She had made it perfectly clear that trying to claim her would be the end of me. But I had never been one to shrink from a challenge. I'd danced on the edge of danger for so long when I served in Inferno Force, but the academy held fewer chances for risk.

Fiona was a risk. If I pushed her, she could cut my throat. If I succeeded in winning her over, I would have to admit that what I truly desired was a human. If I fell for her harder than I already had, I would never recover if she rejected me. If there was ever a lose-lose-lose scenario, I was in it.

CHAPTER

FOURTEEN

Fiona

"It makes no sense," I said under my breath, as I stood at the front of the classroom and stared at my lecture notes on the lectern without focusing on the words. Of course, I wasn't talking about my lecture on using traditional battle formations for battles in space. I was still obsessing over the bet I'd lost against Vyk.

Why did the Drexian want to spend the night with me—aside from the obvious, which he promised he would not attempt? It had always been clear that he hated me, hated my kind, hated that we were ruining his academy. So, what kind of twisted mind wanted to submit himself to my presence and force me to spend time with him when I'd made it equally clear that I would rather do just about anything else? Hell, if we were going to get real, I would rather do just about any*body* else.

76

I frowned at this, realizing that it wasn't entirely true. As much as I hated Vyk for his attitudes toward humans and women, he was exactly the type of growly older guy I'd go for, *if* he wasn't such an ass.

I glanced up when I heard footsteps. The seats that fanned out around me in a half moon were empty, and the light were dim. Cadets weren't even at the academy, but someone was walking toward me, their face obscured by the low lighting. I frowned at the male form that I suspected was Vyk. "Are you here to discuss details?

"I am not."

I instantly recognized the low, deep voice, and my shoulders relaxed. Tivek. Then I realized why he'd probably sought me out, and I bit my lower lip. I'd made Vyk promise not to reveal the terms of our wager to anyone, which meant that I also couldn't reveal it. As much as I wanted to expose the commander, I did not want to expose myself and the impulsiveness that had gotten me into my current mess.

It was a situation that did not look good for a Strategy instructor. Of anyone, I should have seen it coming. I should have known that he was better at Drexian cards than me. I should have known that he would not make a huge wager he thought he had any chance of losing. Now that I had some distance from the game, I could see all my mistakes. I also knew that they were all a result of me being convinced that I was smarter and shrewder than a big warrior who struck me as a hit-first-and-ask-questions-later type. It was hard to admit how badly I'd misjudged him and myself.

When he came fully into view, I attempted to act surprised. "I thought you were someone else?"

"Someone else who needs to discuss details?"

I ignored this. "Did you come to hear about the game? Or did you come because you already heard?"

Tivek joined me at the lectern, his expression revealing nothing. "I only heard that the security chief played well."

I barked out a bitter laugh. "That's an understatement. Vyk clearly knows his way around a card game."

Tivek nodded. "He has a reputation for being good."

Another wild understatement. "You could have told me, you know."

Tivek held my gaze, his eyes penetrating as he seemed to study me. "I have never played against the Drexian. I have heard rumors though. Rumors that he took many credits from his Inferno Force crew mates."

I wished credits were the only thing I'd wagered. "You should have told me that I couldn't win."

The admiral's adjunct cocked his head at me. "Would you have believed me?"

Touché. The Drexian had a point. I had been fully confident in my own strategic skills and talent at cards. I never would have taken anyone's opinion that I could be defeated. If I believed everyone who'd doubted me as a woman in the military, I would never have gotten where I was now. I'd had to assume the hubris of my male counterparts to even the playing field, which meant that I charged in boldly, even if I shouldn't. Not that I regretted this. It had worked most of the time. Until Vyk had literally called my bluff.

I managed to give Tivek a weak smile. "Probably not. Thank you for coaching me. I was able to hold my own against the rest of the players."

He inclined his head to me in an abbreviated bow. "You are very welcome."

"You're sure you didn't get in trouble for taking us into your boss's secret lair?" I was still reeling from the knowledge that the Academy Master had a luxurious study hidden behind the wall of his stark office. But I'd learned not to be startled by any secrets held by the ancient school.

The tall Drexian clasped his hands behind his back. "No. Admiral Zoran fully approved of me helping you. It was his idea."

This made me remember something about Zoran. "The admiral was also Inferno Force. Is he how you heard rumors about Commander Vyk's card prowess?"

"Zoran did not have personal experience playing Vyk, but he has his pulse on much of what happens in the Drexian Empire, and especially in Inferno Force."

The stern Academy Master continued to surprise, and his loyal and enigmatic adjunct was part of the mystery surrounding him. "Did you serve under Zoran when he was part of Inferno Force?"

Tivek's expression quickly shuttered. "I did not."

Before I could ask about the details surrounding him becoming the Admiral's closest associate and confidante, he cleared his throat. "There is another reason I sought you out today."

My curiosity about him and Zoran was pushed aside as he dangled a new mystery in front of me. It wasn't the most skillful change of subject, but I was too interested in what he wanted to tell me to question him further.

"Earth Planetary Defense wishes to send an emissary to assess the success of integration of humans in the Drexian Academy."

"They couldn't ask for reports from the officers stationed here?" I'd thought that was part of our job. We were embedded in the school and would be the boots of the ground who could report back about its success or failure.

Tivek moved his head from side to side. "After the trials, there has been discussion that outside eyes are required."

This made my back stiffen. Earth military didn't trust us. Even though we'd worked tirelessly and often behind the scenes to keep our human cadets safe and the program moving forward, they were second-guessing us. I wondered if this had anything to do with the fact that the highest ranking human officers at the Drexian Academy were women. Would they be sending outside assessors if I was a man?

"The Admiral is okay with this?"

Tivek released a breath as the first few cadets started to enter the back of the classroom. "He does not have much choice. He was notified of the Earth officer's arrival in a few days' time."

It didn't miss me that Tivek had emphasized the word *notified*. It sounded like the Admiral was not pleased with this intrusion, but also that he had little say in the matter. Not if he wished to keep the tenuous alliance with Earth after the disastrous first term. I was all-too-familiar with politics in the military, but even though I was an Assassin, navigating the politics of the Earth Planetary Defense was my least favorite part of serving.

"Did they say who they're sending?" I asked as Tivek started turn away.

He paused and glanced back at me, pursing his lips and twisting them to one side as if concentrating. "His name is Gorman, I believe."

My mouth went dry, and I was unable to ask for a first name. But I didn't need it. I knew exactly who they were sending. Devon Gorman was exactly who'd I'd send if I was in charge. He was tough, smart, and ruthless. He also happened to be the officer I'd ended up in bed with right before I'd left for the Academy. I'd actually snuck from his bed and barely made it to my flight without a single parting word. And now he was coming to the Academy.

Suddenly, Vyk was not my biggest problem.

CHAPTER
FIFTEEN

Vyk

Admiral Zoran stood at the tall, narrow window cut into the obsidian stone of his office. He peered at the Restless Sea in the distance, but I had a feeling he wasn't focused on the crashing waves.

I shifted from one foot to the other as I stood at attention on the other side of his desk. "The reports are inconclusive, Admiral."

"But the Taori believe the swarm is still out there?"

I glanced at my device and the report from our Taori allies, who were on a lifelong journey across multiple galaxies to defeat a menacing alien swarm. "They do, although there have not been any sightings or distress calls from planets."

Zoran grunted and spun around. "One advantage to increasing our defense against the Kronock is that it will provide protection from this swarm."

I heard the disbelief in his voice. It was true that the Sythian swarm had been encountered by our Drexian brothers when they also first met the Taori, but the swarm had gone quiet. It was as if they'd vanished, although I knew that was too good to be true.

"Our deep-space sensors will alert us if any enemy approaches," I told the admiral. "And our pilots have been briefed on battling the swarm."

"Let us hope it does not come to that." Zoran braced his hands wide on his desk and leaned forward. "In the meantime, we have more pressing issues."

I slid my gaze to my security report. We had reviewed every area of concern I had, which had included the upgrades to the perimeter monitoring and more robust alarms on the forbidden tower. I had also briefed Zoran on my plans to remove the remaining beast from the dungeon and transport it back to its home world, although I was awaiting word from an Inferno Force captain on his willingness to transport it. The warrior owed me one after I'd saved his ass from a pair of irate Carrithian warlords on Devos. I had not revealed that particular detail to Zoran.

Had Zoran heard about the game? Had he heard about the wager? Fiona had sworn me to secrecy. She would not have gone to the Academy Master, would she? As I was debating the possibility that I was about to be seriously questioned for a breach of professional conduct, Zoran dragged a hand across his brow.

"The humans are sending an emissary to assess the status of the integration of our staff and our cadets."

It took me a moment to cast aside my defensive arguments and process what he meant. "We are being inspected?"

Zoran huffed out a breath that was more weary than angry. My own feelings were less nuanced.

I curled my hands into tight fists. "They wanted this alliance. They wanted their cadets and instructors to assimilate with ours. Now they wish to judge us?"

"There are concerns." He didn't need to add the words *after the trials*. We both knew they were implied. Earth had been horrified to discover that members of the Drexian High Command had been trying to rid the school of humans. Part of that blame lay at my feet.

I rested my fists on his desk. "If they have concerns, I will assure them."

The admiral slid his gaze to my white-knuckled fists. "Let us assume the visit is only to confirm the positive updates I have provided. At least we are between terms. There will be time to show the visiting captain the academy without the chaos of the cadets."

I straightened and nodded at my superior officer, but my ire was still up. Another human was coming to the Drexian Academy, and this one was coming to judge. I could almost feel the human's critical gaze on me, and my lip curled in response.

"I trust this will not be a problem?"

I snapped my head at Zoran's question. "No problem."

Once dismissed, I strode through the academy, fuming that even more Earthlings were on their way. When would humans ever stop tormenting me? Then I asked myself the crucial question, why did I persist in tormenting myself with the one who consumed every waking thought? Why had I not avoided her at all costs? Why had I insisted on torturing myself with a female I would never have, could never have, should never have?

CHAPTER
SIXTEEN

Fiona

"Let me see if I have this straight." Ariana hunched forward over the table in the staff dining room and lowered her voice, even though we were almost the only instructors there. Only a pair of loud Blades sat across the room from us—too far to hear and too absorbed in their own raucous conversation to care. "Not only do you know the inspector that Earth is sending to check up on how human integration is going at the Academy, but you slept with him?"

I avoided her gaze, as I dragged a spoon through a brown stew that smelled rich and savory. "He's not an inspector, per se. Devon Gorman is a captain, and he was part of the initial team that worked with the Drexian envoys."

"That's the part you want to focus on?" Ariana raised an eyebrow and leaned back in her chair.

"It's better than remembering that I haven't spoken to him since I snuck from his apartment the morning after."

My friend flinched. "Ouch. How did you manage to avoid him? I thought you worked together."

"It's pretty easy to avoid someone if you aren't on the same planet."

Ariana had picked up her forked but dropped it just as quickly, and it clattered to the table. "You slept with him right before you came here?"

I slowly raised my gaze to meet her shocked one. "The night before."

Ariana's jaw dropped. "I don't know if I should high-five you or shake my head. What are the chances that this would be the guy they send?"

Now that I'd had a chance to think about it, the chances were high. Captain Gorman was high-ranking enough to be able to pull rank on others, he had been involved in the Drexian alliance from the start, and he was the kind of officer who would look at things dispassionately. From my experience, he was tough but fair. I hoped that carried over to how he would handle seeing me. "I'm not surprised it's him."

"Do you think he requested the assignment because of you?"

"If you mean so I think the guy is chasing me across the galaxy because he's lovesick, then no. We were never anything but a fling. I'm sure part of him was relieved when he found out I'd shipped out. I saved us both from any awkward conversations."

Ariana didn't look so convinced. "If you say so, but I think you're downplaying your appeal. Any guy would kill to be with you."

I smiled at her, knowing that she fully believed that. "Thanks, but I can be a lot. Not everyone wants a woman as stubborn and bossy as me."

Ariana picked up her fork and stabbed a blue, potato-like vegetable that was cut into cubes. "Then they're the idiots, and if this Gorman guy isn't coming here to tell you that you ruined his life by leaving him and he's thought of nothing but you since that night, then he's also a fool."

I laughed, my friend's blind loyalty cheering me up. I could count on Ariana to make me feel better about myself. She'd been my biggest cheerleader since we'd met on our first day at the Academy. Being the only two human female instructors at the school had created an instant bond, and her willingness to play me at cards even when I almost always won had created another.

"I hope that's not why he's coming. The last thing I need is to deal with is having to tell him that our night together was just that—one night."

Ariana wrinkled her nose. "So, he wasn't very good?" She had her fork halfway to her mouth and she vigorously wiggled her pinky in the air. "Not very impressive, if you know what I mean?"

I rolled my eyes. "I think the Drexians across the room know what you mean."

Ariana cast a look over her shoulder then swung back around. "I don't think any Drexian would connect something as small as my pinky finger with their very large—"

I held up one palm to stop her from revealing any detail about Lieutenant Volten. He might be her boyfriend, but I still had to work with the guy. "There wasn't any issue with that, but as good looking as he is, there wasn't enough chemistry."

Ariana bit into the blue cube and chewed it thoughtfully. She swallowed and pointed her fork at me. "What I'm hearing is he's hot."

I groaned even though I couldn't help grinning. "I guess he's hot, but in a very buttoned up way. Nothing like the Drexians." My mind traitorously went to Vyk and how he'd looked anything but controlled as he'd eyed me last night.

"Too bad." Ariana sighed. "I was hoping to be able to finesse a romance for you since none of the Drexians here are your type." She held up a finger. "Except for Vyk, and you can't stand him."

I considered telling Ariana about the bet I'd made with Vyk, but that would provoke so many questions. Questions I didn't know how to answer. Not yet. Once I'd done my time with Vyk, I would tell my friend everything. Not that there would be anything to tell.

"Speak of the devil." Ariana's gaze drifted over my head to the doorway, and my heart beat erratically as I turned to watch Vyk step inside, scan the rows of wooden tables, and lock eyes with me. Then he walked toward me without lowering his hot gaze.

"Fucking hell," Ariana said under her breath. "He looks...well, like he wants to kill you or—"

"Commander Vyk," I said sharply, so I could drown out her words before he heard them. "I was telling Ariana how I lost all my credits to you last night."

Ariana slid her confused gaze to me but nodded along. "Congrats on the win, Commander."

If he'd been planning on discussing the terms of our bet in front of her, I hoped my statement had dissuaded him. He glanced from me to Ariana and back. "I wished to speak to you about...."

"The upcoming inspection by Earth Planetary Defense?" I added quickly.

He hesitated for only a beat before giving me a curt nod. "That's right. Are you available to meet later?"

My heart pounded as I held his gaze. If I'd thought he might not collect in short order, I was very mistaken. "Later works."

He gave us both swift nods before pivoting on his heel and striding away.

Ariana released a breath. "I would not mention hooking up with the inspector to *him*."

"Not a chance." I allowed myself to breathe normally.

Vyk already did not have a great opinion of humans, so there was no way I was going to give him any more reason to think I was less disciplined or less worthy than my Drexian colleagues. I would just add this to the long list of secrets I was keeping.

CHAPTER
SEVENTEEN

Vyk

I paced across the floor in my quarters, hating myself for more reasons than I was willing to admit. I had not told Fiona how to find my quarters, although I had a feeling that an Assassin instructor would have no problem securing that information. I had also not specified a time, which meant that I had been waiting alone in my spartan quarters since I had finished dinner.

Stopping at the foot of my bed, I gave a cursory glance around the space. As the academy's security chief, I had been granted larger quarters than most of the staff. It wasn't as large as the Academy Master's suite, but it dwarfed the dormitory rooms that housed the cadets and even the regular staff quarters.

Like the rest of the school, the walls and floor were black stone, which sucked up the light and any warmth that attempted to linger. It was why I kept the fire burning in the hearth that was inset in one of the ebony walls. At least the artificial flames sent golden light dancing across the ceiling, although the heat from the cavorting fire could only be felt if you stood close, which I often did.

I walked to the fire now and held out my hands, letting my palms absorb the warmth and allowing the hypnotic sight of the flames calm me.

She would come. She had agreed to come. Not only that, she had lost a bet, and I sensed that the captain was the kind who always paid her debts.

Despite my original hostility toward the humans at the academy, and especially toward the females, I had noted that they were honorable and diligent. Not a single human had displayed any of the weakness I had expected. None of them had complained that the academy was too tough or that the accommodations were too stark or the distance from Earth was too great. None of them had been at all what I had anticipated.

Especially not her.

I had been watching Fiona since the first time we had met, and she had ended up storming away from me. I had been startled that she had not shown me the deference I was due, but I was even more shocked when she'd put me soundly in my place.

"I don't have any idea who you are, but where I come from, respect isn't handed out like candy. If you want me to respect you, then you'd better respect me." Her words still rung in my ears. Then she'd mumbled something about a Grandad and had flounced away, leaving me to stare after her and try fruitlessly not to ogle her twisting ass.

From that moment on, I'd kept a close watch on her. I'd seen her glare daggers at me during the all-staff meetings. I'd watched her give me dismissive side-eye glances at academy dinners. And I'd been on the receiving end of murderous stares after the trials. And with each dark look, I'd become more and more fascinated by the woman.

It was rare that anyone challenged me. I was accustomed to Drexians falling in step behind my orders and shuffling aside to let me pass when I strode through the corridors. But Fiona did none of that. She was not afraid of me, and it was not because she hadn't heard my reputation. She was an instructor in the School of Strategy. She would have done her research on me. But still, she refused to shrink from me, and that was intriguing.

Being curious did not mean that I wanted anything more from her than answers. I only wished to know how she alone did not fear me. That was all.

I had vowed never to take a human as a mate. I had promised myself that I would never trust another human female. They were too capricious, too unreliable, too indecisive. But none of those words would describe Fiona.

I turned to warm up my back, sweeping my gaze across the space that held little besides my large bed draped in gunmetal gray, a pair of armchairs angled to face the fire, and a bare desk. As I looked at my quarters through eyes not my own, I was struck by how unwelcoming it appeared. Aside from the fire, there was nothing that could be considered inviting.

With a grunt of frustration, I crossed to the bed and snatched one of the pillows from the top. I used both hands to punch the sides in an attempt to fluff it up. I returned it to its place, moderately pleased that it was no longer flat. I seized the other and clapped the sides with even more vigor. Fluffy pillows were not much, but they were something.

I tossed the pillow up and crushed the sides together with both open palms, but instead of puffing up like it had seconds earlier, the seam on one end popped. Bits of fluff exploded into the air, flying up and then drifting down, as I stood in shock at the white down that was snowing down onto my bed and floor.

"*Grekking* hell," I growled, as I blew away a bit of fluff that had landed in my open mouth. My quarters might have been stark, but at least they had been clean. Now it looked like a flock of birds had exploded inside my room.

I desperately swept my hands across the bed to gather all the loose down, hurrying to the attached bathroom and peeling the feathery poofs off my now-damp palms and into the trash. The rest, I kicked under my bed, hoping that she would have no reason to look down.

My heart pounded as I rubbed my hands down the front of my pants, then groaned and attempted to flick off the fluff I'd deposited onto my dark uniform pants. How was it possible that I was more nervous about Fiona coming to my quarters than I was about going into the deadliest of battles?

I snorted out a rough, garbled laugh. "Give me an attacking Kronock fleet any day."

I knew how to handle a direct assault by an enemy combatant. Females were another matter entirely.

My door beeped, alerting me that there was someone on the other side. At least she had not pounded her fist. That was a good sign, wasn't it?

I shook out my arms as I went to the door and pressed my palm to the side panel. When it slid open, I was ready for the woman on the other side.

I was not ready for her hard gaze to land on me and soften before the edges of her mouth quivered. Was she fighting off the urge to laugh?

Fiona stepped forward and raised her hand to my face. Instinctively, I caught her wrist and held it.

She raised her eyebrows, but she didn't try to wrench her arm from my grasp. "You don't trust very easily, do you?"

"I am a security chief for a warrior academy that was once sabotaged from within."

She held my gaze as I held her wrist, the steady thrumming of her pulse sending heat up my arm. Then she tipped her head to one side. "Do I look like the enemy?"

I could not tell her that she looked very much like the creature who had damaged me more than any Kronock. I could not tell her that I feared that damage more than any broken bone or bloody gash.

We breathed together for a few moments before I slowly uncoiled my fingers from her wrist, my gaze never leaving hers. Instead of dropping her hand, she gently touched the side of my face and then pulled it back and held up a puff of white fuzz. "I like the silver, but you're not ready to go full Santa Claus yet."

I took the fluff she dropped in my hand and remained motionless as she sidled past me into my room. What was a Santa Claus?

CHAPTER
EIGHTEEN

Fiona

T'd come to Vyk's quarters ready to unload on him. I'd even had a list of grievances ready to list out, starting with his outrageous demand that I spend the night with him. Then he'd opened the door with his usual stern expression and bits of white down stuck to his beard. It had been impossible to stay livid when the guy looked like he'd buffed his cheeks with a gosling.

I couldn't imagine how the stuff had gotten there, since I could tell from even the most cursory of glances that his quarters contained nothing that wasn't black or dark gray. But I also couldn't pretend that it wasn't there. It would be like letting a woman walk around with a strip of toilet paper clinging to the bottom of her shoe. It wasn't in me to ignore it.

When I reached up to brush it from his face, he'd reacted as if I was going to strike him. I froze, choosing not to struggle. One, he was considerably bigger and stronger than me. I could already tell from the strength of his grip that he could shatter my wrist if he wanted. But I also didn't want him to think I was a threat. I thought about reminding him that he was the one who had requested—no, required—my presence, but that seemed overly aggressive, considering my position.

I searched his eyes, noting for the first time that they held traces of fear, although I had no idea why the Drexian would ever fear me. "You don't trust very easily, do you?"

He did not glance away. "I am a security chief for a warrior school that our enemy would love to destroy."

I steadied my breath, even though the touch of his flesh was sending tingles across my skin. It was all I could do not to imagine the gruff warrior holding both of my wrists as he pinned me to the bed. Instead, I tilted my head. "Do I look like the enemy?"

For a moment, I thought he might say yes. His gaze roamed my face, as if searching for treachery. I didn't know all of Vyk's story, but it was clear the guy had been through enough shit to make him suspect everyone, even a woman half his size. I wondered if the fact that he had been part of a plot at the academy against humans made him even more wary of me. Did he think I'd been biding my time to take revenge on him?

Come to think of it, that wouldn't have been a bad idea, if I was the vengeance type. But grudges had never been my style. If I'd held onto grievances as I'd worked my way through the military, I would have been nothing but a ball of fury held together with hairbands and mascara. It wasn't that I didn't remember what the commander had done, but I wasn't willing to let it eat me up.

As if he'd finally realized that he could snap my wrist if he sneezed too hard, Vyk released my arm. I reached over and plucked the fuzz that had snagged onto his beard, being careful to be gentle and not make sudden movements. I handed it to him. "I like the silver, but you're not ready to go full Santa Claus yet."

Then I slipped past him into his quarters, heading straight for the fireplace. I guess being the security chief had its perks, or maybe all the Drexian staff members had bigger rooms than mine. All I knew was that the rooms in the female tower where all the human women stayed did not have fireplaces with sitting areas like this.

I released a contented hum as I stood facing the flames. If I'd known he had a fireplace, I might not have been so reluctant to come, although I wasn't going to say that out loud. I also wasn't going to tell him that his fireplace reminded me of a smaller version of the one in Admiral Zoran's hidden study. That would mean explaining why I was there—to improve my card game—who had taken me—the Admiral's adjunct, and who had given his approval—Admiral Zoran himself.

I slowly spun to warm my backside. Only then did I see that Vyk sat in one of the chairs facing the fire watching me. I bit back a sharp comment. It wasn't like there were lots of seating options. The room might be bigger than mine, but it wasn't cavernous.

"What is a Santa Claus?"

His question caught me off guard, and I blinked at him a few times. "What?" Then I remembered that I'd told him he wasn't ready to go full Santa Claus, forgetting that the Drexians didn't have Christmas or Santa. "Oh, it's an Earth thing. He's a fat elf with a white beard."

He scowled. "You think I could be a fat elf?" He drummed his fingers on the arm of the chair. "What is an elf?"

I exhaled. I hadn't thought I'd be explaining human customs like Santa, and I hadn't known how hard they were to explain without any context. "It depends on your preference. If you want to go with the Christmas version, they're short little creatures who wear pointy shoes. Except for Santa, who is inexplicably chubby and human-sized. Or you could go with the Tolkien version, in which case elves are tall, immortal, and incredibly hot. Oh, and both versions have pointy ears."

He stared at me. "You are making this up."

I laughed and shook my head. "I am not. Ask anyone. I mean, ask any human." When his glower didn't fade, I added, "I only meant that the white fluff made your beard look white, like Santa. That's all."

He grunted and gave a curt nod. "Earth is a strange place."

"Sometimes, but I'll bet Drexians have customs that seem normal to you but would seem weird to an outsider."

"We do not."

His certainty that his culture made total sense should have annoyed me, but it only made me laugh more. "Whatever you say."

I didn't know why the guy was so hostile and defensive. He was the one who'd wanted me to come to his quarters. I slid my gaze to his bed and the one fluffy pillow and the one deflated one. Suddenly, I understood the source of the white fluff. "You want to tell me what the pillow did to piss you off?"

Vyk jerked his head to the pillow that still had remnants of its insides poking out the frayed end. He emitted a low sound of frustration.

I got the sensation of being locked in a cage with a wild animal who'd been agitated. All that was missing was him stalking back and forth with a tail twitching. Since I had no intention of being pounced on, I decided to change the rules of the game.

"Our deal was that I would owe you three nights. I don't know about you, but I usually sleep at night." I kicked off one boot and then the other as I sauntered toward the bed. "I don't like overly filled pillows anyway, so I'll take the flat one."

I tugged back the gray blanket and slipped into the bed, curling to the side and facing away from Vyk. I was taking a huge chance by turning my back on someone who was big enough to overpower me in a heartbeat, but for some bizarre reason, I was sure that he was more afraid of me. I closed my eyes and forced myself to ignore the sounds of him standing and moving toward the bed.

Had I made another bad gamble?

CHAPTER
NINETEEN

Vyk

I watched Fiona slip under my blanket and flip her body to face away from me, tucking her bent arm under her head. Was she truly planning to sleep? I took determined steps toward her, stopping when I reached the side of the bed. Now that I stood over her peaceful form, her body rising and falling as she breathed deeply, I wasn't sure what to do.

What had I expected her to do after requiring her to spend the night with me? I had promised that I would not force myself on her, and it was true that I had no intention of doing that. I had never used force for a female's pleasure, and I never would. But I had never thought Fiona would arrive and crawl into my bed to sleep.

I stood watching her, unable to think of a single thing to do in response. I could get in bed next to her, but I was too restless to contemplate sleep. She had made me restless. Anticipating her arrival, worrying she would not come, and then reacting to her unexpected touch had left me wired and jumpy.

I could sit by the fire until my nerves calmed. And then what? Would I watch her sleep? Would I sleep in a chair like a parent keeping an eye on a child? I grunted at this, not enjoying the reminder that I was old enough to be Fiona's father. Since Drexians lived longer than humans and aged slower, I could probably be her grandfather, but that was something I would never admit.

I lifted a hand, reaching for the golden hair that spilled across the dark pillow. As much as I wanted to touch it, run my fingers through it, tangle my hands in it, I hesitated. Fiona had no idea that she drove me to the edge of reason. She had no clue that thoughts of her consumed my mind. I needed to keep it that way.

It was all too clear that she did not share my feelings, and that she was only in my quarters to fulfill her end of the bargain. She had no interest in shedding her beliefs about me or discovering that I might not be as cruel or brutal as the tales would lead her to believe. And I could not bear the rejection of another female, another human who found me lacking. The battles might not break me, but Fiona rejecting me would.

I snatched my hand back and curled it into a fist. It had been so long since my tribute bride had rejected me and chosen to be unmatched, but the years had not dulled the pain. My heart twisted as I tried to purge the dark memories that rushed to the surface. The years should have blurred the memories of the beautiful human and the fear in her eyes as she'd shaken her head and declared that she would never be my mate. But they hadn't. Her face was just as clear in my mind, and the stabbing pain in my chest was just as fresh, still making my breath catch as her words rang in my ears.

I pressed a hand to my heart and turned away. I had barely known the woman who had been chosen for me back then when I was a young, brash Inferno Force warrior. All I'd known was that she was beautiful and desirable and would be eager to be my mate, like all human women were when presented with a brave Drexian warrior. I almost choked on a bitter laugh. I had been painfully young.

"Maybe age has not made you much wiser," I grumbled under my breath as I glanced back at the woman I'd tricked into my bed.

The only glimmer of hope was that Fiona was nothing like the woman who had supposedly been my ideal match. For one, Fiona would never have been a tribute bride. She was too focused on her career, too high up in her planet's military, too connected. But that was not what drew me to her. Fiona did not look at me with fear in her eyes. She never had. She had never trembled in my presence or looked at me like I was a monster.

She had looked at me like she would like to kill me, but I preferred hate to fear. Hate was passion. I could work with hate.

The pain in my chest was not only an ache, but my thoughts continued to swirl. I would not be able to sleep like this, and watching another sleep was not something I enjoyed, especially if it only reminded me what I would rather be doing with them. What I had sworn not to even attempt.

Fiona's breath had deepened and lengthened. She was asleep. I did not want to dwell on how the female could fall asleep in my bed without a second thought. As glad as I was that she did not fear me, this made me think I might be going too soft.

I strode to the door, pressing my hand to the side panel and stepping into the hallway after it glided open. I did not pause as I took purposeful steps through the silent corridors of the slumbering school, jogging down twisting stairways and keeping my gaze fixed ahead as I crossed stone bridges between towers. My boots echoed off the vaulted ceilings, the sound dissipating once I passed through the main hall and its soaring ceiling.

I did not flick my gaze to the stone arch above the entrance to the School of Battle. It might not have been my school when I had been a cadet, but I knew it well. I had many Blade friends who had challenged me on the sparring mats. They were one of the reasons I had been ready for the challenges of Inferno Force. Between my battle skills and my engineering prowess, I had been a formidable asset to the elite fighting team.

It was muscle memory that led me to the tall, arched doorway. It was not that sparring mats I needed now. I stepped inside the darkened room, my heavy breath echoing back to me. I breathed in the distinctive scent of chalk and sweat, as memories from my cadet days rushed over me. Brushing my hand across the lighting panel, I gazed at the climbing walls towering over me. My fingers twitched in anticipation of gripping the holds.

When I climbed, there was no space in my brain to think of anything but the next hold. There was no time to dwell on regrets when one misstep could send me hurtling to the ground. There was no thinking about the woman asleep in my bed, wondering what I had been thinking, or why I would even consider trusting another human with my heart.

I plunged my hands into the round holes in the wall and waited for powdered chalk to be diffused onto them. Then I pulled them out and clapped them as I crossed to the wall, sending tiny white particles flying into the air. Time to stop thinking.

I swung my arm onto a high hold and hoisted my body flat against the wall. "Climb on."

CHAPTER
TWENTY

Fiona

he light flickered behind my eyelids, and I snuggled deeper beneath the blanket. It got cold at the cabin, which was why I liked to sleep around the fire in the living room with my younger brother. We would set up our sleeping bags so our heads would face each other and then we would stay up whispering long after our parents scolded us for not going to sleep.

My brother would always drift off first, even though he insisted each time that he wouldn't. I didn't care. I just cared that Jack was with me, and sometimes I'd keep whispering to him long after his breaths had become snores. I slipped one hand from the warmth of my cocoon to touch his head, but my hand only touched something hard and cold. I felt around without opening my eyes, sure I'd feel his mass of curls, but there was nothing. He wasn't there.

I jerked up quickly, my heart racing as I gasped, the truth rushing back to me in a punch to the gut that knocked the breath from me. Of course, he wasn't there. He hadn't been there for over a decade.

I clamped a hand over my mouth to keep from crying out as my gaze swept the room. I wasn't in the cabin. I was in Vyk's quarters at the Drexian Academy. The last time I'd seen him, the commander had been by the fire, but now he was nowhere to be seen. I dropped my hand as the heart rate slowed, grateful that he wasn't there to see my confusion and grief.

I raked a hand through my hair as I swung my feet from the bed and to the floor. The cool stone was bracing even through my socks, but I welcomed the shock. Anything to bring me back to the present. Dwelling in the past, as lovely as it seemed at the time, only meant pain when I returned to reality and realized that Jack would never be there again.

Now that I had shrugged off my dream, I took a deep breath and straightened. Where was Vyk? I must have been asleep for a while. I never dreamed about my brother until I was in a deep sleep, and it rarely happened anymore. Only when I was exhausted and stressed—or both. Having to come to Vyk's quarters and discovering that my former colleague—and one-night-stand—was en route to the academy had been a one-two punch that had brought my childhood memories out in full force.

Whatever happiness I experienced by remembering Jack was fleeting and almost instantly obliterated by the crushing weight of sadness that now tinged all my childhood memories.

Even the most joyful recollections were painful because they were a reminder that he'd been snatched from us too young. It was why when I'd left home, I'd gone far away and rarely ever returned. It was easier to forget if I didn't have to see the place where we'd grown up and walk by the room my mother had preserved, his racecar comforter pristine and his trophies faithfully dusted.

"Time to get the hell out of here," I muttered to myself, as I shoved my feet into my boots. It didn't matter where Vyk was. I'd done what I'd promised. I'd stayed in his quarters for the night. Now it was time to hope no one spotted me as I slipped out and slunk back to the female tower.

I stomped my feet to jam my feet deeper into my boots as I made my way to the door, looking down the whole way. I was so focused on my feet that I didn't notice the door slide open until I'd walked into a wall. But it wasn't a wall of rock, like most of the academy, it was a wall of muscle.

Looking up, I stepped back, trod on my boot's laces and started to fall.

Vyk reached out and grabbed me by the arms before I hit the floor. He righted me before he let go, then he eyed me. "You were leaving?"

It was impossible to ignore the fact that the commander wasn't wearing a shirt as he stood in the open doorway, blocking me from escape. His chest looked as solid and muscular as it had when I'd walked into it. There was a black cord necklace hanging from his neck that had always been obscured by his uniform and a swirling tattoo covering one side of his chest that looked like flames chasing more flames.

"Fiona?"

Him saying my name snapped me to attention, and I tore my gaze from his bare skin. I squared my shoulders. "Yes, I'm leaving. It's morning."

"It's the middle of the night."

I opened my mouth to argue with him but then I stole a glance at the window in his quarters and the moonless, inky sky. Why hadn't I noticed that before?

Because you were too distracted by your memories of Jack.

I shook this off and folded my arms over my chest. "I woke up, you were gone, so I thought I might as well leave." Then I noticed the sweat rolling down his neck to the hollow of his throat and a strange sensation pulsed through me. "Where were you getting so sweaty in the middle of the night?"

He met my gaze, his mouth curving slightly. "Would you rather I stayed here and got sweaty?"

I opened my mouth in outrage, then closed it, then opened it again. "No, of course not."

He stepped closer so I had to tip my head back to keep eye contact. "You are sure?"

There was no way in hell I was going to admit that he looked good enough to devour or that sweaty guys were a turn-on for me. Just like I was never going to tell him that the thought of him getting sweaty with someone else made me want to go on a rampage. I could despise the guy and still find him hot. I could know that he was off-limits to me while also hating the thought of any other woman touching him.

I put a hand on his bare chest and pushed hard enough that I could sidle past him. "I'm absolutely sure."

"I was on the climbing wall," he said, as I stepped into the corridor.

I hesitated and pivoted to face him, relief making my shoulders uncoil. I glanced at his back and the raised bumps running along his spine, fighting the urge to reach out and touch one. Don't even think about it, I told myself before tearing my gaze away. I couldn't think of anything sensible to say, and he still looked slightly amused by me, which was annoying as fuck.

"Next time, I will stay in the room, so you do not get jealous."

"I was not..." I spluttered, but he was already turning and unfastening his pants as he headed toward his bathroom, giving me a full view of his muscular back and the long column of nodes that ran the length of it. I didn't wait for him to drop his pants before I spun away and stormed off down the hall. "Infuriating, arrogant Drexian."

I rubbed my fingers together where they'd touched his slick chest, my skin betraying me by tingling. It wasn't lost on me that he'd said "next time," and it wasn't lost on me that I didn't mind.

CHAPTER
TWENTY-ONE

Vyk

I could not reach the shower fast enough, shedding my clothes as quickly as I could, flipping on the water, and stepping behind the stone half-wall before it warmed. The cool stream poured down my shoulders as I planted my palms on the wall and bowed my head.

I opened my eyes to see if the spot on my chest where Fiona's hand had made contact had left a mark; not from the force but from the heat that had seared into me from her touch. Not even the woman who had been matched to me long ago and was supposed to be my ideal mate had provoked such a powerful reaction in me. I touched my chest, relishing the buzz even as the water cascaded over me and cooled my skin.

The water was gradually warming, and I slid my hand down the length of my body until I could fist my cock. The climbing wall had been an excellent distraction, but it could only do so much to burn off the tension that had been building inside me all day. If I was being truthful, the tension that had been building since I'd made the wager.

I groaned as I squeezed the base and felt my cock thicken even more. I was desperate for any release, even if it was not the touch I craved. I stroked my hand up and down my shaft as I closed my eyes and allowed my mind to wander. And it wandered right back to Fiona.

This time I stood beside the bed and did not walk away. This time, I tossed back the blanket. Fiona rolled over so that she was on her back, but she did not scream at me or sit up and slap me. She arched a brow and smiled, before nibbling her bottom lip.

"*Grek* me," I husked, as even the thought of Fiona looking at me with anything less than rage made me nearly explode.

I curled the hand that remained on the stone wall, fisting it as I stroked my cock with my other hand and imagined a different Fiona. A Fiona who did not hate me, did not believe I reviled humans, did not know of my involvement in the trials. This Fiona still had the challenge in her eyes, but not the fury.

"What are you waiting for?" Her voice was a purr as she reached for me and pulled me on top of her.

In this alternate reality, I did not hesitate. I did not worry about old fears, new conflicts, or the ramifications of seducing a colleague. I only cared about that moment, and for that moment, that completely fabricated moment, she was mine.

I crushed my mouth to hers, startled by the softness of her lips and the eagerness of her tongue. Even in my imagination, Fiona was challenging me, which sent hot pulses of desire pounding through me. When her soft moans matched mine, when she arched her back so that her breasts pushed against my chest, and when she curled one hand around my neck to pull me closer, my cock throbbed.

Squeezing my eyes tight as I slid my hand faster down my slippery, rigid length, I allowed myself to surrender to the fantasy, a fantasy I had little hope of ever realizing. Not when the woman could not speak to without spitting fire.

But the Fiona in my mind pulled back and whispered in my ear, *"I hope you made that wager because you wanted to fuck me."*

I managed a mangled sound.

She let out a husky laugh. "Because I want you to fuck me hard and deep, Commander."

Then I threw back my head as my cock jerked, pulsing hot against the wall as I trembled. My breath was ragged, and my legs were shaky. Even an imagined encounter with Fiona was better than most of my encounters at alien pleasure houses. The woman truly had me under her spell.

CHAPTER
TWENTY-TWO

Fiona

"Where were you last night?"

I jerked my head up as I sat at my desk studying star charts, and my cheeks warmed instantly at Ariana's question. How had I not heard her coming into my office in the School of Strategy? "What? Asleep in my quarters. Where else would I be?"

Her brows popped up high as she sat in the single chair across from me and leaned back. "Touchy, touchy. I only ask because you look like you slept in your clothes, and your hair could generously be described as windswept."

I put a hand to my hair, cursing inwardly that I'd forgotten to brush my hair. I'd actually forgotten to do a lot of things, since

I'd come directly to my office from Vyk's quarters. There had been no point in going back to my quarters, not when I'd known full well I wouldn't be able to fall asleep. Not after that dream. I could never sleep after dreaming about Jack.

It hadn't helped that Vyk had walked in all sweaty, making me wonder where he'd been and even getting irate that he might have been with someone else. That, of course, was ridiculous. There were scant few females at the academy, and the only ones who weren't taken were cadets. He would never go for a cadet, and I knew for a fact that every female cadet was too terrified of the imposing Drexian to even look straight at him, much less sleep with him.

So, why had my mind instantly gone to that? Did I truly believe that every male was incapable of loyalty? Did I think they were all like my dad, so weak that they would run off when things got tough? That was what my father had done after Jack had died. My mother had been consumed with grief, and my dad had been determined to move on, which he did with a younger woman who wasn't always sad. He'd moved on from Jack, from my mom, and from me. And I had never forgiven him for any of it.

I dragged a hand through my hair as I gave my head a shake and tried to rid my mind of thoughts of the past that had been bombarding me since I'd woken. "I didn't sleep well, so I came here early to work." That much was true.

Ariana sat forward, her eyes pinching together. "Is everything okay?"

My friend's genuine concern made my throat tighten. I might have a hard time trusting guys, but I had never been betrayed by one of my female friends. It had always been other women who had gotten me through rough patches, and I knew I could rely on Ariana no matter what. If only I could tell her about Vyk and our deal and the dark emotions it was stirring up.

But I'd made him promise not to breathe a word, and I owed him the same discretion. Besides, there was nothing happening between us, and nothing ever would.

When I didn't answer right away, Ariana glanced over her shoulder to the open door, as if someone might be lingering outside the door and listening, which I seriously doubted. It was still early, and there were no classes and almost no cadets left to wander the halls. "Is it the visit from that inspector from Earth? The one you slept with and ditched?"

"I didn't ditch him," I protested, even though the words sounded hollow to my own ears. "It was a one-night deal. We were both clear on that. He never expected anything more."

"Mmmhmm." Ariana sat back again. "And it's just a coincidence that he's the one coming to check on the integration of humans at the academy."

"It could be. Like I said, he was involved with the program."

Ariana flicked her short, red fingernails through her hair. "And you're sure there isn't anything between you, any potential for something?"

I shook my head before giving her questions any real consideration. It didn't matter if there was potential with Devon, or if he was exactly the kind of steady, successful guy I should be going after. I had zero interest in long-term relationships. I'd seen how they ended. I preferred my encounters to be fast and fun, with no chance of heartbreak.

Ariana held up her hands in mock surrender. "Okay, then I hope for your sake that this Devon guy feels the same way you do, and he's not coming here expecting you two to pick up right where you left off. I hope he hasn't been pining away for the best sex of his life since you snuck from his bedroom and hopped a transport to the Drexian Academy."

I groaned. "Hardly. This guy is a captain who can get any woman he wants and often does. I wasn't his first fling, and I can guarantee you I wasn't his last. I'd be surprised if he's thought about me at all since I left."

"Yep," Ariana deadpanned. "You are exactly the kind of woman that men forget—tall, blonde, drop-dead gorgeous, stacked and rocking a great ass."

I grinned at her. "You think my ass is great? I'm touched."

She rolled her eyes. "If I notice your ass, you can bet that every guy who walks by you does. I think you forget how hot you really are, Fi."

"And I think you've very biased, but I appreciate it."

She shook her head. "Think what you want, but I will eat of bowl of those slimy Drexian popping things if this inspector from Earth isn't still into you."

Considering my recent luck with wagers, I really should have known better, but my competitive nature made it possible for me not to bite, especially when I was just as certain that Devon would be all business when he arrived. "I'll take that bet."

"And if I'm right, and he's still into you?"

"I'll eat a bowl of the slimy popping things." Even as I said it, I shuddered. "But trust me, you're going to be the one digging in."

Ariana wrinkled her nose. "You'll be honest, right? You won't try to hide it if he's still interested, will you? I really hate those jiggling poppers."

"You know I would never lie to you." I put a hand on my heart and met her gaze, meaning every word. "I might like to play hard, but I never cheat."

Ariana released a breath. "I know." Then her smile returned. "Do we know when he arrives? I hate having the possibility of eating that disgusting dish hanging over my head."

I actually didn't know, but I suspected it would be soon. "Don't worry. I won't make you eat a big bowl."

She stood and walked to the door. "Trust me, Fi. It's not going to be me, but I'll go easy on you, too. I'll ask the kitchen for ones that aren't as jumpy."

I swallowed, trying not to think of choking down the Drexian dish comprised of still-moving, snail-like creatures. I honestly wasn't sure which was worse—the arriving captain wanting to resume some sort of relationship or having to eat the hoppers.

Once Ariana had left, I slumped into my chair and released a breath. I hadn't been successful at focusing on my work, so maybe I should take my friend's not so subtle hint and go shower. I might not want Devon to be into me, but I didn't want to look like a hot mess when he arrived.

The heavy footsteps outside my still-open door made my pulse trip. They did not belong to Ariana, that much I knew for sure. Who had tracked me down to my office?

CHAPTER
TWENTY-THREE

Vyk

My hair was still damp on the collar of my shirt as I left my quarters. I'd dressed in a hurry, barely shoving the dark shirt into my uniform pants and jamming my feet into the boots I'd kicked off before stomping down the corridor. The lights in the sconces flickered, sending shadows twisting along the black stone since there was no sunlight peeking in through narrow windows yet.

It was early, but I could not wait. I needed to find Fiona. I needed to talk to her.

I raced down a flight of stairs, my feet barely touching the worn rock, determined to find her and determined to explain myself. Her visit to my quarters—her first night with me—had not gone according to plan. Not that I had planned how it would go, when the female who was forced to spend time with me because she lost a wager arrived. How did you plan that?

I had not even planned on making such an outrageous bet, but I had and then she had lost. Which meant she would be spending more time in my quarters. More time I had no idea how to fill.

I clenched my teeth as I thought about what I'd said to her when she'd asked me where I'd been.

Next time, I will stay in the room, so you do not get jealous.

I had actually accused her of being jealous when she had made it very clear I was the last Drexian she would ever be with. Of course, she had called me arrogant because I sounded every bit the overconfident warrior convinced of my own superiority. I sounded like exactly what she most despised.

I crossed the main hall, grateful that I did not encounter anyone. Not that many staff members would be up so early. Not when there were no classes to teach or cadets to corral. The time between terms was a respite for instructors and staff, although it seemed to be just as fraught and difficult for me.

Did I know how to be a part of a team without ruling with an iron fist? It had been a long time since I had been a Drexian who was not known for being ruthless and deadly. My ferocity was what had given me my reputation in Inferno Force, and it was a reputation I was loathe to abandon. Without it, I would go back to being a no-status Drexian who was rejected by the tribute bride matched to him, and I wanted to forget that version of myself forever.

That Drexian had not been worthy. He had been cast aside. Even now, the memory stung.

"That was the past," I reminded myself as I took another staircase two steps at a time. "Fiona is not her."

Not only was the Strategy instructor not the tribute bride who had rejected me, she could not be held responsible for my dislike and distrust of human women that sprung from that rejection. It was no more her fault than it was any female currently at the academy.

Shedding long-held prejudices was not so simple or so easy, but it had to be done. It was those beliefs that had made me an easy target for High Commanders who needed a co-conspirator and scapegoat for their plan of sabotaging the trials, and it was the same backward thinking that had made Fiona despise me. If I wanted her to see me differently, I needed to apologize.

The wind whipping across the open-air bridge between towers cooled the wet tendrils of hair at the nape of my neck and sent a shiver down my spine. I could see the hint of sunlight teasing the horizon, but a chill clung hungrily to the night air, unwilling to release it until the light burned it off in a burst of gold.

Once I'd entered the female tower, I hesitated. I had never entered the domain of the human women. I had never needed to do so, but I felt compelled to speak to Fiona. I needed to explain everything to her so she would not think of me as a monster for one more moment.

With a deep breath, I raced up the stairs to the first landing where I knew her quarters to be, and located her room. I didn't hesitate to rap on the door, knowing that if I allowed myself to think about it, I would lose my courage. There was no answer, so I rapped again. Nothing.

Frustration surged through me. Where was she? Then fear tickled the base of my spine. Had she not gotten back to her room safely? I cursed myself for letting her run off in the night. The academy was deserted. There should be no danger, but it was the academy. There was always some amount of danger.

My heart pounded as I thundered down the stairs and back across the stone bridge, ignoring the blowing wind and the growing light in the sky. I did not slow my pace to drag in a deep breath of salty air. I did not even glance at the sun touching the Restless Sea.

Where would she have gone if not to her room? I practically ran through the silent hallways, the sound of my boots slapping stone echoing back to me, as I made my way down into the bowels of the main building to the kitchens.

"Has a human been here?" I barked at the cooks who were kneading bread and stirring vats of steaming stew. "A female with gold hair?"

There were startled shakes of heads and mumbled assurances that she had not been there. But Fiona had not been a cadet at the academy. Sneaking food from the kitchens was not something she would have known to do. It was something a Drexian would do, a Drexian like me who had spent years at the academy and had found solace in nabbing extra bread.

"Where would a human go?" I asked myself as I trudged back up the stairs, flicking a glance at a dank corridor leading to the dungeons. She would *not* go there, especially after her tirade at me about keeping a remaining beast below. "So where?"

From what I knew of Fiona, she worked hard and was devoted to her friends. If she was not in her quarters, she would either be working or she would be with one of the other females, most likely Ariana. But Ariana would have been asleep when Fiona left my quarters. Fiona would not have awakened her, especially if it meant explaining why she was up.

By the time I reached the main hall again, there was movement in the school. One of the inclinators swirled down from the top of the spiraling hall, and a Blade instructor nodded at me as he strode toward the entrance to his school. I did not go up the wide stairs to my own office. Instead, I passed under the stone arch with the emblem of a mask speared with a dagger carved into it, and I walked with determined steps down the wide hallway leading to the School of Strategy.

It was time to come clean with the Assassin.

CHAPTER
TWENTY-FOUR

Volten

I stretched my arms overhead as my boots slapped the stone walkway leading to the shipyard. The morning light was barely warming the sky, and the air still carried the chill of the night. I sucked in another breath, grateful for the fresh air, then I hesitated as I picked up the scent of freshly fired fuel.

My pace instantly slowed as I scanned the rows of ships and recognized a transport that had not been there the day before. I had been briefed on the arrival of the Drexian ship carrying the human envoy, but I had not anticipated it arriving so early.

I drew myself up to my full height when I spotted the figure walking toward me. It had been so long since I had seen someone not in academy uniform or the school-issued workout clothes that I tilted my head at his mismatched black pants and brown shirt. The hat that perched on his short hair seemed peculiar for a warrior, and I could not imagine the purpose of wearing a flimsy, fabric head covering into battle.

"Are you the welcoming committee?" The man laughed at what I assumed was Earth humor when he reached me and extended his hand.

I remembered the human custom of gripping hands and moving them briskly, so I took his hand and jiggled it. The man's eyes widened, but I continued to wiggle my hand as I spoke.

"I am Lieutenant Volten, an instructor in the School of Flight. Welcome to the Drexian Academy."

"Volten? Then you are Drexian."

He said this as if the significant advantage I had on him in height and breadth did not make that abundantly clear. "I am."

He nodded, flicking his gaze up and down me before looking past me to the academy. "And that is the famous Drexian Academy." He laughed again. "Or maybe I should say, infamous."

I did not understand why this human was laughing so much or what was funny. I decided to ignore his odd statement "You are the envoy sent from Earth?"

He squared his shoulders. "Captain Gorman."

I did not know the salute for officers on Earth, so I thumped my fist across my chest. We were on Drex, so he would get a Drexian salute. "Welcome, Captain. We did not expect you this early or I am certain the Academy Master would have been here to greet you himself."

The captain waved this away. "I wanted to arrive early and see the school without a lot of fuss. I thought I could surprise an old friend."

"You are old friends with Admiral Zoran?" I had never heard the admiral speak about working with humans.

"No, not the admiral. I served alongside Captain Douglas."

I stared at him for a few beats as I processed the name. Captain Douglas? He meant Fiona. Since Ariana was such close friends with the Strategy instructor, I rarely thought of her as Captain Douglas anymore. As a fellow instructor, I did not address her as captain.

"She is an instructor in our School of Strategy," I said, turning and escorting him toward the entrance to the academy. "We call them Assassins."

The human glanced overhead as we walked under the high arch with the four emblems of the schools carved into the ebony stone. "That sounds like Fiona."

He laughed once more, but this time I joined him because I was starting to feel odd letting him laugh alone. We passed through the wide doors and down the entrance corridor until we reached the main hall, the captain swinging his head to look at the weapons on the walls and the vaulted ceilings.

"It is still early, and we are between terms, so our instructors do not have set schedule like we do when classes are in session," I told him once we were in the large open space with the stairs that wound up. "I do not know if the captain is in her quarters, eating breakfast, or in her office."

"It doesn't matter. I'm happy to wait for her if you point me in the direction of her office."

I was relieved he had not asked me to lead him to her quarters, so I pointed to the arch leading to the School of Strategy. "Down that corridor. I believe her office is the third door on the right."

He tipped his head to me. "Thanks, Lieutenant."

I watched him stride beneath the Assassin arch and disappear down the dimly lit corridor, nerves fluttering in my chest. I had not made a mistake in pointing him in the direction of Fiona's office, had I? Protocol would normally dictate that I take him directly to the admiral, but he had seemed eager to see Fiona.

Now that I was thinking about it, he had spoken about the captain with a good deal of familiarity. I knew little of Fiona's past, but it was clear that this envoy was a part of it.

"I'll have to ask Ariana later," I said to myself as I spun on my heel to return to the shipyard, only glancing over my shoulder when Vyk stomped through the hall toward the Assassin building, his jaw tight and his stride purposeful.

Did he already know about the captain's arrival? Did he know where the man was heading?

"That was fast." A shiver went through me as I thought that the commander really did know everything that went on in the academy.

CHAPTER
TWENTY-FIVE

Fiona

My gaze was fixed to the doorway, and my breath was lodged in my throat. I was sure it was Vyk who'd found me. I was sure he had come to give me a hard time about leaving his quarters in the middle of the night, and I was all set to argue with him about it.

The words were almost on my lips when a head poked around the doorframe. "Dev—Captain Gorman?"

The officer with short, sandy-brown hair smiled broadly as he entered the room. "Why am I not surprised to see you working so early?"

I stood, not sure whether to salute him because he'd once been my superior office or hug him because I'd once seen him naked. He was in his Navy uniform, but not his dress blues, and it didn't take much power of recollection to remember helping him quickly remove a similar pair of black pants and khaki shirt. I settled on walking around the desk and extending my hand. "You know what they say about the early bird."

He took my hand and shook it without giving me any strange looks or without trying to pull me into a hug. "I hope that the worms are only metaphorical, even at an alien academy."

"There are no worms served here, sir."

The captain gave a wave of his hand. "Please, I'm not sir, just Devon...to you."

Twinges of warmth teased my cheeks, but I assured myself that he was being friendly. Besides, before we'd ended up in bed together, we had been pretty solid colleagues. Almost verging on real friends. Of course, our drunken night together would have spoiled that if I hadn't left, but since I had, maybe we got a do-over on the friends part.

I sat on the front edge of my desk as he swiveled in place and took in my office. "I was surprised to hear that you were the Earth envoy sent to assess the human integration here."

He pulled his gaze away from the bare, black-stone walls and stacks of books and unrolled parchments scattered across my desk. "I did have involvement in the program before the first cadets and instructors were chosen. Did you know that at one point, I'd been considered for your position?"

My mouth fell open a bit. Devon had wanted to come to the Drexian Academy? He was such a fixture at the base on Earth that it never occurred to me that he had aspirations to leave it. "I had no idea."

"I ended up turning it down." He met my gaze and worked his black cap in his hands. "I guess I'm too fond of Earth." He glanced around the office. "Do you miss it?"

I tried to ignore any subtext that might be lurking beneath the surface. "A bit, but I enjoy the challenge of a new place, Captain."

He groaned. "You aren't going to call me that for my entire visit, are you? Of anyone, you should call me Devon."

I tried not to be bothered by the phrase "of anyone." We had been friends, after all, so it was natural to use first names. Honestly, it would be odd if we didn't. "And you should call me Fiona, of course."

This made him grin and his shoulders visibly relax. "I have to say, you look just the same."

I touched a hand to my hair, which I knew needed brushing, and then glanced at my rumpled clothes that had actually been slept in and my face heated. I might look just like he'd remembered me, but that was only because he'd last seen me sweaty and rolling around in bed. I wished with every fiber of my being that I didn't look like a hot mess. It would have been so much better if I could have impressed the man by looking put together and rested.

"I normally don't look this casual, but we're between terms and there are no classes taking place." I crossed my arms in front of my chest and eyed him. "I'm surprised this is when Earth wanted to send someone to inspect the program. You won't see what the academy is like when it's buzzing with cadets."

Devon shrugged on shoulder. "That's okay. This way I get to spend more time talking to the human instructors and cadets." He leaned forward and winked at me. "I get to spend more time interrogating you."

I laughed, since he was clearly teasing me. He'd always been one of the looser officers, so I wasn't sure if he was teasing me like he would anyone, or if this was about that night. Part of me was glad he hadn't mentioned it, but another part of me felt like it was the elephant in the room. Were we really going to pretend we hadn't slept together? Were we going to act like the last time I'd seen him I hadn't been tiptoeing from his bedroom while he still lay tangled in the sheets?

I spread my arms wide. "Ask me anything. I'm an open book."

He cocked his head to one side. "The enigmatic Captain Douglas is an open book? Then you have changed."

I inwardly flinched at this. Had I been difficult to get to know on Earth? I guessed it was true that I hadn't shared tons of personal information, but that wasn't unusual, especially with male colleagues. As one of the few female officers in any department in which I'd served, I had to maintain a tough exterior, or I'd be walked all over.

It wasn't so different here. I was tough and stern with cadets and around the Drexian instructors. It was only with my fellow female officers—my new friends—that I could be myself.

"I'm still the same officer I was on Earth." I sat up straighter. "But I will happily tell you anything you want to know about life and work at the Academy. That's why you're here, isn't it? To gather information about how the human cadets and instructors are faring at the alien training school."

Devon nodded, his gaze searching my face. "And how are you doing here?"

The way he phrased it made me believe that the question he was asking was much deeper and more personal. He wanted to know how *I* was, not all the humans.

I gave him a bright smile and ignored the subtext of his question. "Coming into an all-male and all-Drexian academy has not been without its challenges, but I would say that every human here has integrated well. And as you are no doubt aware, no humans were lost during the trials, and all human cadets were chosen for schools. I would call that a success."

The man nodded thoughtfully as he took a step closer to me. His legs almost brushed my knees as I perched on the edge of the desk, but there was nowhere for me to go unless I flopped backward on my desk, which seemed a bit dramatic.

"The adjustment hasn't been difficult? No one has experienced bouts of homesickness or has expressed a desire to return to Earth before they graduate?"

"None." I placed my hands behind me on the desk so I could lean away from him.

"No one regrets leaving their life behind?" His gaze bored into me, his expression no longer light and cheery. "No one regrets the way they left things?"

My stomach bottomed out. There it was. Of course, he hadn't forgotten me sneaking out and leaving the planet. Who would forget that? What red-blooded man wouldn't take that personally? I had been an absolute idiot to think that Devon would come here and not want to talk about it, not want an explanation. Running off to a planet all the way across the galaxy clearly hadn't been far enough to escape an awkward conversation about my bad behavior.

I swallowed hard as I searched for the words that would defuse the situation and ensure that his entire visit wasn't torturous. But my gaze caught on movement behind him, movement in the doorway.

Vyk took up most of the doorway with his broad arms folded over his chest. From his fierce expression, I suspected that he had heard at least part of my conversation with Devon. I was positive he'd heard the last bit, which meant he'd heard Devon asking me if I regretted the way I'd left things. Anyone with half a brain would know what the man was implying, and as much as I thought Vyk was an arrogant ass, I knew he wasn't dumb.

There was no reason I should have felt guilty as I stood with Devon in front of me waiting for an answer and Vyk watching. I owed the Drexian nothing. Then why did I feel like I'd been caught doing something I shouldn't? Why was my heart racing and my palms itchy? Why did I have an urge to insist that there was nothing between me and Devon, aside from the fact that there wasn't? But I didn't have a chance to so much as open my mouth before Vyk stepped into my office, the heavy thud of his boots making Devon whirl around and snap to attention. I watched both military officers draw themselves up to their full height in a matter of seconds like two animals posturing before a battle.

I held my breath, knowing better than to step into the middle of a battle.

CHAPTER
TWENTY-SIX

Vyk

I heard the voices before I reached the door.

Voices.

Not Fiona's voice alone, or the silence that I had expected at the early hour, but two voices. And not two female voices. Not Fiona and the flight instructor, Ariana, who seemed to be by her side most often. Not even one of the female cadets from her school who I had seen with her. The other voice I heard drifting through the open doorway was deep and resonant, slipping into my bones and firing a possessive heat in the depths of my core.

"No one regrets leaving their life behind? No one regrets the way they left things?"

That I heard clearly as I reached the doorway, pausing as I quickly assessed the situation. Captain Bowman was not talking to a Drexian or one of the human males at the academy. The human who stood so close to her that she had to lean away from him was no one I had seen before.

His uniform was not one from the Drexian Academy—dark and form-fitting. It was different colors, with a shirt that puffed out from the pants. Instead of heavy combat boots, his shoes were glossy and looked unsuitable for any kind of battle. Did humans fight in these uniforms? I saw no blaster or blade hanging from his waist, which explained why the Drexians had protected Earth for so long. Soldiers like this would never survive against the Kronock.

All these thoughts flitted swiftly through my mind. Just as briskly, I gathered that this human was the inspector from Earth, and that Fiona knew him. Not only did she know him, but there was also something between them. Something that made tension hang heavy in the air and her jaw tighten.

I considered lunging between the two. The sight of him so close to her sent rage coursing through my veins. I did not have to know anything more about the human to know that he was unworthy of her. The way he stood, the way he looked at her, the way he questioned her all told me that he was undeserving of someone as strong as Fiona.

I stood in the doorway waiting for her to snap back at him like she would at me. I waited for her to put him soundly in his place. Instead, her gaze darted over his shoulder and landed on me. There was an instant of surprise, of regret, and then of relief.

I took her expression as an invitation. If she wished me to leave, I knew from experience that she would have no problem telling me off. She wanted me there. She wanted me to intervene.

I stepped into Fiona's office, the thudding of my feet announcing my presence better than my voice could. The human pivoted to face me, his stance changing in a flash. He stood taller, squared his shoulders, and leveled a questioning gaze at me.

He was not small, but I still stood a head taller than him, and I was well aware that my Drexian uniform only made my shoulders appear broader. Even if I was not the only one armed, the human would not have stood a chance against me.

As if assessing all this within the few breaths he took, the man extended a hand and strode toward me. "Captain Devon Gorman. I'm the special envoy from Earth."

I took his hand, remembering the unusual human custom of shaking appendages, and pumped it up and down vigorously. "Commander Vyk of Inferno Force. I serve as the Academy's security chief. Welcome to the Drexian Academy."

Captain Gorman pulled his hand away with a tight smile as he wiggled his fingers. "Thank you."

"You are a brave soldier to venture into the lair of the Assassins," I said, sliding a glance to Fiona, who had taken a few steps to the side, so she now stood halfway between the two of us.

Gorman cocked his head to one side. "I meant to ask, Assassins?"

"That's what they call us in the School of Strategy," Fiona said, her voice an octave higher than usual. "Assassins."

Gorman gave her an indulgent smile. "The schools have cute nicknames?"

I stifled a growl. No one had ever dared to refer to a Blade or an Assassin as cute before.

"It's part of the ancient lore," Fiona said, before I could answer. "The Drexian schools were formed around the various types of warriors and skills. Before it was the School of Strategy, the Drexians had warriors who excelled at battle plans and probably at sneaking into enemy territory."

"The Assassins were once deadly assassins. The Irons long ago forged creations and weapons from iron, although our engineers now work with more sophisticated tools." I did not expect a human to understand the long and glorious military history of my people, but I would not tolerate him laughing at it. Not when Drexians had been protecting Earth since before he was born.

"Interesting," the captain said, his voice telling me he thought it was anything but. He turned his attention to Fiona. "I had no idea you were so into military history."

This made me frown. He must not know Fiona very well. Even I knew that the instructor favored ancient battle strategies and taught them often to her cadets. It was one of the things about her I had approved of, even when I did not approve of her presence at the academy.

I cleared my throat to draw his attention back to me. "I am sure you are eager to get a tour of the academy and learn about the security measures that have been put in place to protect the humans under the academy's protection."

The officer opened his mouth, and I wondered if he was searching for a reason not to agree with me. But if he was truly at the academy to inspect it and assess the success of the integration of humans into the school, there was no way he could.

I suspected that his visit to Drex had just as much to do with Fiona as it did with his purported mission, which was why I was determined to thwart him. Fiona might not be mine. I might not have any claim on her. But that did not quell the jealous haze that had settled over me like a heavy blanket that prickled my skin and quickened my pulse.

I did not care what claim this man might have on her. If she had ever been his, she was not his now. That much was clear from the way she avoided his gaze. And if I had anything to do with it, she would never be his.

It took considerable self-control not to flatten the man to the ground or, at the very least, challenge him to a battle of honor. I inhaled deeply and reminded myself that he was an envoy from Earth—a guest of the Academy—and the Admiral would be severely displeased with me if I bloodied him. That was fine. There were other ways to make him suffer.

"Come." I motioned to him with one arm. "I will give you a tour and tell you every detail of our security protocols."

"I don't want to impose—"

I slapped the man hard on the back, sending him stumbling forward and then catching him before he fell. "I insist."

I glanced back at Fiona as I steered the captain from her office. She did not look angry, but she did not look pleased. It was a mystery to me which of us had irritated her more. I would usually have guessed that it was me, but I got the sense she was glad I was taking the man from her presence.

I hoped so, because I intended to keep the human much too busy or too exhausted to bother her again.

CHAPTER
TWENTY-SEVEN

Fiona

I stood in a state of shock after Devon and Vyk left. Had that just happened? I'd been glad for Vyk's arrival, since it saved me from a very awkward conversation with the captain, but I had not been comforted by the look in the commander's eyes as he'd led Devon away.

I sat on my desk and released a long breath. Should I go after them? Should I join the tour of the academy's security systems to make sure the two guys didn't end up in some kind of stand-off? No, my presence definitely would not help with that. Besides, Vyk had no reason to flex his authority over Devon. It wasn't like I was anything to him, after all. And Vyk wasn't a brute.

I winced at that thought. He had been Inferno Force, and he'd been known for ruthless interrogations. Not that he had any reason to interrogate Devon. Keep telling yourself that, I thought.

"He wouldn't do anything to the man," I said out loud, more to convince myself than anything. Would he?

The sound of steps in the hallway made my pulse quicken. Were they back so soon or had Gorman managed to escape? Then I realized that the footfall wasn't heavy and determined, it was light and quick.

"There you are, hon." Reina's towering blue hair popped around the doorframe before the rest of her appeared. Her snug fuchsia dress hugged her angular frame and reached below her knees, which explained her short stride. The contrast between her hair and dress was striking, and seemed even more dramatic since everyone else in the school wore dark uniforms. "I thought I might find you here. I did check the female tower, the staff dining room, and the Stacks before coming here, so it wasn't my first guess, but here you are!"

I managed to return her bright smile even though my heart was still hammering from the appearance of first Gorman and then Vyk. "What can I do for you?"

"Not a thing, hon, but I thought you might have seen the Earth envoy."

"Captain Gorman?"

Reina nodded her head and her vertical swish of hair bobbled. "That's the one. I heard that

you know him."

"Barely," I said, the words rushing out so quickly that the Vexling's eyebrows shot skyward. I tempered my voice. "I mean, I do know him but not well."

"Then you haven't seen him yet?"

"Actually, I have." My cheeks warmed. Why did I feel like I was on the receiving end of a

very skillful interrogation and losing? "But he's not here now."

Reina's smile didn't falter. "Do you know where he is? Noora was hoping to give him an official welcome alongside the admiral."

The thought that Admiral Zoran and his wife would be waiting on Devon while Vyk toured him around the school made me twitch with guilt, although I also knew that it wasn't my fault. I hadn't asked Vyk to show the captain around.

"He's with Vyk."

This surprised the lanky alien, and she steepled her thin fingers in front of her face. "I suppose it makes sense that the security chief would want to elaborate on all the safety improvements at the academy. I suppose Noora can wait to officially welcome him at the banquet."

"Sorry." I didn't know why I was apologizing but I felt responsible for the missing captain. Then I blinked a few times. "Banquet?"

"We have to welcome him to the academy properly. I know we don't have a full house of cadets, but a dinner with those remaining and the staff should impress him."

How had I missed the memo about that? As long as I wasn't assigned a seat next to Devon, it shouldn't be too awkward.

"I know we can count on the Earthlings to make our visitor feel welcome. He is here to assess the exchange program, after all. We want to give him the best possible impression of life here at the academy."

I stifled a groan. I had a sinking feeling that Vyk did not have impressing the captain at the top of mind. He might want to impress something on him, but I doubted it was anything that would help the case of the exchange program.

Reina cocked her head at me. "Is everything okay, dear? You look a bit green. I wouldn't worry if you were a Vendelen, but the shade isn't as flattering on Earthlings."

"Totally fine," I lied, as I walked her to the door of my office, "but I should probably get back to work."

"Of course." Reina fluttered her hands at her throat. "I'll see you tonight."

I waited until her brisk steps had faded before stepping into the corridor myself. I needed to find Gorman and Vyk before, well, I didn't know what, but I had a gut feeling that it wouldn't be good for the captain.

CHAPTER

TWENTY-EIGHT

Fiona

"I don't understand." Ariana gave me a side-eyed look. "What do you mean you can't find him?"

I rubbed my hands briskly over my arms and wished I'd thrown on a jacket before rushing outside. The wind off the water was biting, and even though the water was striking the bottom of the nearby cliffs, I could hear the crashing waves from where I stood.

I'd found my friend in the shipyard, inspecting one of the fighter jets and chatting with the Drexian pilot who'd transported Devon to Drex. After briefly meeting the pilot and thanking him for making all the jumps from the space station, I'd yanked her behind the nearest fighter and told her that I had no idea where Earth's envoy had gone.

"I mean that I've looked everywhere, and there is no sign of him or the security chief."

Ariana wrinkled her nose. "Why are you looking for Commander Vyk?"

I huffed out a breath, more impatient with myself for not telling my friend the entire story than at Ariana for being confused. "He's the one who ran off with Devon."

Ariana's eyes widened. "Now, that's a twist I didn't see coming."

"Be serious."

"I am. I did not think Vyk was the type of Drexian to run away with anyone, male or female. He's too stern for that."

I wasn't sure if I agreed with her assessment. Lately, I'd started to see glimpses of emotion in the commander, and when he'd interrupted me with Devon, I had been sure that I'd picked up a flash of something dark and dangerous in his eyes, which was why I was looking for Devon. I didn't want Vyk to have the wrong idea about me and Gorman and somehow take it out on the guy.

"I don't mean ran off like that." I steadied my breath. "I mean that Vyk insisted on taking Comm—Captain Gorman around the academy and telling him about all our security measures."

Ariana patted the side of my arm. "There you go, then. If he's showing him the entire academy, it could take a while, especially if he's going over all the security protocols. I'm surprised I haven't seen them come out here yet. This is where we launch the perimeter patrols."

"So, they haven't been out here?"

She shook her head. "Nope, and I've been here since I left you in your office. I actually saw Gorman's ship arrive, but I was too busy tinkering with an engine to say hi. I figured I'd meet him later."

If he survives that long, I thought, letting dark thoughts swirl in my brain.

Come on, Fi. Commander Vyk is not a homicidal maniac. He's not going to throw the guy out of a tower just because he isn't a big fan of humans.

"The towers." I snapped my fingers. "I haven't checked all the towers yet—or the maze."

"Why would he show him the maze?" Ariana eyed me like I was unhinged. "Are you sure you're okay?" She dropped her voice and cut a glance over her shoulder, even though the whipping wind made it impossible for anyone to hear us from more than a few feet away. "This isn't about you being nervous about how you left things with the guy from Earth is it? Did he mention it yet?"

"Not directly," I admitted. I wasn't going to tell her that Vyk walked in on him before he could press me further about how I'd left. Not yet, at least. First I needed to make sure the guy wasn't being tortured by the security chief. "We don't have a torture chamber at the academy, do we? Do you think there's an old one in the dungeons?"

"You're starting to scare me." Ariana squeezed my arm. "Why would you think that Vyk is doing anything but exactly what he said he was going to do and give the guy a grand tour?"

I knew that it would sound crazy if I explained it, but I had the craziest feeling that Vyk had been jealous of Devon. Of course, that was absurd. There was nothing between me and Vyk but resentment, judgment, and now a wager.

He had never shown the slightest bit of interest in me. Even what I would have normally perceived as heat from a guy, I could easily assume was just his anger at me for being at the academy. There had never been any love lost between us...and yet, I would have bet money that he had looked at me like a jealous boyfriend would have when he'd seen me talking with Devon.

The craziest part? I'd felt like a cheating girlfriend by just allowing Devon to stand so close to me. When I'd seen Vyk, my first instinct had been to explain my innocence, when I didn't owe the Drexian a single explanation.

I rubbed a hand across my forehead. Maybe the fact that I'd slept in his bed—although completely alone—had made me feel some misplaced loyalty to him. I had felt a surge of jealousy when he'd come back all sweaty, even though he owed me as little explanation as I owed him.

I blew out a breath and managed a smile. "You're right. I don't know why I'm so worried. Maybe because I know Devon, and he's here to write up a report on the integration of humans into the Academy. I guess I want his visit to go well so nothing changes."

Ariana released my arm. "If Devon is fair-minded, none of us have anything to worry about. The beginning might have been bumpy, but I think we've adapted to the Academy beautifully."

I shot her a look. "You're just saying that because you're banging your boss."

Ariana sucked in a breath. "He is *not* my boss. Volten is my colleague. I'm banging my colleague, thank you very much."

I laughed at this, already feeling better. "My bad."

"It's a good thing Volten is such a big—and I do mean big—distraction. Otherwise, it would be hard for me to stay here with Sasha still out there."

I pulled her into a fierce hug, kicking myself for being so paranoid about Devon when she was dealing with a sister being held by the Kronock. "You know we're going to go get her as soon as we have a target."

When I leaned back, Ariana's eyes were glassy. "I know. Maybe don't tell your buddy from Earth about our rag-tag rescue team. I have a feeling it wouldn't be authorized by Earth Planetary Defense."

It hadn't occurred to me to keep that a secret, but now that she mentioned it, I knew Ariana was right. Nothing we were planning was authorized by Drexian High Command or Earth Planetary Defense. It was why we had assembled our own team that included cadets, and why we'd solicited information from Inferno Force warriors on an unofficial basis.

I made a motion of zipping my lips. "You know I would never do a thing to risk our mission. My lips are sealed."

Ariana forced a laugh. "Not that it will be an issue if Vyk has thrown the guy into the dungeons with that beast."

"Right." I laughed along with her as I turned back toward the Academy, hoping that we were both very wrong, and that the security chief was giving the captain the world's most boring security briefing.

CHAPTER
TWENTY-NINE

Vyk

"Another round?"

The human captain braced his hands on his knees as he bent over and sucked in breath. "What do you call this again?"

I inhaled the familiar scent of sweat that permeated the massive room in the School of Battle. Even when the cadets were not in session, the dark mats and enormous apparatus held remnants of their toil and struggle. "The gauntlet. It is a favorite of mine."

He tipped his head up and nodded, sweat trickling down the side of his red face. "I can see why. It's...fun."

I slapped his bare back, which was slick with sweat, and appraised the obstacles that made up the course. "I thought you might enjoy seeing how Drexians relax."

The captain straightened and managed a tight smile. "I had no idea the tour would be so thorough."

I put a hand to my own bare chest. "Apologies if I was too enthusiastic. I thought you wanted to see how the human cadets are being trained."

"I do." He rested a hand on his side, flinching a bit. "How often do cadets do this gauntlet?"

"If they are Blades, they do it regularly. If they are in the other schools and it is not the first term, they will only do it occasionally. Any cadet may use it recreationally, of course, just as may any member of staff."

He nodded, his expression telling me that he did not consider this recreational.

"If you wish, I can also let you try our climbing walls, although ours do not use ropes to keep you from falling."

"You climb walls without ropes?"

"Knowing that you cannot fall makes the course less challenging and the cadets less alert."

He blinked at me for a few beats before giving his head a shake. "I do not need to experience all elements of the cadet experience."

"No?" I twitched one shoulder, as if this surprised me. "Does that mean you do not want to try out the caged sparring rings?"

He shook his head so quickly and firmly that some sweat flicked off his face and onto me. "I think I should probably meet with the Academy Master."

Guilt twinged at me. I had been so determined to keep him busy and away from Fiona that I had forgotten that the man was at the academy for a legitimate reason. How long had I been dragging him through the school, and how long had we been running the gauntlet?

I had not been lying that I went through the gauntlet as a way to relieve stress and burn off energy, but I also knew very well that the human had not been prepared for it. Not only had he just arrived on Drex, but he had also endured a journey across the galaxy that included multiple jumps, which left some feeling ill. If he had not felt bad before my tour, he did now.

My behavior was not rational, and even as I stood next to him with my chest bare, I had little to defend myself except that I had been compelled to challenge the man. It had not been my initial plan to make him show his mettle on the gauntlet, but I would not deny that I had enjoyed every time he fell from one of the swinging platforms or rotating rings. It had been a long time since I had gotten as much pleasure from anything as I had when he had face planted on the warped wall before sliding down it.

I stifled a grin. This was not the behavior of an honorable Drexian. I knew this, but I also knew that I did not like this human, and I did not like whatever relationship he had with Fiona. It might have been petty for me to put him through physical tests I knew I would win, but I would deal with any retribution for my competitive nature later.

I eyed the human, realizing that I had pushed him to his limits and made my point. If he had any doubt that I could defeat him in any physical battle, despite being twice his age, I had put that question soundly to rest. Fiona did not have to know. He knew. I knew. That was enough.

"Please accept my sincere apologies for taking up so much of your time." I turned toward the ladder leading down to the floor. "Come. I will take you to Admiral Zoran."

The captain released an audible sigh as he followed me down the ladder and toward the pile of shirts and shoes we'd left by the door.

I snagged a pair of towels hanging on a row of pegs next to the entrance and tossed one to the captain. "So you do not go to the Admiral covered in sweat."

He made a grumbling sound as he swiped the towel over his face and then his chest and back, although it would take more than a cursory wipe to make him look as neat and presentable as he had when he'd arrived.

The door slid open, and we both stepped back as a Drexian entered. It was not a Blade coming to work out or get in extra practice. It was Tivek, the admiral's adjunct, and it was clear from his narrowed gaze that he had found the object of his search.

"Captain Gorman." He gave the human a salute with his fist thumping across his chest. "I heard you arrived and have been looking for you."

I ignored the pointed look he shot me.

"Admiral Zoran was hoping to give you a proper welcome."

"It's my fault," Gorman said before I could explain. "I should have found the Academy Master when I arrived, but I went to see an old friend instead."

Tivek again looked at me, startled that I might be this old friend.

"Captain Douglas," the man said. "Fiona and I served on the same base together before she came to the Academy."

Tivek shifted his gaze to me and barely lifted one brow, but his question was obvious. How had he ended up with me, half undressed, on the other side of the school?

"I offered to show the captain around the academy. I thought he could benefit from a tour of the schools and an understanding of the security protocols that are ensuring the safety of the human cadets."

Tivek's gaze remained on me. I had not explained why that would bring us both to the gauntlet and why I would run a guest through the arduous obstacle course, especially a human one.

"I also thought the captain might be interested in some of the unique features of the academy, like the gauntlet."

By this point, the captain was hurrying to dress and was not adding anything to my weak explanations. Maybe because he knew as well as anyone that I did not have to make him run the gauntlet. Although I had not forced him. I might have challenged him to a friendly competition, but I had not held a Drexian blade to his throat like I might have if he had agreed to go into the sparring ring with me.

Tivek's brow furrowed, and he finally turned his attention from me and focused fully on the human. "Why don't I show you to your quarters so you can rest before meeting the admiral?"

"Thank you." The captain followed Tivek without another glance back at me, moving swiftly as if he wished to put as much distance between us as possible.

I feared that I might have to answer for my actions later with Zoran. I thought about the human's face smacking the wall again and grinned to myself. For once, I had no regrets.

CHAPTER

THIRTY

Fiona

I let out a long breath as I reached the archway leading into the School of Strategy. That did it. I'd made a complete circuit of the academy, and there was no sign of Vyk and Devon. I hadn't gone to the maze, but I'd convinced myself that the commander wouldn't drag a visitor out there. Not after what had happened and his involvement. Especially since Devon was at the academy to assess the human exchange, and that had been a black mark on the attempt to integrate the school.

"No, they aren't there," I muttered to myself.

Then where were they? The bigger question was why I cared so much. I'd been anxious about Commander, check that, Captain Gorman visiting, but now I was searching for him like he was a long-lost relative.

It was the look in Vyk's eyes that had me dashing about like a madwoman. It hadn't taken an empath to see that the Drexian didn't like Devon and really didn't like that I knew him. He'd been much too eager to take the man on a tour of the school, and I did not trust his motives. Since I'd been hunting for them for hours, my concern seemed warranted.

But Vyk wouldn't actually harm the guy, would he? My stomach did an uncomfortable flip flop as it hit me that I didn't know. I didn't know enough about the Drexian to know whether he was truly dangerous, or if it was all hype.

It was true that the warrior had a reputation for being fierce, but he hadn't so much as touched me when I'd been in his room. He'd made a scandalous wager with me, but then he'd promised he would never force me. So how scary could he be?

I put my hands on my hips and rapped one toe on the stone floor. "Scary enough to vanish a military officer from Earth."

"That does sound scary."

I spun at the high-pitched voice to find that Reina had come up behind me. Somehow the willowy Vexling floated around the academy without making much noise, since she didn't wear heavy battle boots like everyone else. Even though she surprised me, I was glad to see her.

"Don't mind me." I tried to wave away my words. "I'm talking to myself."

Reina big eyes were unblinking as she nodded thoughtfully, her blue twist of hair quivering. "I do that all the time, hon. Sometimes I think I'm the only one who really listens."

I laughed. "I feel that."

"Did someone truly vanish?" Reina asked, placing a bony hand on my arm.

"Not really. At least, I don't think so." It wasn't fair to dangle something like that and not explain. "The envoy from Earth arrived this morning. We used to be stationed together before I left for the Academy, so he stopped by my office to say hi. That was the last I saw of him, and I've been looking everywhere."

"Young fellow with light-brown hair and different-colored clothes?"

I thought about the uniform of black pants and a khaki shirt that he'd been wearing. "That sounds like Devon. Have you seen him?"

Reina bobbed her head, smiling brightly. "Not too long ago."

I exhaled loudly, my entire body relaxing. I'd been ridiculous to worry so much about the guy. I was embarrassed that I'd suspected Vyk of doing something bad to him. Had I really believed that the Drexian security chief would get rid of the visiting envoy? Now that I knew Devon was fine, my fears seemed crazy.

"Were you worried he got lost?" Reina patted my arm. "The Academy can be confusing if you don't know the layout."

"Not really." No way was I going to admit what I'd actually thought. "Commander Vyk took him on a tour and then I couldn't find either of them. I guess I wanted to make sure the captain was settling in okay."

Reina nibbled the corner of her lip. "I don't know about settling in, but the tour must have been quite comprehensive."

"What do you mean?"

"When I saw the human, he was with the admiral's adjunct and they were near Zoran's office, so I assume..."

"Tivek?" How had he ended up with him when he'd left with Vyk? The back of my neck started to tingle, as if sensing that I wasn't going to like the rest of what Reina had to say.

The Vexling nodded, but her gaze darted to the floor. "He was escorting the human, who looked like he had been through some kind of battle. Perhaps he came from a battle on Earth? He is a warrior, right?"

I thought about Devon and wondered the last time he'd been in an actual fight. "He did not come from a battle on Earth. When I saw him this morning, he looked fine. His uniform didn't even look as rumpled as mine does."

Reina glanced at the clothes I'd slept in and still hadn't changed out of, and she shook her head. "Oh, no. His clothes were sweaty, and one side of his face was slightly bruised."

"Bruised?" My embarrassment at thinking the worst about Vyk quickly morphed into fury. Had he attacked Devon? "How did he get bruised during a tour of the school?"

Reina giggled nervously. "I'm sure there's a perfectly logical explanation, hon. He might have tripped or—"

"Or our security chief punched him," I finished Reina's sentence for her, the sharp words bursting from my lips.

Reina reared back. "Why would he do that?"

"Don't ask me! Ask the maniac who tried to sabotage the maze and who's had it in for humans since we stepped foot in this place. Why wouldn't he do something to Devon? It's totally on brand for a human-hating grump like Commander Vyk!"

Reina glanced around as if the Drexian might appear from the shadows. "I don't think that's true, hon. Sure, the Drexian made mistakes, but he's changed since the trials."

I pulled away from her. "Has he? Well, I guess I'm going to find out when I ask him what the hell he did to our guest."

Then I stormed off, with Reina's voice calling after me. I didn't care what I'd wagered, Vyk was going to regret messing with *this* human.

CHAPTER
THIRTY-ONE

Vyk

I stepped from the bathroom with water trickling down my back and dripping onto the stone floor. I'd wrapped a towel around my waist after rubbing it quickly over myself, but I was by no means dry. It didn't matter. It would have to do. I needed to return to work or, in today's case, start work.

Now that I was not with the human envoy, the reality of what I'd done gnawed at me. At the time, it had felt reasonable—necessary, even—to knock him down a few pegs and show him what it meant to be a cadet at the Drexian Academy. How could the man assess our school if he had no idea what the cadets, including the humans embedded with us, experienced.

I did not know if Admiral Zoran would agree with me. I could tell from the look on Tivek's face that he had not been impressed when he'd found me putting the captain through his paces. Seeing the human bare-chested and bruised had not been what he'd expected.

"I will answer for that," I said to myself, as I snatched a fresh uniform from the standing wardrobe and laid it out on the bed.

My gaze lingered on the bed that was still rumpled from Fiona's abrupt departure earlier. I hadn't slept after she'd left, although part of me had wanted to slip beneath the blanket and feel the warmth her body had left behind.

I scowled at myself, shaking my head in disgust. What was wrong with me? I had spent decades living on cold battleships with other Drexian warriors. I was used to being alone. I preferred it. So why was I preoccupied with the human female? If I had seen another Inferno Force warrior luring a female into his quarters and obsessing over her, I would have taken him to task. But I could hardly take myself to task when I had no idea why I could not purge myself of thoughts of her.

I clenched my teeth as determination pulsed through me. "I will conquer this."

What I would rather do was conquer her, but I forced that thought to the back of my brain as I dropped my towel to the floor and stepped into my snug boxer briefs and then my dark uniform pants. A thumping on my door made me turn and stifle a groan.

I would be answering for my actions sooner than I expected. I had no doubt that Tivek had come to summon me to speak to the Academy Master, so I did not glance back. "Come. It is open."

I picked up my shirt as the door slid open behind me.

"What the actual fuck did you do?"

The voice was piercing, sharp, and female. Not Tivek.

My entire body tensed as I turned, shirt still in hand. Fiona did not wait for me to invite her in or finish putting on my shirt. She didn't even glance at me as she stormed into my room, her fists tight by her side and her face flushed.

"I did not expect to see you again so soon." I managed to keep my voice steady, even as my heart pounded.

She whirled on me, her eyes flashing fury. "Well, are you going to answer me?"

She'd come in on a whirlwind of rage and caught me off-guard, and I had little memory of what she'd asked me. Luckily, she had no intention of letting me answer.

Fiona flung one arm wide. "Did I hear correctly, or was the envoy from Earth, the captain sent to assess how the exchange of humans is progressing, the man who will determine my future here, barely on the planet for an hour before you beat him up?"

I bristled at this accusation. Not that I would not have relished beating him. Not after the way he'd stood so close to Fiona, eyeing her like she was something to be devoured. But I had not laid a hand on the man. "I did not touch the captain."

She barked out a derisive laugh. "Then how did he end up with a bruised face?"

I flinched but fought to keep my expression measured. I had enjoyed seeing the human smack the incline wall, but now the moment of triumph felt hollow and small. "I showed him the

163

gauntlet in the School of Battle and offered to run it with him. He fell."

Her eyes became slits. She did not believe me. I did not blame her. That was hardly the entire story. "You thought the tour of the academy should include him testing out the apparatus that humbles most Blades? I'm surprised you didn't send him through the maze."

I clenched my jaw to keep from responding. What could I say? Her anger was justified, not that I would admit that. If I confessed that I had relished seeing the human struggle, that I had savored his sweat and strain, then I would have to admit why, and that I could not do.

The gauntlet was a punishment for him knowing you, touching you, invading your space like you would never allow me. The bruise was his payment for being someone you do not reject and despise.

"I treated him as if he were a Drexian," I finally said. "I am sorry if that was wrong."

Fiona crossed her arms over her chest and loudly expelled a breath. "So, mistakes were made?"

I did not answer that. As we stood staring at each other, her gaze drifted to my bare chest, as if she had just noticed that I was not fully dressed. She bit her bottom lip and jerked her gaze away. "Are you going to put on a shirt?"

"You did interrupt me," I reminded her.

She pressed her lips together as if biting back a response, but I sensed she would not continue talking until I dressed.

I did not rush as I slipped my arms through the sleeves of my shirt. "Who is he to you?"

Her eyes widened. "What?"

"You heard the question, Captain. It is evident that you know this human. How well?"

She spluttered for a few moments, pink splotches coloring her cheeks. "We were stationed on the same base before I left to come to the Academy."

I buttoned my shirt, never taking my gaze from her. "I have been stationed with many warriors. I have shared close quarters with many of them, but none have ever stood as close to me as he was to you."

"I am not involved with the captain."

That had not been what I had asked, but I did not challenge her. It was clear that there had been something between her and the human. "I will have to take your word that whatever was between you is over."

"I do not lie." She practically spit the words at me.

"Then I will be honest with you. I do not trust the captain. I do not believe he is here to give a fair assessment of the human integration at the academy. I think he is here because of you."

Fiona was silent, but concern flitted across her eyes. She did not disagree with me. Not enough to argue.

"But his arrival changes nothing," I husked, stepping closer to her. "The terms of our wager have not changed."

She drew in a quick breath, as she tipped her head to hold my gaze. "I never said it did. I don't welch on deals."

I gave a single nod. "Good. I will expect to see you tonight."

Fiona released an exasperated sigh and flounced from my quarters with almost as much outrage as when she'd arrived.

What are you doing, Vyk?

I did not know how to answer myself. All I knew was there was a threat to my plan, a threat to Fiona's place at the Academy, and a threat to my world.

And the only way an Inferno Force warrior knew how to handle threats was head on.

CHAPTER
THIRTY-TWO

Volten

"Did you hear?" Kann did not wait to be fully seated across from me before the question burst from his mouth.

I looked up from my bowl of *chidi* berries and grinned at the enormous plate of fried padwump he placed on the table between us. The salty, savory smell wafted up and teased my nose. "Did I hear that the kitchen is now out of padwump?"

He rolled his eyes at me as he picked up a strip of the crispy meat and took a loud bite, sending shards onto his lap. "No. Did you hear that the inspector from Earth has arrived, and that our security chief made him run the gauntlet?"

I cocked my head at my friend. "Vyk made the human envoy run the gauntlet in the School of Battle? Is that some sort of strange new security protocol?"

Kann swallowed and his grin widened. "Doubtful. My theory is that Vyk has gone so long without torturing anyone that he snapped."

I had heard plenty about the commander's reputation in Inferno Force as a ruthless interrogator, but I had also thought that he had been given a short leash by Admiral Zoran, especially after the fiasco of the trials. "Are you sure about this?"

Kann sat back, glancing around the deserted staff dining room. "One of my fellow Blade instructors saw Tivek leaving the gauntlet with the human and then Vyk walking out. He said that the human did not look like he had enjoyed the experience."

"Welcome to the Academy," I said under my breath. I could not imagine arriving from Earth after enduring multiple jumps through vast amounts of space and then being challenged to the gauntlet. I enjoyed scaling the climbing wall, and I had favorite holo-chamber programs, but never having to do the gauntlet again was one of my favorite things about being a Wing.

"Vyk isn't even a Blade." Kann chomped on another strip of padwump. "I cannot imagine why he thought the gauntlet would be a good way to introduce our guest to the school."

I could think of one reason a Drexian would want to put someone through the gauntlet, but I could not think of a reason why Vyk would want to humiliate an envoy from Earth that we should be trying to impress.

"If Tivek was with the human, then he must be meeting with the admiral now." I wondered if Zoran knew of Vyk's plan, or if he had authorized it, but that seemed unlikely. Admiral Zoran was no fool, and he wished the integration of humans and Drexians to be a success. He had fought for the program. Why would he jeopardize it?

"I saw Zoran stalking the corridors earlier." Kann waved a fried strip at me like a pointer. "Now I know why. He must have been looking for the envoy."

If that was the case and Tivek had retrieved the man to escort him to Zoran, I did not want to be Vyk. "Why would Vyk do something like that?"

Even though we were the only ones sitting at one of the long wooden tables, Kann dropped his voice. "Especially after, you know..."

I did know. I had been the one Vyk had told of the planned sabotage before the maze. I had been the one he'd enlisted to help him reveal the plot. It did not mean we were close, even though we had included him in the card game. The gruff, older Drexian was still a mystery to me.

I straightened as I spotted Ariana walking in, my heart tripping in my chest. It did not matter that we spent every night together, the sight of her still made my breath catch and my pulse quicken.

She smiled at me as she crossed the room, ignoring the back table laden with platters of food. "I thought I'd find you here."

Kann beamed at her as she sat next to me. "The early Drexian gets the padwump."

She eyed the mountain of the crispy meat and shook her head. "You have the metabolism of a hummingbird."

Kann wrinkled his nose, probably wondering about the strange Earth birds that hummed. "Help yourself."

Even though Ariana's demeanor had dampened since learning of her sister's imprisonment by the Kronock, she managed to find moments of lightness. It helped that our plan to find Sasha was already being implemented by Inferno Force recon teams. That was the only reason she hadn't commandeered a ship and taken off to find her sister on her own.

She took a slice of padwump and nibbled the end neatly. "I thought I might find Fiona here."

"You weren't looking for me?" I teased her with a look of manufactured pain.

She elbowed me in the side. "I rolled out of your bed only a few hours ago. Don't be greedy."

Kann leaned back. "Is Fiona missing?"

She shook her head. "She found me in the shipyard a little while ago, but she was searching for the officer that arrived from Earth. I wanted to know if she found him."

Kann's eyes popped wide. "I do not know if she found him, but I do know that Vyk did."

Ariana's brow furrowed.

"Commander Vyk put the envoy from Earth through the gauntlet," I explained.

She didn't look any less confused. "The gauntlet?"

Kann released a mournful sigh. "You Wings know nothing about the academy if it doesn't fly."

I shot him a look, although it was not altogether false. The only reason I knew of the gauntlet was because of my years as a cadet. Otherwise, there was no reason for a Wing to be in Blade territory. "It is a series of physical challenges in the School of Battle. It is not easy."

Ariana's brows lifted. "As if anything in this place is easy." She rested her hand on top of my leg. "Why would the security chief take him there?"

Kann shrugged one shoulder. "Who knows? The good news is that he survived with minor bruising and is with Admiral Zoran now."

Ariana's hand on my leg was making it hard to focus, especially since she was moving it up and down absently.

"I guess that answers the question of where Vyk took him," she said.

"What?" Kann and I asked at the same time, as we swung our heads to Ariana.

"When Fiona was looking for him, it was because Vyk had gone off with the man to give him a tour. Fiona couldn't find them, and for some reason, she suspected that Vyk might throw him in the dungeon or something."

"She wasn't far off," Kann said.

I placed my hand on top of Ariana's so she wouldn't rub my leg to the point that I would be unable to stand without terrifying my friend with an enormous hard-on. She glanced at me and smiled, as if she'd just realized what she'd been doing. She squeezed my leg, then twisted her hand so that she could interlock her fingers with mine.

"I should probably find Fiona and tell her that her friend is okay." She gave my hand a final squeeze and stood.

"Friend?" I asked. "Fiona knows the envoy?"

"She does." The tone of Ariana's voice told me that there was more to the story, but I didn't press her. I would get to do plenty of that later that night.

As she walked from the room, I traced her steps and made no secret of watching her swaying ass. Then I cursed at myself and shifted on the wooden bench. I would not be standing for a while.

CHAPTER
THIRTY-THREE

Fiona

I hesitated outside Admiral Zoran's office, lifting my hand to the door and then dropping it. When I'd rushed from Vyk's quarters, it seemed like finding Devon was the best idea. After all, I needed to see for myself that he was okay, and that the insane security chief hadn't roughed him up too badly.

I cursed under my breath as I thought about Vyk. I could not figure him out. One minute, I was convinced that he was cold and unfeeling, and the next minute I was just as certain that there was some kind of weird, inexplicable heat between us. But if there was heat, it was nothing either of us wanted or needed in our lives, that was perfectly clear.

Besides, Vyk hated humans.

"Which is why he thought it would be fun to torment Devon," I said, as I shook my head. Part of me still felt responsible for what had happened, although I wasn't the one who made things weird in my office—Devon—or who gave the captain the worst tour ever—Commander Vyk. Now that I thought about it, the only ones to blame were the guys who clearly had too much testosterone for their own good.

Before I could debate further on whether to knock or not, the admiral's door slid open, and Devon emerged. I took a few steps back as I took in his appearance. Like Reina said, he looked like he'd been through the wringer, and knowing the Drexians, their gauntlet might in fact have an actual wringer as one of the challenges.

Despite the bruise blooming on his cheek, the captain smiled. "Fiona, were you coming to speak with the Academy Master as well?"

I shook my head. "Actually, I came to find you." Before he could get the wrong idea, I added quickly, "I wanted to make sure you were okay."

The man squared his shoulders, even though he shifted from one foot to the other. "Do you mean what happened in that gauntlet of theirs?" He laughed. "That was all in good fun."

"Was it?" My gaze flicked to his cheek. "If I had any idea that the tour of the academy was going to include you being forced to—"

"I wasn't forced to do anything. The security chief showed me all the facilities in the School of Battle, which are quite impressive. I said that the gauntlet looked intriguing."

I had a feeling that Devon was trying to save face, but if he wanted to insist that it had been his idea to compete in physical challenges right after a trip through space, I wasn't going to fight him on it. "If you're sure..."

"I am sure." He tilted his head at me. "If it got you to come here then I would gladly do the gauntlet again."

I fought the urge to groan. "As long as you're fine, I won't bother you."

The captain grabbed my elbow before I could turn away. "We didn't get to finish our conversation this morning."

"No?" I tried to play dumb, but my voice came out high and squeaky, just like it always did when I wasn't being honest. Of course, I remembered what we'd been talking about when Vyk had walked in. It was the only reason I wasn't entirely upset that the commander had interrupted us.

"No." Devon's expression became serious, and he kept his hold on my arm, although it wasn't firm. "We haven't talked since before you left for Drex, and that night we didn't do much talking."

My cheeks warmed as flashes of that last night rushed back to me—desperately pulling each other's clothes off as we'd fumbled through his apartment on the way to the bedroom. He'd tasted like beer and smelled like a blend of the smoke that had permeated the bar and the remnants of a spicy cologne. My head had been swimming, but I remembered thinking that as much as I wanted him at the moment, as horny as I was, I would regret it one day.

Hello, one day.

"Right." I steadied my voice. "That seems like forever ago."

The corner of his mouth twitched. "It does feel like you've been gone for a long time, Fiona. You know, the base isn't the same without you."

"Thanks, Devon, but I'm sure that's not true. Besides, coming here was a good move for me. I have no regrets."

"None?"

Now I regretted that night and coming to find him. I should have left well enough alone. He was a big boy. Why did I think I needed to check up on him? Now, he'd think that I cared, which I did, but not in that way.

Good going, Fi. This visit by the captain wasn't going to be awkward at all.

I patted his arm as I slid my elbow from his grasp. "It's so good to see you, Dev, and I'm really glad that you're here so you can see how well things are going."

"I'm glad too." He shifted his gaze around the empty corridor. "After what happened first term, there was a lot of talk about bringing you back and killing the exchange."

My gut clenched. That was exactly what I'd been afraid might happen. And now I had to make sure he returned to Earth with a positive view of the program, which meant not pissing him off or making him hate me. I was not great at diplomacy or gracious exits, which was evident by my running off and ghosting the guy.

"I promise you that everything is great now."

He nodded. "Then I look forward to you telling me more while I'm here."

I was on the verge of telling him that as much as I wanted to tell him all the reasons the integration was a success, I wanted to do it as the good friends we'd always been, the door slid open again and Tivek stepped into the hall.

Fuckity-fuck.

"Captain Douglas?" He looked confused to find me there. "I was going to show the captain to his quarters before the welcome dinner tonight."

"Welcome dinner?"

"Admiral Zoran thought it would not be a problem since we are between terms and a smaller number."

I slapped on my brightest smile. "Sounds perfect." I took a few steps back and pointed a finger at Devon. "I guess I will see you at dinner."

I walked briskly away without a second glance. I needed to find Ariana and Jess and the rest of my girls and explain to them why they had to run some serious intervention for me with the captain. This was going to be fun.

CHAPTER
THIRTY-FOUR

Vyk

I breathed in the savory scents as I strode toward the banquet hall, scowling despite my stomach rumbling. I did not wish to be heading for a dinner in honor of the visiting captain. I might be hungry, but I was in no mood to dine with the staff and our visitor. I wished to have a quiet dinner in the staff dining room and then retreat to my quarters to await Fiona's arrival.

"But that will not happen now," I grumbled.

The quiet dinner was out, and I was not even confident that Fiona would show, despite her assurances. Had she remembered the banquet when she'd said she would come?

I snarled at the thought that this human captain was ruining everything. Not that there was anything to ruin. Not yet. My plan of getting to know Fiona and showing her that I was not the heartless creature she believed me to be had been derailed by the arrival of Earth's envoy, although I could not blame him for injuring himself on the gauntlet.

Fiona's irritation at me was entirely my fault, although I would not take it back. Replaying the human captain landing on his face was worth all of her outrage. Even now, a smile teased my lips at the thought.

The golden light from the wall sconces cavorted on the ebony walls as I took the wide, sweeping stairs two at a time to the second floor. There was not the same buzz of hundreds of voices spilling from the tall doors like there was at the weekly academy dinners, but I could tell from the smattering of conversation that I was not the first to arrive.

I drew in a breath, tempered my frown, and walked through the doors. Instead of rows of long, rectangular tables for cadets with the staff and instructors seated on the raised dais, the hall had been set up with tables arranged in a U-shape and only benches running along the outside.

Admiral Zoran and his wife stood at the center of the U as they spoke with the visiting human. He no longer wore the dirty and disheveled clothes I'd left him in, although he was in another military uniform, this one with medals attached to his chest.

A part of me wished I'd donned my Inferno Force uniform with my commander's sash, but another part knew that would be overkill. Not even the admiral was wearing his dress uniform.

You are an Inferno Force Commander, I reminded myself. You have nothing to prove.

I scanned the rest of the attendees, noting almost instantly that Fiona was not there. The other instructors had arrived, and they had congregated at one end of a long side of the table along with the smattering of cadets who had remained during the break. Volten and Torq glanced up at me, both acknowledging me with subtle nods.

"I guess he survived your tour."

I swung my head to see Kann walking up behind me. Did every Drexian know what I had done?

"It's the Drexian Academy," he added, as if sensing my thoughts. "Word travels fast, and I saw him emerging from the gauntlet looking like he had not been victorious."

I thought about explaining that the human had expressed interest in the apparatus, but Kann would not believe me. He might be a Blade, but he was no fool.

Kann crossed his arms over his chest as he stood next to me and looked across the room. "I am aware that you outrank me and that you could have thrown me out an airlock for insubordination if we were serving on your battleship..."

"But...?" I prodded.

"But you should not make your dislike for humans so obvious. Especially after..."

He did not need to finish that thought. I knew of my reputation at the academy.

"This had nothing to do with my feelings about humans serving at the academy." This was true. My dislike of the captain had nothing to do with his species.

Kann tracked my gaze that was locked onto the human envoy. "You just dislike a human you'd never met until today?"

I thought about my instinct about the captain. One of the things I had honed during my time on Inferno Force was instinct. I could size up an opponent almost instantly, and I had assessed the human when I'd seen him with Fiona and when I had escorted him around the academy. I could not say precisely why—and I refused to believe that it was only because of his connection to Fiona—but my gut told me that the man was not to be trusted.

"I do not dislike him," I said. That would have been personal. This was not personal. This was a warrior's instinct.

Kann shrugged. "For your sake, I would do a better job of pretending."

He left me to join his friend Volten, and I turned his words over in my head. The Drexian might be a Blade, but his comment was astute. I could not let the rest of the academy know that I distrusted the human envoy. Not when everyone else seemed to be charmed by him. It would only give everyone another reason to dislike me.

No, I would need to find a reason for my distrust, a reason my gut told me the captain was a danger. Which meant that I would need to spend more time with him, not less. I could not avoid him if I wished to uncover his true motives. I would need to be his shadow.

I steeled myself as I strode forward. Time to make the human into my new best friend.

CHAPTER
THIRTY-FIVE

Fiona

I released a whoosh of air as I spotted the women walking toward me. "I've been looking for you."

Jess glanced at Morgan. "You have? Is this about the mission to find Sasha? Has something happened?"

I immediately regretted my breathless voice and urgent tone. "No, nothing like that, but I do need your help."

Jess flicked her fingers through the dark hair that swept across her forehead. "You can count on us. Is this Assassin business?"

I swept my gaze to include Britta, an Iron, who stood by their side with her silvery-blonde hair pulled into a high ponytail. "No. It's not even official academy business."

Morgan lifted her eyebrows. "Even more intriguing. What's up?"

I swiveled my head to make sure the corridor was empty, but it was just as deserted as the rest of the school. Not only were there not the throngs of cadets that would normally fill the halls, but the few of us who were left were probably at the welcome banquet.

Before I could speak, Jess narrowed her eyes at me. "Is this about the envoy from Earth who arrived earlier?"

I nodded, trying to think how to word this so I didn't undermine my authority with the women. After all, they were still cadets, and I was their instructor. In the case of Jess and Morgan, I was an instructor in their school. "The envoy sent by Earth is someone I know. We were stationed together right before I left to join the academy."

"Small world," Britta said.

Too small, I thought.

"So, you know him?" Jess asked.

"I do know him."

"How well?" Morgan asked with a smile twitching the edges of her mouth.

Leave it to an Assassin to read between the lines. Of course, these women would pick up on the real issue. "Let's just say we were very close right before I left, and I might not have given him closure."

Britta's eyes widened. "You ghosted him?"

I shifted from one foot to the other, starting to regret sharing this with anyone. "I don't think it can be called ghosting if I'm on the other side of the galaxy. I left and he stayed. There was never going to be anything more."

Jess cocked her head at me. "Did he know that?"

"Maybe not." I let out a half sigh, half groan. "I feel awful about it, but I never thought I'd see him again. No time soon, at least."

"And you never imagined that he would be the one sent to evaluate the human integration into the academy," Morgan said, her hint of a smile fading.

"Not even a little bit." I gave them a tentative smile. "This is where you all come in."

Jess linked her arm through mine and started walking me in the direction of the banquet hall. "So, what's the plan?"

I hadn't come up with a specific plan, but the cadet was right. We needed a plan. "I'm afraid that the captain might have come here hoping to start things up again."

Morgan hooked her arm through mine on the other side as we walked four astride. "And you do not want that?"

I thought about Devon and our night together. It had been fun —hot, even—but I was sure that was because I'd been leaving the next day. The fact that he was my colleague, and I wouldn't be seeing him again, had combined to make a potent cocktail of forbidden and last-chance love. It had been great, but I did not want to go back for seconds. "Not even a little bit."

Britta leaned forward to catch my eye. "Has he told you he wants to start things up again?"

"Not in so many words," I admitted. "But I get the feeling that he does and he's waiting for a moment to get me alone."

"Then our job is to make sure he never gets you alone," Jess said, squeezing my arm closer to hers. "We run interference."

Morgan snapped her fingers with her free hand. "With the three of us, we can keep the guy distracted while he's here."

My throat tightened. "You would do that for me? Are you sure?"

"Of course, we're sure," Jess said. "It's not like it will be hard with three of us. We'll take turns. Right, girls?"

Britta and Morgan nodded and grinned.

"There's one more thing," I said, hesitant to add more to their plates. "Vyk has it out for the captain."

Morgan shuddered. "The security chief has it out for everyone, doesn't he?"

"He's not so bad," Britta said. "He's an Iron, so he pops into our school every so often. He's not as scary as I used to think."

Jess made a face. "He might have saved me in the dungeons, but I would not want him on my bad side. So, we need to distract the captain so he can't get you alone and we need to keep Vyk from getting him alone?"

Britta shook her head so hard her ponytail swung around her face. "Commander Vyk would never hurt a visiting envoy from Earth."

I thought about the bruise on Devon's face. "All I'm saying is to watch out for Vyk. I don't trust him around Devon."

All the women eyed me curiously as I used the envoy's first name, and my cheeks warmed under their scrutiny.

"Keep the visiting captain distracted and keep Vyk from killing him." Morgan twitched one shoulder. "That should be simple enough."

"You don't need to worry about Vyk."

We all looked up as Ariana rounded the corner in front of us.

"I was looking for you," I said, noticing that my friend had changed from her oil-stained uniform to a clean one.

She jerked a thumb behind her. "I went to the banquet but saw that you all were missing. I came to tell you to hurry up."

"We were just getting marching orders from Fiona," Jess said. "To run interference so the Earth envoy can't get her alone."

Ariana grinned at me. "Sounds like a plan. I'm in."

"Why were you saying that we don't have to worry about Vyk going after Devon?" I asked.

Ariana pivoted on one foot and joined us in walking toward the banquet hall. "Because I just saw the two of them in the banquet. Vyk seemed to be having a great time talking to the guy. He was even laughing."

I almost tripped at this. "Vyk was laughing?"

Morgan let out a low whistle. "I don't know if I've seen the Drexian smile, much less laugh."

Only earlier in the day, the commander had told me that he didn't trust Devon. Plus, he was the reason Devon sported a bruise on his cheek. How had Vyk gone from glowering at the man to laughing with him?

186

"I guess that's good, right?" Britta asked. "One less thing to worry about?"

I nodded, but I was far from sure I agreed. A stubborn Drexian like Vyk would not change his tune so quickly. The commander was up to something, and I had a bad feeling that it was going to bite me in the ass.

CHAPTER
THIRTY-SIX

Vyk

"I hope you do not hold it against me for the brutality of the gauntlet," I said as I patted the human captain on the back. "You made an impressive showing, especially for a first attempt. Most cadets do not make it as far as you on their first go."

Captain Gorman had looked both alarmed and hesitant when I had first approached, but I was doing my best to appear jovial and friendly. Now that I had decided to win the man's trust, I had to change my strategy. I no longer wished to humiliate him and show him up. I wanted to prove that I was his friend.

"The gauntlet was not so bad," he said, managing a laugh.

"I should not have taken you so soon after you arrived. Jumping is hard on the body." I did not add that it was harder on humans because they were naturally weaker and less resilient. "I was too excited to show you all of our academy."

"I hold no ill will. The training facilities in the School of Battle are impressive."

I leaned closer to him and dropped my voice to a conspiratorial whisper. " Next, I will have to show you the holo-chambers. They are very entertaining."

Concern flickered across his face. "Don't you also use the holo-chambers for military training?"

"The Blades do, but I prefer to enjoy different simulations." I nudged him with my elbow. "The pleasure planet Pariza is especially enjoyable."

His brows popped up. "Pleasure planet?"

"They have devoted themselves to being a destination for traveling warriors so there are sunny beaches and warm seas. Not to mention the barely dressed females and males eager to show visitors of all orientations a good time."

His mouth gaped. "This is a holo-chamber program?"

"It is a real planet that had been recreated for our holo-chamber. Access is restricted, otherwise cadets would do nothing but disappear into the holo-chamber, but as the security chief, I have access."

He cleared his throat. "I would be very interested in seeing that."

The human no longer looked wary in my presence. There was nothing like dangling the idea of a pleasure planet to redeem myself.

Admiral Zoran took his seat at the top of the U-shaped table with his wife taking the seat next to him. I knew that our guest of honor would be on his other side, so I steered Captain Gorman toward his seat so I could take the one beside him.

Once we were seated, I picked up my goblet. "As the chief of security for the academy, I am the one you will want to talk to when it comes to the safety of the cadets, human and Drexian. Since we will be spending a lot of time together, we should get to know each other." I nudged him again. "Aside from our visits to the holo-chamber."

He chuckled as he reached for his own goblet. "My visit is not supposed to be a long one."

I forced myself to look sad. "That is too bad. I understand you are acquainted with one of our human instructors."

He took a drink, hiding behind the rim of the goblet as his gaze darted around the room.

Fiona was not here yet. I knew without even glancing. I would feel her if she was. Her energy shifted something in the air when she was near me.

Gorman replaced his goblet onto the wooden table. "I was stationed with Captain Douglas before she was assigned to come here."

"Captain Douglas," I repeated, as if I did not know exactly who she was, as if I had not been prodding him to speak of her, as if I was not manipulating him for information.

He bobbed his head up and down. "You came into her office this morning."

"Ah, yes. The Strategy instructor. Do you know her well?"

Something dark crossed his gaze. "I thought I did, but I don't think she's the type to let anyone know her well."

I nodded as if I knew what he meant. "I hope your reunion was pleasant and she welcomed you to the academy."

He choked back a laugh and picked up his drink again. "Not the way I hoped she would."

I took a swig from my own goblet, the tart Drexian wine preventing me from speaking, which was probably a good thing. Taking a drink also prevented me from planting a fist in the man's face, which would not have helped me make friends with him. I would have to ignore his innuendo, even though the suggestion that he had hoped for an intimate welcome from Fiona made my blood simmer in my veins.

"One thing I have learned about human females is they are unpredictable."

Gorman swallowed a gulp of wine and barked out a laugh. "Then you've learned all there is to know about them. Don't ever think you understand women, because I promise you that you don't."

A frisson of energy tickled the back of my neck, and I looked up to see Fiona walk into the room flanked by several other females. I recognized one as an Iron, one as the flight instructor dating Volten, and one as Torq's mate. But I only knew Ariana and Fiona by name.

I attempted to glance away before Gorman noticed, but I was too late.

"Speak of the devil," he muttered.

"You believe she is an evil deity?" That seemed extreme, even for a stubborn, hot-tempered human like Fiona.

"It's a figure of speech," he said, not taking his gaze from her as she and her friends took seats at the far end of the table. "I don't think she's evil, even if she did sleep with me and ditch me."

My back bristled as I absorbed what he'd let slip. "You were involved with the captain on Earth?"

He jerked his gaze from her and focused on his goblet of wine. I should have warned him that Drexian wine was known to be potent, and humans should go slowly, but looser lips would give me the information I wanted. "I would not say involved. It was one night. I hoped it would be more, but she left for here the next morning." He took a drink of wine and shook his head. "She did not even bother to tell me. I woke up, and she was gone. Then I heard that she'd shipped out—way out."

Part of me felt a rush of satisfaction that Fiona had left the man without a backward glance, but another part of me wondered what she had been running from. I slid my gaze to her and found her shrewd gaze pinned to me. Was the captain the only secret she did not want following her to the academy?

CHAPTER
THIRTY-SEVEN

Fiona

T he scraping of silverware and the clunking of goblets on the wooden table had slowed as the welcome banquet came to an end. I'd managed to push enough of my food around my plate, so it looked like I'd eaten when I'd really just nibbled on a roll of warm, yeasty bread.

Ariana leaned closer to me on my left side. "Don't think I don't see what you've done."

I sighed. Of course, Ariana had noticed. She might not be an Assassin trained to notice small details, but she was my closest friend at the academy, and she knew I loved eating. "I'm not that hungry."

She eyed my plate. "When are you not hungry, Fi?"

"When Vyk and Devon are sitting next to each other and acting like they're best buds."

Ariana followed my gaze across the room to the head of the table to where the Drexian and human were talking and laughing. I'd seen the way Vyk had looked at Devon when he'd walked in on us that morning. I'd seen the hardness in Vyk's eyes when he had told me that he didn't trust him. And now he was acting like they had known each other for years?

"Maybe they've found common ground," my friend suggested. "They are both military officers."

More like that common ground was me, I thought. What was Devon telling Vyk about me? What about my past was he revealing, courtesy of the powerful Drexian wine?

"Have you ever seen Vyk like this?" I asked Ariana. "Have you ever seen him laughing, even with Drexians he knows?"

Ariana hesitated, nibbling the corner of her lip. "No, but that doesn't mean anything."

I gave her a side-eye glance. "So, it's just a coincidence? I don't believe in coincidences."

Admiral Zoran slid his chair back, the legs scraping loudly on the stone floor. He'd already given a welcome toast to Devon at the start of the meal, but he looked poised to do it again. Would this night ever end? I was still supposed to pay Commander Vyk a visit, although I dreaded it now.

"Thank you all for joining me in welcoming Captain Gorman, and I trust all of you will help me show him the best of the Academy during his stay."

Everyone lifted their goblets one last time, and I tossed back the remnants of my wine, glad I'd already developed a tolerance to the stuff. The last thing I needed now was to be drunk.

Zoran did not sit again, but instead, he pulled out his wife's chair for her and gave her his hand to help her stand. That was the signal for everyone else to stand, as well.

I lost no time in pushing back my chair and jumping to my feet. "At least that's over."

Ariana stood, but she was distracted by Volten slipping his hand in hers, so I turned to Morgan, who'd been sitting on my other side.

"That wasn't so bad," she said, touching a hand to her stomach. "The food was good, and we were all the way across the room from the guy you wanted us to keep away from you. This task isn't going to be hard after—"

A sharp elbow in the ribs caused her words to drift off, but a glance to one side told me why. Devon was making a beeline for us, for me.

"*Grekking* hell," I muttered, finding the Drexian curse oddly satisfying.

Before the captain could reach me, Jess stepped into his path. "We haven't met yet. I'm Jess, short for Jessica. I'm a cadet in the School of Strategy, and I would love to tell you all about my experience being a human at the academy."

Devon blinked slowly at her, as if trying to focus his gaze. "What?"

"That's why you're here, isn't it? To find out how the integration is going." Her voice had become much more bubbly than usual, and she hung on his arm to prevent him from walking forward, a fact that prompted her boyfriend, Torq, to glare at the captain.

"There might be some flaws in this plan," I said, as Torq drew himself up to his full height.

Before I could step in and prevent Devon from being attacked by a jealous Drexian who had no idea why his girl was suddenly simpering over the visiting captain, Morgan pushed Jess aside.

"If you really want to know what's going on, I can tell you. I'm also an Assassin, but I'm..." she cast a glance at Jess, "more available for intimate conversations."

"Assassin?" Devon mumbled, clearly forgetting the nickname of the School of Strategy.

Britta came up and flanked the captain on the other side, causing him to swing his wide-eyed gaze to her. Then she and Morgan spun the captain around, and proceeded to walk him away from me, chattering eagerly about how much they had to tell him.

I backed away and made a dash for the exit, knowing that I would owe my friends big for this. Whatever future favors I owed them were worth it for not having to deal with a wine-soaked Devon with more questions than I had answers. I didn't even stop to say goodnight to Ariana as I slipped away, grateful to escape the banquet hall without being spotted.

I'd just stepped into the corridor when I was yanked backward, and a hand clamped over my mouth.

"Did you really think you could run?"

CHAPTER
THIRTY-EIGHT

Jess

"That was awkward." Morgan sidled up to me, as the crowd in the banquet hall dispersed.

I released a sigh of relief. "I was wondering how far you were going to take it." I swept my gaze around the long room that echoed with chatter, even from the few of us remaining. "Where's Britta?"

Morgan ran a hand through her blonde hair. "Taking one for the team?"

My jaw fell open. "Not really?"

My friend grinned. "No, but she was going to walk the captain to his quarters. I don't think the guy could find them on his own."

"At least he isn't pestering Fi, although I'm not sure how long we can keep distracting him. At some point, he's going to be more sober and figure it out."

I nodded, wondering why Fiona didn't just tell the captain that she wasn't interested. Normally, the instructor was a tough-as-nails ballbuster, but the arrival of the envoy from Earth had rattled her.

"Maybe by then he'll have already given the human integration a good review."

My stomach tightened. "You don't think he would let his deal with Fiona color what he reports to Earth, do you?"

My friend angled her head at me. "Do I think a guy would make a decision based on his bruised ego and be petty enough to punish an entire program to get back at one woman who rejected him?"

I groaned. "You're right. Forget I even asked." Then I straightened. "But that's not going to happen, because we're going to make sure the captain is way too distracted to get dumped by Fiona—again."

"What happened to you thinking we couldn't keep this up for too long?"

"If it means saving the program, we can."

"Saving what program?"

I pivoted to face Torq, who did not look pleased.

"Does this have anything to do with you falling all over the human envoy?" His expression was stern, as he stood with his arms crossed over his chest.

I almost laughed at how irritated he was. I was still not used to having a Drexian boyfriend, and I'd never had a guy act jealous over me before. Even though he was wrong, I secretly loved that he had a possessive streak. It wasn't very liberated of me, but since I'd never had much male attention before, I couldn't help but revel in the sensation of being desired enough to provoke envy.

"I was *pretending* to be interested in him." I put a hand on Torq's arm. "I was helping Fiona."

His rigid stance softened. "You were pretending?"

"Of course." I leaned closer to him. "Why would I be interested in him when I have you? You're bigger and hotter, and you're a badass Blade."

Torq's chest swelled, and a grin teased his lips. "That is true." Then he narrowed his eyes at me. "Wait, are you flattering me to change the subject?"

"Not a big, dumb Blade after all," Morgan whispered so only I could hear her. "Nice try, though. You're getting way better."

I fought the urge to shoot my friend a look. She knew of my previous inexperience with men and had been coaching me on how to handle a boyfriend, especially since Drexian males were so dominant.

"I'm not changing the subject." I squeezed Torq's arm and smiled at him. "I'm telling the truth. Fiona asked me to help keep the captain occupied for her."

Torq returned my smile, unfolding his arms and pulling me to him. "Good. I did not enjoy seeing you flirt with someone else. Do not do that again, please."

Despite the fact that he was much taller and broader than me, Torq was still a cadet, and he was not far away from his boyhood. It was easy to forget that he could be fragile when he looked so tough and was a badass Blade.

"I am not interested in anyone but you." I touched a hand to the side of his face. "I promise."

"This is my cue to leave," Morgan mumbled as she stepped away. "I'll catch you later, Jess."

I gave her a finger wave as Torq exhaled and curled his arms around my back. "Now what is this about you helping Fiona and saving a program?"

I cringed. I had hoped he'd forgotten overhearing that part.

I tried to laugh it off. "Fiona knows that captain from Earth, and she wants to make sure he doesn't get the wrong idea about them."

"There is a *them*?"

Ugh. I was digging myself into a hole. "No, there isn't."

"So, why would an Assassin instructor need you to flirt with the human envoy? That seems like a lot of effort if there is no relationship."

Torq was a lot quicker than anyone expected, sometimes including me.

I hesitated, but finally decided to loop him in. I hated lying to him, and I would just have to trust him to keep the secret. The one advantage I had was the powerful sense of Drexian honor. If I made him vow not to tell, he would not. "If I tell you, you cannot reveal this to anyone." I pinned him with a stern gaze. "Drexian honor."

"I would never betray you," he said solemnly.

I knew he wouldn't. "The truth is that Fiona knows the guy from being stationed together. He likes her but she isn't interested. Now, she's worried that if she rejects the guy outright he might take it out on the human-Drexian exchange program."

Torq nodded as he absorbed this. "You and the other human females have been tasked to keep him away from her?"

"It's a girl code thing. We help each other like this."

He lifted a hand to my hair and brushed a loose strand off my forehead. "There is also Drexian mate code."

My pulse fluttered every time he called me his mate, even though I knew that as an independent woman I should not enjoy it so much. "What is Drexian mate code?"

"Your problems are my problems. Your mission is my mission."

I pursed my lips and scrunched them to one side. "Does this mean you're going to start flirting with the captain as a distraction?"

Instead of being shocked, Torq laughed. "That would be an effective distraction and might ensure he remained in his quarters for the duration of his visit. No, what I was suggesting was that I join you in keeping the envoy preoccupied so he will not have time to pursue Captain Douglas."

It took me a beat to remember that he still thought of Fiona as Captain Douglas. "You would do that?"

He pulled me closer to him, and I could feel a very firm testament to his affection. "You know I would do anything for you."

My heart pounded as heat suffused my entire body. Luckily, there was almost no one left in the banquet hall to see us, and those who remained were deep in conversation with each other.

"Do not worry," Torq added. "I will not tell anyone why I am suddenly interested in keeping the Earth envoy entertained. It will stay between us."

I put my hands to both sides of his face and pulled his head down so I could whisper in his ear. "I would say thank you, but I think I'd rather show you my appreciation—in your quarters."

He let out a low rumbling sound. "Then why are we still standing here?"

CHAPTER
THIRTY-NINE

Vyk

"It is me," I husked as Fiona squirmed in my grasp, attempting to elbow me in the side.

She stilled, and I released my hand over her mouth as soon as I was sure she would not scream. Then she whirled around, her eyes flashing murder. "What's with the grabbing? Why does everyone in this *grekking* school grab people from behind?"

I enjoyed hearing her use a Drexian curse, but I could not smile. "This academy was forged from violence and secrecy. It still holds that legacy in its walls."

She glared at me. "It's been a while since battles were fought here. I think we can dispense with the hands over the mouth."

"I thought you might make a scene if I startled you."

She put her waist and jutted out one hip. "How about not star-tling me?"

I huffed out a breath. This was not going the way I'd intended. "My apologies, but I wished to speak with you."

"I'm surprised." She jerked her head toward the open doors of the banquet hall. "I would have thought you were all talked out."

I frowned at this. So, she had noticed that I had talked with Captain Gorman for most of the dinner. "It was a welcome banquet. I was being welcoming."

Her eyes became slits. "What's up with that? You've never been welcoming before. Not when I arrived at the academy with the others from Earth. Not when the new class of cadets joined the school. Not when other Drexian warriors have visited. But you went from not trusting Devon to chatting with him like he's your best friend. What gives?"

"What gives?" I repeated her question, not certain what that exact phrase meant, even though I knew what she wanted to know. I should have expected someone as clever as Fiona, an Assassin instructor, to detect deception.

"You don't like Devon. I know that because you told me, and you put him through the gauntlet to torment him." She held up a hand to quell any protests. "Don't deny it. But you changed your tune by the time this banquet rolled around. I want to know why."

I did not want to lie to her. She might despise me, but I could not stomach the thought of piling lies onto lies with her. If I did, it would be impossible to untangle myself. It would be impossible to move forward. I decided to go with the truth, but not all of it.

"Admiral Zoran expects me to treat our visitor with respect, and he wishes the captain's report to Earth to reflect positively on the human exchange."

She rocked back on the heels of her boots. "Are you telling me that you're cozying up to Devon so you can make sure the humans stay at the academy?"

"That is what I am saying."

She laughed, the sound bouncing off the high ceiling. "Well, that's quite the about-face, isn't it? You went from trying to get rid of the humans to kissing ass to keep us here?"

I blinked at her a few times as I tried to digest her words. "I might have shown the captain hospitality, but I promise that I did not kiss any part of him."

She grinned widely, and I wondered why she was suddenly enjoying our conversation. "It's an Earth expression, but trust me, sweetie, you were."

The term of endearment was surprising, but from her tone I did not believe that she meant it. Humans were so confusing, and their language and expressions made no sense.

Fiona stepped closer to me, and I instinctively took a step back toward the shadows hugging the walls. "Do you want to know what I think?" She did not wait for me to answer. "I think you are keeping your enemies close."

I chose not to respond, since any denial would be a lie.

"It's not a bad strategy," she continued. "It might be what I would do if there was someone I didn't trust. Keeping your friends close and your enemies closer is smart, especially if you're the kind who doesn't trust easily."

Again, the accusation that I did not trust.

"You do know that your plan has a few flaws, though. For one, if you intend to keep this up, you'll have to spend a lot more time with Devon, and I know humans annoy you. And I'm pretty sure you can't do anything with him that will injure him again, which means you're left with safe activities. Drexians are bored to tears with safe things."

"I am an Iron. I do not have to risk my life to enjoy myself."

Her brows peaked. "That's right. I always forget that you're an Iron, because being an engineer doesn't fit with you being an Inferno Force Commander and having a reputation for being ruthless."

I clenched my jaw to stifle the urge to tell her all the things she did not know about me. Instead, I took a deep breath and stepped closer to her so that she had to either back up or tip her head back to meet my eyes. "Maybe you do not understand me as much as you think you do."

She did not step away, so she dropped her head back to continue holding my gaze. "I never claimed to understand you."

"But you have opinions about me. Opinions based on what you think you know."

Pink tinged her cheeks as she folded her arms over her chest. "Why are we talking about me? This is about you and your plan regarding Devon."

"A plan you are certain you understand, even though you admit you do not understand me."

She cocked her head to one side. "You're clever. Now I can see why you were an Iron. But you hide all that shrewd, strategic thinking behind a tough exterior. Maybe I *should* try to find out why, but what I really want to know is if you plan to put the envoy from Earth in danger—again."

"You are worried I will hurt him? You are concerned your captain is in danger from me?"

Irritation flickered across her face. "He isn't *my* captain, but yes, I'm worried that your friendly act is only covering up sinister intentions. You may have wanted to see the back of all the humans since we arrived, but I would really like to stay, so forgive me if I don't trust the intentions of a Drexian who has been against me from the beginning."

Her words were like blades piercing my heart, but they were nothing I did not deserve. "I promise you that I no longer wish for humans to leave the academy."

Because that would mean you would leave the academy. That would mean I would never see you again.

She opened her mouth to snap back, but then turned abruptly when footsteps emerged from the doorway to the banquet hall. I did not recognize the voices, although I could tell one was female and one was male.

Fiona pushed me back into the shadowy recesses of the corridor, slapping a hand over my mouth when I started to question her. "Now it's your turn to be quiet and my turn to be grabby."

CHAPTER
FORTY

Fiona

"So, you are hiding from the captain?" Vyk asked, as he pressed his hand to the panel beside his door and it slid open.

I rushed inside with a furtive glance over my shoulder. "I'm not hiding."

He followed me slowly. "No? Then why did you put a hand over my mouth and drag me into the shadows when he passed by?"

I exhaled loudly. "I just didn't want to deal with him, okay? Besides, Britta was distracting him, and it would have ruined all her hard work if he'd spotted us."

I strode toward the crackling fire, grateful for the warmth. It seemed strange that I'd been in the room not even a full day ago, yet so much had happened.

"You are sure you did not want him to see you with me?"

I snapped my head to him. "It's not you. I promise."

That wasn't exactly true. No one knew about my deal with Vyk. No one knew that I'd lost a bet with him. No one knew that I was forging some kind of bizarre relationship with the gruff security chief. Not even I understood what we were doing, or why I was starting to soften toward the jerk.

He made a noise deep in his throat that told me he believed me about as much as I believed myself, but he didn't press me. Instead, he crossed to a low wooden chest and opened the doors.

I did a double take. "I thought that was for clothes. It's a booze cabinet?"

He turned as he retrieved a bottle of amber-hued liquid. "I have collected bottles from all over the galaxy during my time with Inferno Force." He inclined his head toward a tall cabinet against another wall. "My clothes are in there, but they are not as interesting."

I'd never seen the Drexian in anything but his academy uniform or black clothing for working out, so it made sense that he prioritized his liquor collection. Part of me wanted to peek in his wardrobe and see if the uniforms were as neatly hung as I suspected, but I wasn't bold enough to do that. Not yet.

Vyk poured two glasses and handed one to me. "Zenarian gin. It comes from a small planet that produces vast quantities of spices from their trees. It tastes sweet but it has a kick."

I swirled the drink in my glass, captivated by the way it shifted colors from gold to amber to brown. "Here goes nothing." I slammed it back in a single gulp, gasping as the liquid slid down my throat and burned my stomach.

Vyk took a small sip of his as he eyed me. "I have never seen anyone drink it as fast as you did."

I fanned my mouth as I tried to breathe. "I assumed you chugged it. Don't Drexians chug everything?"

He poured me another glass of a clear liquid. "You have very peculiar ideas about Drexians, considering you have lived among us for a while now."

I took the glass, hesitating.

"You can drink that in one gulp. It is bubbling water."

I gratefully tossed it back, sighing as the cool drink doused the fire. I sank into one of the chairs as the alien gin made my fingers and toes tingle and the room sway a bit.

Vyk took both empty glasses from me and sat in the other chair. "Are all human females as bold as you?"

"Don't you mean foolish and impulsive?" Now that my throat wasn't in flames, I was starting to feel embarrassed for being so overly confident. I was used to being the woman who could drink everyone under the table, beat everyone at cards, and outsmart my opponents on the battlefield. I was not used to being beaten or being bested by an alien liquor.

"If I meant that, I would have said that." Vyk leaned forward and rested his elbows on his knees. "I should have warned you not to drink it in one gulp, although it did not occur to me that a female would do that."

He'd been doing so well until he'd called out me being a woman. "Because females you know are smarter than me?"

"No, because they are too afraid. I do not know any females as smart as you."

Okay, that got him a bit back in my good graces. "Even if you beat me badly at cards?"

He took another sip of his drink. "Even so. You were brave enough to play me, even though you could not have had the decades of experience I do."

"I think we're back to me being overly confident."

Vyk twitched one shoulder, as if dismissing this. "I am Drexian. There is no such thing as overly confident."

I snorted at this and then slapped a hand over my mouth. Well, I was making a truly stellar impression. Then I remembered that I shouldn't care what kind of impression I made. I was here because I'd lost a bet. I didn't owe Vyk charming companionship. Which was good, because he certainly wasn't getting any from me.

"You want to know why I'm so tough?" I asked, fully aware that the booze was loosening my tongue. For some reason, I wanted to tell him. "I had to be. I learned early on that life is cruel and no one will take care of me but me." I thought about losing Jack and then my father walking out. "I trained myself to be so smart and so tough that I could always save myself."

When I glanced at Vyk, his gaze was locked onto me, but I didn't see pity in it, which was good. I despised pity. He said nothing, but there was an understanding in his eyes. He knew what it was like to build walls to protect yourself.

I closed my eyes and leaned back, partially so I could pretend I wasn't embarrassing myself and partly because my body was now tingling all over. He hadn't been joking about the gin being stronger than Drexian wine, and Drexian wine was no joke. I was pretty sure I couldn't walk a straight line, and it was all I could do not to roll off the chair and onto the floor. Especially with the fire warming me and the sounds of the flames lulling me to sleep.

When I felt a hand take mine, I opened my eyes instantly and jerked my hand away.

Vyk stood next to the chair looking down at me with what I would swear was amusement. "I was going to help you stand."

"Oh." I took his hand and let him help me up. "Wait, why am I standing?"

Vyk still had my hand, and he was so close that I could feel the heat from his body pulsing into mine. "It is time for bed."

My pulse jangled. He wasn't taking me to bed as in *taking* me to bed, was he? Then I realized that the thought wasn't so horrible. I wouldn't mind seeing what was beneath the uniform. Or, to be more specific, the uniform pants, since I'd seen him in a towel.

I tipped my head to meet his gaze, startled by the intensity in them. I lifted one hand and ran it across his cheek and then to the nape of his neck. Not only was the gin strong, it seemed to dissolve my inhibitions. Suddenly, I needed to touch him, taste him, feel him.

Scraping my fingers into the back of his hair, I yanked his mouth to mine. His lips were soft, and the short hairs of his beard tickled my cheek as I allowed myself to sink into the kiss. But before I could enjoy the smoky taste of him and the spicy scent of his skin, he was pulling away from me.

"What's wrong?" I asked, feeling dazed.

"This is not you," he gritted out, each word sounding pained.

Before I could tell him to stop being so *grekking* honorable and kiss me, there was a thumping on the door.

CHAPTER
FORTY-ONE

Vyk

Fiona's hand brushed my cheek and then the back of my neck as she peered at me. My heart skipped several beats as she fisted her hand into the hair at the nape of my neck and tugged me forward. I did not fight her, even as I doubted her judgment and my own.

The sensation of her mouth on mine was electric, and the room seemed to sway as I surrendered to the sweet taste of her, the eagerness of her lips, and her quickening breaths.

This is wrong. All wrong.

The voice in my head was sharp and commanding, like the orders I had given so readily over my career. It did not matter that she had kissed me or that her body hummed with desire.

She had been compromised by the gin. She was not herself. I would not allow myself to enjoy stolen pleasures, even if they lit my entire body on fire.

I pulled away, breaking the kiss and sucking in a breath for strength. Fiona blinked at me, confusion etched on her face.

"What's wrong?"

Her breathy voice sent heat arrowing to my cock. I curled my hands into fists by my side as I forced the words from my lips. "This is not you."

She opened her mouth to speak again, and I knew in that instant that I would not be strong enough to resist her if she protested too much. But a hard knock on the door broke the spell between us.

I expelled a heavy breath that dripped with relief, straightened, and took a step back.

Her gaze darted to the door. "Who could need you now?"

It was a good question. This was not an Inferno Force battleship. There were rarely emergencies that required my attention in the middle of the night, even though I was the chief of security. An academy did not deal with the same level of potential danger, which was something I had come to value after years of living on the edge of battle.

"I do not know, but it must be important." No one would disturb me otherwise. Admiral Zoran was no alarmist, and the rest of the staff was too terrified of me to dare disturb my sleep.

Fiona grabbed my arm before I could press it to the panel. "Wait," she whispered. "How are we going to explain me?"

There was no explanation I wished to offer anyone. The truth did not make me look good, and anything else would create more questions.

She pointed to the attached bathroom. "I'll be in here. Just make sure not to offer your guest a full tour."

Fiona darted into the room, disappearing into the darkness as I turned my attention to the door. I touched my palm to the panel as another sharp rap sounded.

When the door slid aside, Tivek stood on the other side. Maybe I had been wrong about Zoran not summoning me, or maybe there was trouble brewing.

"I would not bother you if..." the admiral's adjunct began, then paused. "I thought you might have information about the whereabouts of the Earth envoy."

I stared at him for a beat. "The captain? You think he is here with me?"

"No." Tivek inclined his head to one side. "I thought you might provide insight into where he might go."

"Are you telling me he is lost?" I had not expected *this*.

Tivek held up a hat. "The captain left this behind at the banquet table, but when I went to his assigned quarters to return it to him, he was not there."

"And you thought that since I had spent most of the evening engaging in conversation with the man, I might have greater insight?"

Tivek frowned slightly. "You are the head of security. I think you, more than anyone, would want to ensure that he is safe during his visit."

The rebuke was deftly done. It was my responsibility, and after my lapse of judgment earlier that day, I needed to prove that I could still keep the human safe. "I will find him."

"Thank you," Tivek said. "I have not notified the admiral. I thought this could be handled quietly since it is most likely nothing."

This consideration and discretion were probably more than I deserved. "The academy is cavernous, and more than one cadet had gotten turned around in the labyrinth of corridors. I doubt it is anything more than that."

"Agreed." Tivek allowed himself a breath, and he flicked his gaze around my quarters, landing for a moment on the two empty glasses. If he found this odd or if he believed I was secretly hiding the captain, he did not comment.

"We should search separately to cover more ground," I suggested, knowing that Fiona would never forgive me if I left her in my room. "You take the main hall and the corridors and towers around his assigned quarters. I will make sure he has not wandered to the underground levels."

Tivek gave me a curt nod and turned to go while I let the door slide shut. It had barely closed when Fiona strode from the bathroom.

"He's missing?" She pinned me with a hard gaze. "You had nothing to do with this?"

"How could I? I have been with you since leaving the banquet hall."

She rubbed a hand over her forehead. "Right. Of course. We saw him walking out with Britta together." She snapped her fingers. "Britta!" Then she made a face. "She wouldn't have taken him back to her quarters, would she? I know she was taking one for the team, but I didn't mean for her to do *that*."

"Chances are good he got lost. He did drink Drexian wine for the first time."

She nodded. "I'm still going to check with Britta. Did I hear that you're going to go to the underground floors?" Her expression darkened. "Please don't tell me there are still beasts in the dungeons."

"There are not, but that doesn't mean there aren't tunnels that are unsafe."

She groaned. "This place is a death trap. Why did I think we'd be able to convince anyone from Earth that it's safe?"

I stiffened at her comment. "The academy is only dangerous for those who do not heed warnings."

"I don't know if anyone gave Devon warnings."

I disliked hearing her refer to him in such familiar terms, but I reminded myself that she was more concerned with the damage he could do with a bad report than she was for him.

She raked a hand through her hair. "I hope we find him before he gets into more trouble."

"We will." I eyed her disheveled hair and remembered her fingers tangling in my hair. As much as I wanted more of her, I did not trust myself. Not tonight. "It is late, and this search might take a while. I do not expect you to return here."

I opened the door and stood to the side so she could exit first.

She glanced at me then quickly away. "As you wish."

I hung back for a moment after she stomped out. The woman had no idea what I truly wished. If she did, she would have run.

CHAPTER
FORTY-TWO

Fiona

M y face burned as I hurried from the commander's quarters, and I didn't dare look back. Why was I angry that he'd told me not to come back? I should have been thrilled, right? After all, I'd been outraged by his bet and by being forced to spend time with him. So, why had his dismissal irritated me when it should have made me cheer?

"It's not because of that kiss," I scoffed to myself as my feet thwacked the stone floors in a punishing rhythm.

He was hardly the first guy I'd kissed. Hell, he wasn't even the first superior officer I'd kissed, which was not something I should be bragging about. But I was not some innocent flower who could have her head turned by a single kiss.

But he hadn't kissed me. I'd kissed him. "And then he sent you away."

My eyes burned as I tried to brush off the humiliation. It hadn't been a bad kiss, so if Vyk wasn't into me—or my kiss—then that was his loss. Still, my cheeks flamed as I made my way down one dimly lit corridor and then another.

I had never asked for any of this—the bet, the time with the infuriating Vyk, the blast-from-the-past visit from Gorman— but I was in too deep to get out now. I had to suck it up and move forward, which meant ignoring the fact that I'd kissed Vyk and he'd pushed me away, and focusing on finding Devon.

I welcomed the cold wind swirling around me as I crossed the open-air bridge and caught a glimpse of the moonlight bouncing off the tempestuous waves of the aptly named Restless Sea. The cool was bracing and banished any remnants of effects from the alien gin. By the time I reached the other side, I was completely awake. I was also fired up.

I'd built a reputation for being a tough badass. I could hang with the guys any day, and I'd never backed down from a challenge. It was why I'd adapted to the academy so well. The Drexians rejected toughness. So why had I forgotten that?

I was an Assassin. And as the academy rules stated, you needed to beware of the Assassins. "Both Vyk and Devon should be wary of me."

I practically ran up the smooth, black stairs of the female tower, the echoes of my footsteps the only sound in the silent building. Night had enveloped the tower, and only the faint light from the wall sconces illuminated the empty landing as I reached it.

I strode across toward Britta's room, rapping on the door then pausing to catch my breath.

I waited, hoping that she was taking some time to answer because I'd roused her from bed, not because she and Devon were scurrying to get dressed. I didn't care if Britta got with Devon, but I did not want her to do it because of me.

The door glided open, and I loudly exhaled when I saw the cadet standing alone in the darkened doorway in her pajamas and a sleep mask pushed up onto her forehead.

"What's up?" She rubbed her eyes as she peered into the hallway.

Now that I was standing outside her room, I felt like a bit of an idiot for thinking that she would have brought the captain back to her room. "Sorry for waking you but I wanted to check on something."

"Shoot," she said, not questioning the fact that it was the middle of the night.

"You left the banquet with Captain Gorman, right?"

She nodded. "Jess was talking to him, but Torq looked like he was getting bent out of shape, so Morgan and I stepped in. We got him away and kept him occupied for a while. Then Tivek pulled Morgan aside with a question, and I walked the captain to his quarters."

All that tracked with what I'd seen when they'd emerged from the banquet hall. "How did you know where to find his quarters?"

"He seemed to know, although to be fair, they put him on the instructor hall, and that's relatively close to the main building and easy to find."

And not very far from Vyk's quarters.

"Why?" Britta pushed her pink, satin, eye mask higher on her forehead "Is there a problem?"

"Nothing major, I'm sure." I gave her a thin smile. "He isn't in his assigned quarters now."

Britta frowned. "Weird. When I left him, he seemed eager to get some sleep."

"Was he drunk?"

She considered this, tipping her head back and forth a few times as she thought. "I don't know if I'd say he was drunk. At first, I thought he was, but he seemed pretty sober when I was leading him through the corridors and telling him where things were."

"You gave him a tour?"

She shifted her weight from one foot to the next. "Not an official tour, and it was only of the places we passed, like the administrative offices and the staff dining room. He said he'd been given a tour by our security chief, but they'd only gotten as far as the School of Battle."

That much was true, so it was hard to find fault with the guy asking questions about the school he was tasked to evaluate. Still, he had gone to his quarters and then left again. Why? And where had he gone so late at night? I would understand if he'd had impaired judgment and decided to wander about, but from what Britta said, he hadn't appeared drunk.

My stomach tightened as I thought about one place he might want to go. "Did he ask you about where you lived?"

"He did make a cheeky suggestion of seeing my quarters, but I told him that the female tower was not close."

If he hadn't known that all the women were in one tower, he did now. I glanced over my shoulder at my door. There wasn't any way he could have gotten into my room, was there?

Devon was resourceful and shrewd, but he wasn't bold enough to break into my quarters, was he? How would he even do that?

"Thanks, Britta." I backed away from the cadet. "Sorry to wake you up."

"No worries," she said as she started to slide her eyes mask back down and pivot back to her bed.

I spun around and made a beeline for my own door. If Devon had somehow snuck into my room, it was not going to be pretty. I palmed the side panel, flipped on the lights, and stepped inside.

I glanced at the lump in the bed. "Would you like to explain yourself?"

CHAPTER
FORTY-THREE

Vyk

I did the right thing, I assured myself, as I trudged down a winding staircase. I did the honorable thing.

Then why did I feel so rotten? From the moment I'd sent Fiona away, it had been eating at me. Every bone in my Drexian body knew that it was right to push her away, yet every nerve ending screamed at me.

My body ached as if I'd ripped off a limb, and I could think of nothing but how she'd tasted when she'd kissed me. My ears were filled with her breathy sigh, my nose still twitched from the flowery aroma of her hair, and my lips tingled from the touch of her skin.

I growled as I reached the lower level of the academy and the floor angled downward. It was pointless to obsess over a female like this—a female who I'd always thought despised me.

"Then why did she kiss me?"

The gin, a voice in the back of my head taunted me. It was all because of the gin. She never would have touched you if not for the potent drink.

I clenched my teeth, hating the truth in the mocking voice. "It doesn't matter. You have a job to do."

Whatever had happened between me and Fiona, she would not be happy with me if I didn't find the captain. Even if a part of me would have loved to imagine him wandering lost in the hidden tunnels, I could not let that happen.

I strode down the narrowing corridor, feeling the temperature drop as the floor sloped. The dark rocks beneath my feet were damp, and I scanned the space in front of me for footprints. There were none. I glanced behind me, seeing my own distinct bootprints. He had not come this way.

I turned back, relieved that I would not have to traverse tight passageways in search of the missing human. I made a series of turns until the air warmed, and the loamy, damp smell was replaced by pungent, savory ones.

The kitchens. Had the captain been in search of a late-night snack and found his way down here? It was a long shot, but I had to consider everything.

I stopped outside the doors, poking my head inside and spotting the two cooks bent over long, worn tables and rolling out the next day's bread. "Have either of you seen a human down here?"

The two alien cooks jumped and exchanged a startled glance. "Human? Not for a few days, at least."

I grunted and thanked them, resuming my search. Of course, Fiona could have already found him. Since we had last seen the man with the human cadet, there was a significant chance that he was with her.

I could not help but grin. The captain taking up with the cadet would not be such a bad thing. It might even make him more inclined to give the exchange a positive report. And it would ensure that his attention was fully off Fiona.

I finished searching the lower levels, checking the lock on the dungeon gates and walking down every corridor that wound beneath the school. My eyes were heavy as I walked up the stairs, certain that my hunt was a waste of time.

My bed beckoned me, but I decided to make a cursory spin around the main building. It was where the captain had first entered, it was where the banquet had been held, it was where he'd met with the admiral. Of all the places in the academy, he'd spent more time here than anywhere.

I felt relatively secure in the fact that I would not find him in the gauntlet. I choked back a laugh, even though there was no one to hear me. No, I did not need to search the School of Battle. The captain would stay far from there.

I ran my hand along the cool stone of the banister as I walked up the wide, empty staircase leading to the second level of the main hall. The inclinators that normally zipped up and down the interior of the tall central building were still and silent, like sleeping creatures awaiting the return of the cadets who loved to pack into them on their way to classes.

I stuck my head into the banquet hall, but found it deserted. Then I continued down the hallway, passing Admiral Zoran's office. I turned the corner and stopped abruptly, my breath catching in my chest.

What was Captain Gorman doing outside the door to my office?

I watched him take a few steps away and then turn. I had not seen the door close—and how would he have gotten in, anyway?—but I got the strange sensation that he had not just arrived at my office.

When he saw me, he froze before breaking into a friendly smile. "Commander, I'm so glad you found me. I have been walking in circles."

"You are lost?"

He chuckled. "Very. I'm afraid I left my hat at the welcome dinner but got turned around looking for the banquet hall."

I knew that he had, in fact, left his hat behind, but something about his claims rang false. But why would he want to get into my office? What would be the purpose of learning the strategies for keeping the academy secure? We were allies, after all, and the Earth Planetary Defense was well aware of our upgraded security protocols. He would only have to access the records on Earth to know our joint plans for defending Earth and Drex.

There was no evidence that the human was anything but what he said he was, just as there was no evidence that he was not searching for his missing hat. If I did not know of his connection to Fiona would I not see that clearly?

I gave him an aggressively firm thump on the back. "Your hat is safe. Come. I will take you back to your quarters."

"You know, you aren't at all what I expected," he said, as I led him back down the hall. "Of all the reports I read, yours is the one I think they got wrong."

A trickle of unease slid down my spine. He had read reports on me? Of course he had. I had been involved in the near annihilation of the human cadets. Suddenly, I was not so sure that the envoy was at the academy to assess the exchange.

He was here to pass judgment on me.

CHAPTER

FORTY-FOUR

Fiona

"What are you doing here?"

Ariana had rolled over and jumped from my bed. "Sorry, Fi. I just lay down for a few minutes while I was waiting for you and ..."

"How did you get in here?" I didn't mind my best friend being in my room—I did trust Ariana completely—but I had no idea my room was so easy to access.

"You gave me access a few weeks ago when I needed to grab some stuff for you, remember?"

Now I remembered. I'd gotten an Iron to add her palm print to the ones my door panel would recognize. I just hadn't imagined I'd ever find her sleeping in my bed. "Right. Is there a reason you're crashing in my bed instead of in your own room?" I sucked in a quick breath. "Did you and Volten have a fight?"

She shook her head. "Nothing like that, besides, we usually stay in his quarters, so it isn't awkward for women in the all-female tower. And why would he get to stay in my room if we fought?"

"Good point." I walked deeper into the room and pulled out the desk chair to sit on. "That still doesn't tell me why you're here."

She brushed a hand through her short hair. "It actually does have to do with Volten, but only in a roundabout way."

I crossed my legs at the knees and leaned back, waiting for her to elaborate as I stifled a yawn. "And it couldn't wait until morning?"

"I guess it could have, but I was pretty surprised, and I knew you'd want to know." She gestured to my now-closed door. "I did knock a few times, just so you don't think I'm a total creeper."

I grinned at her. "The jury is still out on that. Spill your news."

She shot me a slightly amused look. "I was leaving Volten's room because he started snoring—"

"He snores?"

"Not usually." Her tone was a bit defensive. "But when he does, watch out. Anyway, I decided I'd rather sleep than listen to a chainsaw and get annoyed. I slipped from his room and was trying to be quiet, although I don't know why since he was so loud."

I gave her a stern look.

"I'm rambling. Sorry." She leaned forward and rubbed her palms down the front of her pants. "I'm explaining why I was tiptoeing and how the captain didn't hear me when I passed his open door. I wasn't trying to eavesdrop."

I sat forward. "By captain, do you mean Devon?"

She bobbed her head up and down. "The door to his quarters hadn't closed all the way. It looked like there was something stuck in the doorway like a strap to a bag, but whatever it was, it made a gap in the door."

"And made it possible for you to hear him?"

Ariana grimaced, as if dreading telling me more. "He was talking to someone, but he was on a device. It sounded like a vid call, probably with Earth. The voice was distant, so I know there wasn't someone else in his room with him."

"It isn't odd for him to making a vid call after arriving here." I hoped he hadn't felt the need to share being put through the literal gauntlet by Commander Vyk.

"Not at all. I didn't think much of it once I got over the shock of being able to hear him and the guilt about lingering outside his door to hear more."

I shook my head, even though I was smiling. "I would have done the same."

She let out a whoosh of breath. "Good. I know it was nosy but since he has the fate of the exchange program in his hands, I wanted to know what he was saying."

My heart tripped in my chest. "And? Did he say anything that might hurt the program?"

"No. From what I could tell, he wasn't giving a report on the academy at all."

"But he was talking to someone on Earth?" Then something occurred to me. Maybe the captain had a girlfriend back home. Maybe I'd been worried about all the wrong things with him. Maybe his call had been personal, which was why Ariana was beating around the bush so much. "You don't have to worry about telling me if he has a girlfriend back home. I was being honest when I said that I wasn't interested in Devon and it had been a one-night thing."

"That's not it. He wasn't talking to a woman. If that was it, I would be relieved. At least then, you wouldn't have to worry about him making the moves on you."

My heart sank a bit. It would have been so much easier if he was romantically involved with someone on Earth.

"Whomever he was talking to sounded like he was a superior officer. He was pretty stern and did not seem happy with your friend."

"Why not?" Devon had always gotten along well with the higher-ups. He was great at kissing just the right amount of ass.

"From what I heard, he was not supposed to come here. He was not the envoy that Earth Planetary Defenses intended to send."

"Then how—?"

"The guy he was talking to pulled some strings to get the mission, and he wanted to make sure Devon knew that he owed him for it."

I groaned and slumped back in the chair. Devon had maneuvered his way to Drex, and I had a sinking feeling it wasn't because of the scenery or a love of long-range space travel.

CHAPTER
FORTY-FIVE

Vyk

I stood over my desk as I scoured the surface with my gaze. Nothing looked out of place, but the captain could have replaced everything to appear just as it had been when he'd snuck into my office the night before.

I had no proof that he had been inside my office. There was no sign that the door lock had been tampered with, there were no indications of forced entry, and there was no sign that anything had been taken. Even so, something told me that the human envoy had not been outside my office door by coincidence.

"But what did he want?" I rapped my fingers on the wooden surface that I kept neat and orderly. There was little that could be taken or moved, which made it easier to reassure myself that all my documents and reports were in order. But because I kept my desk so free from clutter, it would also be simple to restack everything into sharply aligned piles.

I picked up the latest security reports and flipped through them. There was little contained in even the most classified reports that was not also shared with our allies on Earth. Since we now worked in tandem with the humans, we briefed them on all potential threats. Captain Gorman could read any of these security briefings back on Earth, especially if he was ranked high enough to be sent to assess the exchange program.

Sinking into my chair, I tapped my device. There was little good to be gained by worrying over information that was not even secret from our allies. As much as I disliked and distrusted the man, I did not believe he was working for the enemy. No human would be so foolish as to align themselves with the Kronock when the creatures were determined to destroy Earth. No one on Earth even knew how to communicate with the aliens.

No, I did not believe that Gorman was that treacherous. If I was being honest, almost all my suspicion came from his connection with Fiona. It was not true suspicion as much as jealousy. I hated the idea of him with her. The thought of his hands on her, his lips on hers, his body on hers made revulsion pulse through me hot and fierce.

"*Grekking* human," I growled as I swept my fingers across the surface of my device to review the latest reports of long-range activity.

Drexian ships throughout the galaxy compiled data on the Kronock—where their ships were sighted, if their fleet was moving, how close their ships were to our territory—and relayed it to High Command, who then disseminated it to all the stations and to us. I might have been able to improve our planet's long-range sensors, but we still depended on the information gathered by our fleet—and mainly our far-flung Inferno Force ships—to keep us informed of any potential threats.

Now that the Kronock had shown us that they possessed jump technology, it was more crucial than ever to know how close they were, and if they were amassing ships. We could not afford to be surprised again, although the last attack had only happened because the enemy had traitors on the inside. They did not have that advantage anymore.

I scanned the reports, my trained eye noting that Inferno Force was tracking Kronock ships deep in their space, but that there were no unusual movements. Then my gaze snagged on a short postscript at the end of one report.

"An Inferno Force transmissions specialist detected chatter between two Kronock ships," I read aloud, even though I was alone. "Chatter about one of their outposts being devoured."

I reread that word. "Devoured?"

My Kronock was rusty, but that seemed like an odd choice of phrasing. Then again, maybe the phrasing was that of the Drexian who had interpreted the message. Kronock was a complex language that was not easy to translate, especially not when native speakers were talking rapidly, which I was sure the Kronock had been when discussing the destruction of an outpost.

Still, it made me uneasy. If there was a plague sweeping through enemy territory, I did not want it to come anywhere near us.

My door beeped, snatching my attention from the report. I glanced up, wondering who was coming to my office so early, especially since the academy was so deserted. "Come."

The door glided open, and Admiral Zoran swept in. He might not wear the flowing robes his predecessor had, but he still carried an air of authority and command that had me jerking to my feet. I thumped a hand across my chest in salute.

He returned the salute and motioned for me to sit as he drew closer. "At ease, Commander."

Despite his request, I waited until he took the chair across from me until I sat. "Did we have a meeting, Admiral?"

He shook his head, glancing briefly at the weapons hanging on my walls. "We did not, but I wanted to speak briefly about the envoy from Earth."

I stiffened. We had already spoken about my actions the day before, and I had thought the matter was settled.

"I was pleased that you warmed up to Captain Gorman," Zoran continued, unaware or unconcerned by my bristling. "I wanted to thank you for welcoming him so warmly at the reception."

I tried to hide my surprise. It was not common for the Academy Master to make office visits for something so trivial, so I knew this was not the true reason for his visit. But I played along, inclining my head solemnly. "You are welcome, Admiral. It was my pleasure."

"It is crucial that this human captain return to Earth with a positive report. Too much effort has gone into the human exchange for it to be ruined now."

I nodded, knowing this already.

"It is also important that we control what he sees," Zoran continued.

"If this is about the creatures in the dungeons, they are already gone." I did not mention that we owed this to Fiona and her insistent outburst.

His brows lifted, and it occurred to me that he might not have known they had remained. "I am glad to hear it. That would be hard to explain. But what I am talking about is the long-term goals of the program. The Drexian long-term goals for the human exchange program."

This gave me pause. "I do not believe I know the long-term goals for the human exchange program. I thought this was an experiment that only concerned a small group of humans here and Drexians on Earth."

"Originally, it was, but both exchanges have been more successful in more ways than we anticipated."

I frowned at the Academy Master. "I do not think I understand."

"Within a short amount of time, we already have two mated couples in the Academy, not counting me and my bride. Three of the Drexians who have been stationed on Earth have formed mating bonds with humans. Human women who are also military officers."

"This is a good thing?"

"The entire reason we signed a treaty with Earth all those years ago was because we needed females so we could continue our species. The Tribute Bride program has been a success, and it has been an even bigger success since we started taking volunteers. But this exchange is proving to be an excellent way of making compatible matches."

An instinctive protest rippled through me. "You are saying that the long-term goal of the exchange is now to encourage mating at the academy?"

Zoran leveled his gaze at me. "I am saying that the long-term goal of the exchange is to bring more human females as instructors and cadets—and not return them."

I had heard whispers of how the Admiral had brought his own bride to the school. He had used a loophole in the tribute bride contract to bind her to him and force her to come with him to Drex. She had come to love him and marry him willingly, but it had not started with her agreement. "You wish to abduct them?"

He shifted from one foot to the other. "Drexians have never abducted females. Every tribute was part of our agreement, and no bride was ever forced into a marriage. But the fact remains that we need more females on Drex and more in our academy. Too many of our instructors are not mated. If they do take tributes, they usually leave their posts."

"So, the exchange will become more of an acquisition program?"

Zoran gave me a curt nod. "In a way, yes, but only in the sense that our goal will be to provide such a beneficial experience at the Academy to the humans that they will not wish to leave. Most importantly, the captain cannot know. If Earth knew that our objective was to lure their best female officers, they may not be as willing to send them."

"Why would he know this?" I did not add that if I had not known, I doubted the human would find out.

"Because he requested to return with Captain Douglas, and we cannot let that happen."

He had requested to take Fiona back with him? My stomach tightened as I fisted my hands by my sides. "No, we cannot."

FORTY-SIX

Fiona

I wasn't trying to avoid the captain, but I did not see him the next morning at breakfast or in the corridors. By the afternoon, curiosity was eating at me.

"Where do you think he is?" I asked Ariana, as we sat together in the Stacks poring over various rescue plans for when we located Sasha. Crumbly books were stacked on the long wooden table to hold down the curling edges of the unrolled parchments that covered the surface, and the scent of dust and leather permeated the cool air.

Ariana cut her gaze to me, her brow furrowed. "Where do I think who is?"

"Sorry." I gave an absent shake of my head. "I was thinking out loud."

"Is this about the security chief?"

"What?" My voice rose significantly above the usual hush I used in the ancient library. "Commander Vyk? Why would you say that?"

Her lips scrunched to one side as she eyed me. "I don't know. I've noticed the way he watches you. I know you've always hated him but hate and love are two sides of the same coin."

I rolled my eyes at this. "I don't hate him."

Now, her brows shot up. "Really? Since when?"

The conversation had taken a turn that I had not been expecting. "The guy might be surly as hell, but he's just doing his job."

Ariana leaned over the parchment that showed one of the first known renderings of Kronock space. "Does his job include tormenting visiting envoys from Earth?"

Okay, that was harder to explain away. "You know the Drexians. They're always trying to do something badass and dangerous. I think it was Vyk's way of welcoming him."

Ariana mumbled something about not signing her up for a Drexian welcome.

"But it's not Vyk I was talking about," I said, trying to get the conversation back on the rails. "It's Devon."

"Another guy who looks at you like you're a snack."

"There's nothing between us. Not anymore."

"If he pulled strings to get the gig to come here, he's still into you."

I sighed, the sound louder than I intended. "Which is why I need to find him and tell him that it's over. Actually, it never really began. I need to tell him that it was one night—one fun night—but that was it."

Ariana shook her head. "Sounds like a super fun conversation."

She was right. It was not going to be a fun one, but I needed to be honest. Discovering that Devon had pulled strings to come here had been gnawing at me all night. I'd been so consumed by what Ariana had overheard that I'd barely slept. I might not have asked Devon to come here, but I was the one who left without a proper goodbye. I owed him an honest conversation now.

"I need to find him and get this over with." I stood and pushed back my chair, the legs scraping across the stone floor. "Where would an envoy from Earth be?"

Ariana bobbled her head from side to side. "I'd guess that he'd either be with the Academy Master, or he'd be meeting with all the humans at the Academy individually. I assume he needs to interview all of us to hear our experiences."

I considered this. I hadn't heard of him setting up meetings with the human instructors and cadets who'd remained at the school between years, so I suspected he was still in the early stages of his overall assessment. Chances were good he'd be meeting with the admiral or completing his tour of the academy.

I glanced at the papers on the table and cringed. "I promised to help you narrow down the best routes."

She waved a hand at me. "Go. I've got this."

"But you hate battle strategy."

She winked at me. "But I love flight plans, and this is just a glorified flight plan." Her smile faltered. "I wish we would hear back from Kax and Jaxon. I know they sent out Inferno Force warriors to do recon on some of the potential Kronock holding sites, but shouldn't we have heard something by now?"

I squeezed her shoulder. "Once those warriors go into Kronock space, they go silent. Since they have to fly off the radar—literally—they can't communicate until they've reemerged and joined their ships. That will take time, since some of the sites were deep in enemy territory."

Ariana nodded. "I wish we could do something more. I feel useless just waiting to hear."

I nodded to the papers and tablets on the table. "What we're doing isn't useless. We need to be ready to go the moment we have confirmation of a target site. That means we need to create complete mission plans for each different site and the best routes to them. It won't do Sasha any good if we get caught on our way to saving her."

Ariana pressed her lips together for a beat. "You're right. We have to be ready when we get the word. It just feels like it's taking forever."

"That's because you're a Wing, and you like things fast. Trust me that the most successful missions are planned to within an inch of their lives. The more contingencies we anticipate, the better prepared we'll be for whatever happens."

"You're right. I know you're right." She nodded fervently. "This mission to get Sasha has to succeed."

"It will," I told her, believing it deep within my bones. Everyone involved in planning the rescue mission was fully committed and determined to rescue the human pilot who'd been taken by the enemy. Everyone was willing to risk their lives to bring Ariana's sister home.

I gave my friend's shoulder another squeeze. "I'll come back once I've settled everything with the captain."

"I'll be here, trying to imagine that I'm in the cockpit of a plane."

"As long as you don't make flying noises."

She tilted her head at me. "Flying noises?"

I took a few steps back. "You know, shhhhooo, shhhoooo, pew pew pew."

Her eyes widened. "Were those supposed to be what a ship sounds like?" She shook her head slowly. "Sad, Fi. Very sad."

"That's why I keep my feet planted firmly on the ground," I said, before I turned and strode from the Stacks.

I hurried down the ominously silent corridor and through the echoing main hall, my feet clicking on the stone as I jogged up the stairs. I was so focused on finding the captain that I didn't slow down when I rounded a corner and walked right into him.

CHAPTER
FORTY-SEVEN

Vyk

After the admiral left, I tried to focus on my work, but my thoughts were swirling and spinning like eddies in a rushing stream. The idea of the human captain leaving with Fiona had made it impossible for anything to hold my attention. Not the security reports, not the long-distance scans, not even the communications from my former Inferno Force colleagues.

I pushed back from my desk, standing to leave, when my device trilled. I tapped the surface and glanced at the name on the incoming vid call before I accepted it.

"Jaxon." I nodded at the image of the Inferno Force pilot on the screen, his cheeks dark with scruff. "It is good to see you."

"It is good to see you, Commander. I take it things are quiet at the academy with the cadets gone?"

I thought about the visiting Earth envoy and the human instructors and cadets who had chosen to stay. "Not as quiet as you might expect."

He raised an eyebrow but did not press me for details.

I cleared my throat. If he was reaching out via vid call instead of sending a report or standard update, he must have important news. "Is this about the mission to find the human pilot?"

Jaxon grunted, frowning as he glanced at something in his hands. "You know we sent out several Inferno Force warriors on solo recon missions."

I had read the reports about the warriors chosen for the missions earlier. All were battle-tested and had knowledge of Kronock space. "I do. Have they returned with news?"

My pulse quickened. If there was positive news and Inferno Force had located Sasha, then we would need to launch the rescue mission immediately. I would not be sad to leave the academy and the Earth envoy behind.

"In a way." Jaxon pursed his lips and then sighed. "All the warriors have returned, except for one."

I leaned forward, my heart stuttering in my chest. "Was a warrior killed?"

Jaxon gave a curt shake of his head. "We have no proof that he was killed, but he has not returned at his appointed time. The last transmission we received from him was before he entered Kronock space."

My mind raced with possibilities. "There are no reports of explosions or energy anomalies, no enemy chatter about destroying a Drexian ship?"

"Negative, Commander. The Kronock usually do not hesitate to share with us when they take out one of our ships. We have heard nothing."

I tapped my fingers on the desk. "This could mean that he was delayed because he needed time to determine if he had found the missing pilot. It could mean that he is in a position where moving would reveal him to the enemy."

"Or it could mean that he was taken prisoner by the Kronock, "Jaxon added, his expression grim.

The Inferno Force pilot knew plenty about being held captive by our enemy. He had been in a dank alien cell and tortured before we had found him. Even now, I could see the painful memories flicker behind his eyes.

"What do you think happened to him?" I asked.

He released a long breath as if purging himself of the past. "My gut tells me that the enemy has him, but I think they have him because he got too close to something they do not want him to find. I think he located the pilot."

"How can you be sure?"

"I am not." He raked a hand through his shaggy hair. "That is why I am not suggesting we deploy a rescue team. It could just as easily be a trap." He released a bitter laugh. "Knowing the Kronock, it is both."

"You think the Kronock have taken him to lure us into sending more warriors to save him?"

"Like I said, I cannot know any of this for certain, but our warrior was one of the best. He was smart and tough, and he would not have been discovered if he had run the simple recon mission he'd been instructed to carry out."

I leaned back. An Inferno Force warrior who had gone off-script sounded very familiar. The problem with the elite Drexian fighting force was that it was filled with daredevils and heroes who were more than willing to risk their lives to save others. Most Inferno Force fighters I'd served with would have diverted the mission if they'd thought it meant bringing home the missing pilot. "So, either he is in the middle of his own rescue attempt, or he is also a captive of the Kronock?"

"Those are the best options, but either way, I think we have a better idea of Sasha's location."

I rubbed a hand along my beard. "But not enough to justify launching an official rescue mission."

"Not unless you wish chances to be high that it would be a suicide mission."

I did not. "Will you send another warrior in after him?"

"We have a plan that involves a team, with one member who excels at subterfuge and, as she calls it, B&E."

I narrowed my gaze at him. "Do you mean your wife?"

He opened his hands wide. "She is the best, and once she heard that a pilot from Earth was missing, there wasn't much I could do to talk her out of it. I will be joining her on the mission, as well."

My chest tightened. I knew what a sacrifice it was for the Drexian to go back into enemy space after his horrific ordeal getting out. "Your courage is admirable."

"We do not leave warriors behind."

I nodded. It did not matter if the pilot was human or Drexian, we did not leave allies behind. "I wish you good hunting."

Jaxon thumped a fist across his chest, and the transmission ended.

I took a moment to digest what he'd told me before standing again. I needed to tell Zoran. This was not information that should be transmitted or sent in a report.

My nerves jangled as I walked briskly from my office. We were quickly approaching the time when the rescue team would leave the academy and race toward danger ourselves. I could not wait.

CHAPTER
FORTY-EIGHT

Fiona

I braced my hands in front of me as I walked straight into Captain Gorman. He grabbed the sides of my arms to steady both of us, chuckling low as he did.

"I was looking for you," I blurted before I could think how that might sound.

His eyes crinkled as he smiled. "You were?"

Devon wasn't even close to a silver fox, but I did like the smile lines he'd acquired. I had to admit that he was a good-looking guy, which was probably why I'd ended up in his bed in the first place. Not that any of that was relevant now.

"I thought we should talk." I slipped from his grasp and headed down the corridor. "But not in the hall."

He took long steps to catch up to me. "We can go to my quarters, if you prefer a truly private conversation."

I couldn't tell him that my friend had overheard him in his quarters last night, so they weren't as private as he thought. Especially if the door wasn't closed. Even so, I wasn't going to compromise myself by going to his room.

I shook my head. "How about the staff dining room? Have you eaten?"

He frowned. "I'm not hungry, and we shouldn't talk in public."

I stopped and spun to face him. "Why not?"

He swept his gaze around the deserted corridor. "There are things I need to tell you. Things that only you can know."

Well, that was sinister. I eyed him with a healthy dose of suspicion. I wouldn't put it past any guy to make up some dramatic reason as a pretext to get me alone. But I wasn't naïve. I was an Assassin. And I was very uninterested in being tricked.

"Are you telling me that you have some sort of classified intel that is for my ears only?" I folded my arms over my chest. "Are you serious?"

His expression was solemn, and for a moment, I wondered if he was telling the truth. But it made no sense. I wasn't an intelligence officer. I hadn't been sent to the Academy as a spy. I was an instructor of Strategy at the Drexian Academy, which meant that I technically worked for them now. Why would Earth Planetary Defense have intel for me alone? We were allied with the Drexians. If there was something crucial to know, the Admiral should be the one told, not me.

"You have to trust me, Fiona."

But I didn't trust him. I barely knew him. Sure, we'd been colleagues at my last base, but I hadn't been there very long. It wasn't like we had years of friendship I could draw on to know he was being truthful. I'd known too many male officers who were either more concerned with their career advancement than the truth, or more interested in getting in my pants.

It was true that Devon had already gotten in my pants, but I could not be sure that he wasn't still nursing a bruised ego from my leaving. A man with a fragile ego was a dangerous thing.

"Okay, Devon. Tell me one thing. Why were you sent here?"

He jerked back slightly. "What do you mean?"

"I mean, evaluating programs isn't what you do. This is a little below your pay grade, if we're being honest. Why did they send you?"

He cleared his throat, and for a moment, I thought he might confess. But he squared his shoulders and met my gaze. "I was pulled into the program because I've been working with the Drexians who were sent to Earth as part of the exchange. It made sense for me to come here and see if the programs have parity."

"You didn't request the assignment?"

He expelled an impatient breath. "Are you suggesting I chased you here?"

That was not an answer, but I already knew the answer.

I changed my tactics and relaxed my stance. "Devon, you know I always liked you as a colleague. We got along great at the

LEGEND

base, but what happened between us was a one-time thing. It was fun, but it was never going to be something bigger."

He stepped closer to me. "It could be. We never got the chance to find out."

Even though we were in a public corridor, his closeness unnerved me. "Because I left to come here, which is where I work and live now. Unless you've come to tell me that you're transferring here to teach...." I hesitated. "You aren't, are you?"

Davon wrinkled his nose. "No. I don't know how you stand it here. It's so dark and cold and it feels like being in an old castle that's about to collapse."

"You get used to all of that, and I promise you it won't collapse. This school has been standing for millennia."

He rolled his eyes. "I've heard all about the glorious legacy of the Drexian Academy and how it was built from stone forged from a faraway mountain, although why you would want everything to be black stone is beyond me."

I cocked my head at him. "Do you have something against the Drexians?"

His eyes flashed malice. "Do I have a problem with the aliens who think that just because they're bigger and stronger and have more advanced tech that they can take our women in secret for decades?"

Whoa. I'd had no idea Devon had an issue with Drexians and their tribute bride program. He wouldn't be the first. There were plenty of people who'd been outraged when we discovered what the Drexians had been doing for years. Even more infuriating for some was that it had been authorized by our governments.

"The Academy doesn't have anything to do with the tribute brides," I told him in my calmest voice. "Everyone here wanted to come, and we can all leave at any point. Some of the cadets returned to Earth after the year ended."

"You didn't," he spit out. "You stayed. Is it because you're fucking one of them?"

I reared back. "What the hell? No, I'm not fucking one of them, but even if I was, it wouldn't be any of your *grekking* business."

He clenched his teeth and a muscle ticked in the side of his jaw. "You even sound like them now."

"I don't know why you're so angry right now, but this isn't the Devon I know. This isn't you, and I'm not going to talk to you when you're like this." I turned from him and started to walk briskly down the corridor. Before I could turn the corner, a hand snatched my arm and spun me back around.

"You can't leave." Devon looked manic, as he held my arm in a vise-like grip. "I told you I need to talk to you."

I tried to shake off his hand. "Let go. You're hurting me."

He squeezed tighter and pain shot up my arm. "Not until you listen to me."

Before I could throw a kick, a blur of motion came from around the corner, a massive fist punched through the air, and Devon was knocked onto his ass. I stumbled back and hit something huge and rock-hard, peering up and over my shoulder to see Commander Vyk glowering at the man on the floor.

It took me a moment to realize that he'd knocked him out, and another second to mutter about men being ridiculous, before I stomped away. I needed to be away from all guys, and I needed a drink.

CHAPTER
FORTY-NINE

Vyk

I opened and closed my fist as I stood over the human captain, seeing red and trying to steady my breath. I tasted blood, but it might have been the metallic scent of it from the flecks of crimson dripping from the human's mouth. My nostrils flared as I breathed it in, and my heart pounded in response.

The primal beast within me wanted more. I wanted to feel his flesh beneath my fists, hear his bones crunch, watch his blood spill. I wanted to punish him for touching her. I wanted him to beg for forgiveness.

He groaned as he started to stir, rolling his head slowly even though his eyes remained closed. I felt like groaning along with him as the red blurring my vision faded.

This was not good.

I had attacked a guest of the Academy. I had attacked the human envoy sent to pass judgment on the exchange program. I had attacked the very man I had promised not to torment.

I watched the captain move, but I did not offer to help him stand. I did not trust myself. Not after I'd seen him grabbing Fiona. Not after I'd heard the pain in her voice as she'd told him to release her.

He had hurt her, and I regretted nothing. Correction, I regretted not punching him hard enough that he would stay down longer. I was going soft. In my peak form with Inferno Force, one punch would have knocked him out cold for half a day. Still, his jaw was red and would no doubt bruise vividly, even if it was not broken. That would have to be enough. For now.

I gave him a final dismissive glance and stepped over him. I had better things to do than coddle a human who had proven that he was not worthy to be walking the halls of the Drexian school. I needed to find Fiona.

I'd acted so quickly, so impulsively, so instinctively that I had not stopped to think how punching her former colleague might upset her. I'd been blinded by rage that the captain was hurting her and consumed by a possessive fury that he was touching her.

It was unreasonable to think that Fiona was mine. One kiss did not make her mine, but I did not care. I knew in the core of my being that she belonged to me. She belonged by my side. She was mine. And no puny human was going to touch her—ever.

I stopped and pressed one palm against the cool stone wall, sucking in a greedy breath. Where was I? I had stormed through so many passageways that I had to take a moment to get my bearings. The only sound was my ragged breathing and the distant sound of crashing waves.

The Restless Sea.

I was near one of the open-air walkways that connected the towers. I forced myself to continue forward and take halting steps across the walkway as the wind whipped my face.

The cold air sobered me, and I gripped the low stone walls as I dragged in a salty breath and stared across the turbulent surface of the water. The natural forces that surrounded the school—the sea, the mountains, the wind, the storms—were a good reminder of greater things beyond the walls.

I crossed the rest of the way and hesitated at the bottom of the tower. I had not planned to come directly to the female tower, but my feet had taken me there. I did not even know if I would find Fiona in her room, but I needed to try. I needed to explain.

With a burst of resolve, I bounded up the twisting staircase until I reached the landing that held her quarters. I knew which room was hers. I knew who lived in every room. It was my job to know where everyone in the school lived and how to find them. But I had taken special care to remember Fiona's room.

I didn't allow myself to linger before knocking, rapping quickly on the heavy door. I waited, almost relieved that she might not be there. I had not rehearsed what I wanted to say, and I had learned that the female was not one you wanted to spar with unless you were well prepared.

"Not here," I said under my breath, as I turned to leave.

Then I heard the door glide open. "It's you."

I pivoted to face her, noting that she held a bottle of alien whiskey in one hand. "I came to—"

"Let me guess, you came to tell me how you didn't mean to go after the captain—again."

That might have been what I had originally intended to say, but seeing her hands trembling as she set the bottle onto her desk banished those words from existence. She was trying to appear tough, but her chest heaved and there were red marks on her wrists from where the human captain had grabbed her.

I would not be apologizing now or ever.

"No," I growled, stepping inside her room. "I came here to tell you that the next time someone—anyone—puts their hands on you, I will not just strike them down, I will end them. I do not care if they are from Earth. I do not care if they outrank me. I do not care if I get thrown in the dungeons. I will never let anyone hurt you again." I held her gaze as her eyes widened. "That is a promise."

I waited for her to snap back at me and tell me that I was out of line and that it was not my job to protect her, that she did not need protecting. But instead, she launched herself into my arms and curled her legs around my waist as I caught her.

She crushed her lips to mine in a hard kiss, pulling back to lock eyes with me for a moment. "I need one more promise from you."

I managed to nod even though I was too stunned to speak.

"Fuck me hard."

A snarl escaped from my mouth as I ran one hand through her long hair and fisted it. "I promise."

CHAPTER
FIFTY

Fiona

My entire body trembled as Vyk held me, one hand tangled in my hair and his eyes blazing with a hunger that almost made me think twice. There had been no doubt in my mind that giving in to my own desires was playing with the most uncontrollable type of fire, the kind that spread indiscriminately and scorched everything in its path.

But I didn't care. I'd wanted Vyk since the moment I'd seen him. I'd wanted to run my hands through his silvered hair, I'd wanted to feel the scratch of his beard on my cheeks, I'd wanted to let the husk of his voice slide down my spine and send shivers through me. And it didn't matter to me that he wasn't a fan of humans, or even that he'd been a colossal ass to me.

I still wanted him. I needed him. I needed to burn off my irrational desire for him.

Vyk held my head back and locked eyes with me. "You are sure?"

I gave a frustrated twitch of my head and felt the sting of his fingers knotted in my hair. "Yes, I'm sure. I need you to fuck me now."

With a growl, he set upon my neck, his teeth scoring my sensitive skin as he alternated between kissing and biting. I tightened my legs around his waist, arching back and moaning. Every touch of his fingers, his lips set my flesh ablaze and jangled my pulse.

I couldn't be still, so I raked my own fingers through his hair, scraping hard until he loosed a deep, rumbling sound and raised his head to meet my gaze.

"Flexing your claws, I see," he murmured as he walked me over to my bed and dropped me on it. I bounced, but before I could reach for him, Vyk flipped me onto my stomach and pinned me down by straddling my hips.

I twisted around to protest, but he bent forward and captured my mouth in a kiss that startled me with its ferocity. He parted my lips and tangled his tongue with mine, stroking it as he curled a hand around my throat. His hand slid down the length of my neck and dipped below the neckline of my top, his fingers slipping beneath the fabric of my bra and gently teasing one of my nipples as he continued to kiss me.

I moaned, bowing back as he moved his hand to my other breast and circled the tight peak until I was groaning into his mouth. But just as forcefully and suddenly as he'd started to kiss me, he stopped. I gasped, breathless but hungry for more.

Vyk moved off me as I tried to regain my normal breath, but he was not done with me. He grabbed me by the hips and pulled me up so that I stood flush to him. Then he spun us both around and turned me to face him. He lifted my face to his, kissing me gently before moving me a few steps away from him and sitting down on the edge of the bed.

"Undress for me."

I stared at him for a few moments, suddenly awash with self-consciousness. "You don't want to do it?"

He gave a curt shake of his head, his eyes molten as they seared into me. "I want to watch you."

My heart caught in my chest, but then I locked eyes with him. Desire radiated off him in waves, and as I saw myself through his eyes, I started to move.

I unbuttoned my shirt, never looking away from him as I teased him by slowly slipping it off my shoulders and letting it fall to the floor. I ran my fingers over my bra, circling my hard nipples until they strained against the sheer black fabric. "Like this?"

Vyk's pupils were so huge they'd swallowed every bit of the iris as his gaze traced my movements like an animal stalking his prey. His jaw was tight, a muscle throbbing on the side when I slipped my fingers beneath the fabric of my bra and softly flicked my nipples. He grunted without forming a word.

Watching his reactions gave me even more confidence, so I unhooked my bra slowly and only let it fall away when I'd covered my breasts with my hands. I gave them a squeeze, which dragged a desperate moan from Vyk's throat.

"I didn't know you liked to watch." I finally slid my hands down my body and slowly unfastened my pants. I wiggled my hips to shimmy them over my hips, and my breasts jiggled until my pants were a heap on the floor.

Vyk's lips were a thin, white line as he watched me without moving, but his entire body was like a coil about to be released. "I like to watch you."

I curled my fingers under the sides of my black panties and nudged them down a bit. "What else would you like to watch me do?"

He reached for me, pulling me forward by the waist. He took my wrists and wrapped them behind my back, holding them together with one of his large hands. "I want to watch you spread your legs for me." He kissed his way down my stomach. "I want to watch you take my cock." He trailed one finger down one side of my panties until he slid his finger beneath the fabric. "You are soaking wet for me."

I wiggled my hands behind my back, but he held them tightly. "There is no escaping now. Not until I've given you what you want."

I lifted my chin in challenge, even as my breath was uneven and my juices were trickling down my thighs. "And what do I want?"

He dragged his finger through my slickness, muttering Drexian curses I didn't know. "Your body is begging to be fucked, Fiona. You need my cock to fill you, don't you? You want me to pound you until you beg for mercy." He slid his finger inside me as I sucked in a breath. "But I have no intention of showing you mercy. Not after you have begged to be punished by my cock." He moved his finger in and out slowly as I whimpered. "Not when you are so hot and ready for me. Not when you need to fucked so badly."

I gripped my hands on his shoulders, digging the nails into his flesh. "Then what are you waiting for?"

He slid his finger out, and I instantly wanted it back, needed it back. "First, I need something else."

"What?" My voice sounded desperate, but I didn't care.

He grabbed the sides of my panties, ripped them off me, and reached around me to grab my ass with his palms. He fell back on the bed and took me with him, but then he used his hands on my ass to scoot me up so that I was straddling his face. "First, I want to feel you come on my tongue."

CHAPTER
FIFTY-ONE

Vyk

I pulled Fiona so that her legs opened above me, and I slid my tongue inside her as she lowered herself fully on my face. I kept my hands on her ass, squeezing it as I tilted her forward to reach more of her. The sweet taste of her, the slickness of her on my tongue, the petal-softness of her skin all made the blood rush loud in my ears and my heart knock against my ribs.

Fiona gasped as I worked my tongue until I found the spot that I had heard Drexians talk about for so long. Any Drexian male who had taken a tribute bride or a human as a mate spoke of their bodies with reverence, but it was the magic bundle of nerves between their legs that had always mystified me. Drexian females had no such thing, but it could drive a human female wild.

Now that I had found it on Fiona, I could not get enough, especially when she started writhing her hips in response to my tongue's flicking. I watched her above me, her lush body moving with the rocking of her hips and her breasts bouncing.

My cock ached as her sounds became faster and more desperate, but I could not stop until I'd felt her come, until I'd experienced her release. Even as I imagined my cock deep inside her and feared it might rip my pants as it strained against the seams, I continued to hold her to my mouth and work my tongue.

Fiona ran her hands over her breasts, thumbing her own peaked nipples as her gasps gave way to cries and her body jerked on top of me. I gripped her ass to keep her on my face as her hips gyrated. She threw her head back and her entire body convulsed before she fell forward and caught herself with her hands.

"Vyk," she panted, when I finally released my grip and let her roll off. "How did you know how..."

"Your magic buttons are well-known in the Drexian world." I sat up as she flopped on her back beside me. "I have been eager to experience one."

Her chest heaved as she glanced at me. "But you don't like humans."

I sat up and unbuttoned my shirt, quickly tossing it to the floor. "You believe I do not like humans after that?"

Her gaze trailed to my chest and then dropped farther as I stood and unbuttoned my pants, shedding them just as swiftly. "Haven't you heard of hate fucks?"

When I was in only black snug boxer briefs that barely contained my rigid cock, I grabbed her ankles and tugged her toward me. "This is not a hate fuck."

Her blonde, wavy hair fanned out behind her as she lay naked with her chest flushed, her pink nipples pebbled, and her sex slick. "I thought you said you needed to punish me with your cock."

I bit back a groan. "Only because you need to be taught who this belongs to, Fiona." I spread her legs and gripped her hips, pulling them up and close to me. "You need me to fuck you hard enough so you know that you belong to me now."

She opened her mouth, and I was sure she was on the verge of protesting. The woman loved to argue, even when her legs were open, and she was wet and ready for me.

I yanked down my underwear so that my cock sprang up, the crown swollen and glistening. Whatever she had been prepared to say was forgotten as her mouth fell open and her eyes widened. I dragged the tip of my cock through her before pausing at her entrance. "You can fight me about this, but you will lose."

I pushed inside her, holding my breath to savor the tightness as her body stretched to take me. Fiona's mouth opened wider as I drove myself all the way in, and her eyes watered as she sucked in a breath.

I bent over her as I held myself deep, kissing her softly and feeling her body tremble. "See how well you take me?" I murmured as I nipped her earlobe. "See how perfect you are for me?"

She nodded as I slowly started to move. "You don't have to worry that you'll break me."

I pulled back so I could meet her gaze. "I thought you wanted me to break you."

Her eyes glinted as she wrapped her legs around me. "I want you to fuck me hard. I want you to make me scream."

A possessive growl rumbled in the back of my throat. "Only if you promise to scream my name."

"I don't scream anyone's name," she shot back.

"You'll scream mine."

She curled her arms around my back and her fingers stroked my nodes, sending fresh waves of desire pulsing through me. "You first."

I almost laughed. The female could not resist challenging me, even when I was filling her, even when she was pinned beneath me, even when I was going deeper with every thrust. I loved it but was going to love making her scream my name even more.

I sat back and held her hips again, but this time when I pulled out I did not drive back inside her. I flipped her onto her hands and knees, kicking her knees apart and powering into her from behind. Fiona fisted her hands into the sheets on the bed as I tipped her ass higher and thrust into her.

I snatched her arms and pulled them behind her, pressing them to the small of her back and holding them with one hand. Her cheek was against the bed as she struggled against me, but her wiggling ass only made me want to pound her harder.

"That's right," I rasped. "Fight me, Fiona. I will only fuck you harder."

"Bastard," she said, but her eyes were glittering with pleasure as she leaned her ass back for more.

"That's not my name." I reached my free hand around and slipped it between her legs. I circled one finger lazily around her swollen nub as I fucked her from behind.

"*Grek,*" she muttered as she closed her eyes and arched into my hand, eager for my touch.

"Greedy girl." I gave her a little spank before I stopped moving my finger, but I did not stop thrusting inside her. "Close, but no."

"Please," she rocked her hips forward as her body trembled around my cock. "I'm so close."

I brushed my fingertip over her skin. "Tell me who this belongs to, Fiona. Tell me who you belong to. Tell me that you're going to spread your pretty, long legs for me every night and take my cock like you were always meant to."

"Yes," she groaned. "I belong to you. Please, Vyk."

I returned my finger to her slick flesh, circling it as her body detonated beneath me. Her tight heat clenched around my cock like a vise, and I held myself as she jerked and moaned. But it was more than I could take, and as her body trembled, I thrust hard two more times before losing all control and exploding inside her.

I released her wrists and slid my hand up her back, which was damp with sweat, then I folded over her and sank onto the bed to one side. I curled my body around hers as we both fought to breathe normally again.

"I didn't scream your name," she said between shaky breaths.

"You said my name."

She nuzzled into me as I wrapped an arm around her waist. "But I didn't scream it."

My still-hard cock twitched inside her. "Who said that we were done?"

FIFTY-TWO

Fiona

My legs were still shaky the next morning when I stepped from my room and glanced at the other doors on my floor. All closed.

I let out a heavy breath, relief coursing through me. Everyone was still sleeping or had already headed to the dining room. Small talk might have been beyond my capabilities after the night before.

I sighed again as I thought of last night. Hands down the best night of my life, but what the hell had possessed me? I'd spent most of the first two terms either avoiding the security chief or being livid at him. How had I ended up in bed with him?

My pulse jangled and my heart stuttered in my chest as images from the night before flashed through my head. I had always imagined that he would be dominant, but I'd never anticipated how much I would like it.

I was known as a ballbuster, a tough woman who was used to getting her way and used to being obeyed. So why did I love letting the Drexian take control? Why had I relished in submitting to him?

A shiver went through me as I remembered him pressing my wrists to the small of my back to hold me in place. I would have killed anyone else who tried that, but the not gruff commander. With him, I'd only wanted more. At least I hadn't begged for more. I had that point of pride left. And I hadn't screamed his name, even though he'd done his best to make me.

My door slid shut and even that soft sound echoed in the silence. Was there any way we hadn't been heard by the other women on my floor? I had no idea how soundproof the walls in the tower were, although they were stone, so I hoped that counted for something. The thought that my colleagues and cadets might have heard my moans sent heat straight to my cheeks.

One small favor was that I wasn't trying to leave with Vyk or attempting to sneak him out. He'd left my quarters sometime in the night after we were both spent, slipping from my bed and dressing while I'd watched him. I hadn't protested, even though my bed felt empty without his huge body curled around mine.

I'd never particularly wanted a guy to stay the night. I was the kind of girl who liked to wake up in my own bed by myself in the morning. But I wouldn't have minded waking up with Vyk, even if I was glad I wasn't having to worry about being seen with him creeping from my room. I should be grateful that he'd left unseen, and no one would have to know if I didn't tell them.

"It was a one-time thing anyway," I whispered to myself as I smoothed my palms down the front of my pants and squared my shoulders.

It had to be a one-night deal. As hot as I found the commander, he was still an irritant who'd done nothing but offend and annoy me since I'd arrived. He was arrogant and grumpy, and he'd made it abundantly clear that he wasn't a big fan of humans.

He seemed fine with you being a human last night, I reminded myself. In fact, he'd seemed fascinated by everything human about me.

I gave my head a firm shake. Why did Vyk have to be so confusing? Just when I was sure I understood him, he said something that made me think the complete opposite.

"It doesn't matter. We work together. It can't happen again."

I had experience sleeping with a colleague, and Devon's presence at the academy was evidence that it did not end well.

Devon.

I groaned as it hit me that I hadn't seen the man since I'd stormed off and left him lying on the floor after Vyk had punched him. I hadn't even bothered to ask Vyk if the man was okay. Not once during the entire time Vyk had been in my room had I thought about Devon.

I guess that told me all I needed to know about my feelings about the captain. Not that there had been any doubt. I'd never wanted anything more with him, and I owed it to him to tell him that directly—even if it meant he got upset and even if that meant that he tried to give the exchange program a bad review.

I headed for the stairs, newly determined to sort out the mess that I'd made.

"Wait up!"

I paused at the top of the stairwell and turned to see Ariana hurrying toward me. Then I remembered that I'd left her in the Stacks with the promise that I'd return. I slapped a hand to my mouth. "The Stacks. I was supposed to come back to the Stacks."

She grinned at me. "Don't worry. I figured that you got distracted when you went to talk to Captain Gorman."

"Gorman?" I shook my head at her knowing smile. "It was nothing like that, I promise."

She looked me up and down. "Fi, I'm not blind. You look like you've been fu—"

I held up a hand to stop her. "It wasn't Gorman. I told you that we were a one-night stand and nothing more."

She eyed me like she didn't believe me. "So, you found him and told him that?"

I thought back to my conversation with Devon. I'd tried, although he'd been so full of anger and resentment toward the Drexians that he hadn't been listening to what I'd said. He'd been insistent that I listen to him. So insistent that he'd left bruise marks on my arm from where he'd grabbed it. Bruises that had made Vyk growl when he'd seen them last night. I forced thoughts of Vyk from my mind as they stirred heat in my core.

"I tried," I told my friend as we started walking down the spiraling stairs, "but things got a bit...complicated."

Ariana tilted her head at me. "Complicated how?"

"Commander Vyk might have come across Devon grabbing me, and he might have knocked him out."

Ariana's eyes flared wide then she nodded as if everything made sense. "That explains it."

"Explains what?"

She fluttered a hand at me. "You. The flushed cheeks. The muffled sounds I heard through your door when I came back to the tower last night. I should have known that couldn't have been a human guy." Without waiting for me to confirm or deny, she leaned closer to me. "So, is the silver fox as good in the sack as I'm thinking he is?"

FIFTY-THREE

Torq

"Where is he?" I said to no one, as I walked through the hallways searching for the envoy from Earth. I had promised to help keep him distracted so that task wouldn't fall so heavily on the human women, especially Jess. Seeing her flirt with Captain Gorman had not been an experience I wanted to repeat anytime soon.

I had expected to find the human in the staff dining room, but he had not shown up the entire time I'd waited. He had also not been with the admiral or the security chief, although no one had answered Commander Vyk's office door, so I could not be certain they were not together.

Crossing the main hall, I cast a questioning glance at the entrance to the School of Battle. Vyk would not have taken the captain back to the gauntlet or challenged him to the climbing wall, would he? I shook my head and tried to convince myself that the Drexian would not be so foolish.

No, the captain must be somewhere else in the academy. Somewhere I had not yet searched. He was supposed to be conducting a review of the human integration, which I assumed meant a full inspection of the school, which meant he could be anywhere.

My stride faltered as a figure emerged from the entrance to a stairwell. His gait was slow, but I recognized the uniform.

"Captain Gorman." I made sure my tone was artificially upbeat, as if I was thrilled to see him again. "I have been looking for..."

My words faded as he stepped into the light and revealed that not only was his cheek bruised from the incident on the gauntlet, but his other side of his face was now swollen and purple.

"What happened?" I could not help myself. His injury was too pronounced to ignore, and I had to know how he'd managed to acquire another bruise so quickly. I had always been told that humans were not as tough as Drexians, but then I had met the human cadets and been disabused of this notion. Until now. Unless this human was especially fragile, he was setting an all-time Academy record for the most visible injuries in the least amount of time.

"I was attacked," he rasped, his voice rough and cracking.

I wondered if his windpipe had been damaged, since his voice was so hoarse, but even so, I had a hard time believing what I heard. "You were attacked? Here? In the Academy?"

He glowered at me, clearly disliking my tone of disbelief. "Yes. I was attacked. Do you not think your Drexian colleagues are violent enough to do something like this?"

I knew that any Drexian could easily do that much damage, but I also knew that we were supposed to be welcoming the human envoy, not wounding him. "Can you tell me who did this?"

He shifted on one foot and then winced. "I did not see my assailant, but Fiona will know. She was with me."

My pulse quickened. The Strategy instructor had been with him when he was attacked? "Was she hurt?"

He dropped his gaze. "I do not know. She was gone when I came to, and so was whomever struck me."

I blinked at him. Something was not adding up. If Captain Douglas had seen her friend be attacked, she would not have left him, and if a Drexian had struck him, he would not have left his victim wounded and alone. But no Drexian I knew would launch an unprovoked attack. The human was not being honest.

"So, you were with the captain when you were unexpectedly attacked by someone you never saw and when you came to, the captain was gone? Did you not think that she might have been injured, too? Did you not worry about her?"

He had still not raised his eyes to meet mine. "Why would she be attacked? She is one of you now. I was obviously attacked because I am an outsider coming here to pass judgment on your beloved academy."

I was starting to understand the individual who had attacked the envoy. This human was begging to be put squarely in his place. And as someone who had also needed to be knocked down a few pegs, I felt like I could say this with confidence.

I folded my arms across my chest. "I do not think the captain would claim to be a Drexian just because she teaches here, although she has done an admirable job adapting to our ways. And I was unaware that your role was to judge our entire school." I gave him a cold smile. "After millennia producing warriors who have been fighting across the galaxy and protecting your planet, I did not know we required your approval."

The human cleared his throat. "I did not say—"

"We should not worry about that right now." I bestowed a broad smile on him, switching my persona quickly to knock him off-guard. "I should be getting you to the surgeon."

"Surgeon?" His eyes went as wide as they could, considering his facial swelling. "I do not need surgery—"

"That is what we call our med bay here, and you should have a medical professional look at those injuries."

I took his arm and steered him toward the surgery, before anyone else could see him in his current state. Our surgeon could do something about the swelling and make the human look like he hadn't endured a very powerful hit by what I suspected could only have been a Drexian. I needed to get him to the surgery, instruct the surgeon to keep him sedated until his face looked normal, and then make sure Fiona hadn't also been hurt.

Then I needed to find out from her who had attacked the captain and why. There was more to this story than the lies the human had spun for me—and I was going to find out what they were and what he was hiding.

CHAPTER
FIFTY-FOUR

Fiona

"I don't know when I've seen you eat so much." Ariana sat across from me, eyeing me as I ate my fourth strip of fried padwump.

I paused with the crispy strip of salty meat inches away from my mouth. "What can I say? Vyk wore me out."

Ariana grinned at me. "I could not be happier for you."

"Why? Because I had a wild night with a Drexian who's driven me crazy since I got here? It's not like this could ever be something real."

I didn't have to worry about anyone overhearing us because we were the only people in the staff dining room. Since classes weren't in session, instructors kept erratic hours, and the long tables were almost never full.

I had been a bit dismayed when we'd walked in, but did I truly expect that Vyk would be there? He was probably still sleeping it off, since he'd left my quarters in the middle of the night. Even so, a part of me wanted to see him again and wanted to get our first public encounter out of the way.

Ariana leaned forward and braced her arms on the table. "Why not? Some of the best couples start out hating each other or at least annoying the living fuck out of each other. Take me and Volten. We started out with him insulting me. Torq was a cocky asshat to Jess before he fell for her. Even Admiral Zoran had a bumpy start with Noora and look at them now." She tilted her head and scrunched her lips to one side. "Come to think of it, not a lot of Drexian-human couples start out liking each other."

I bit off the end of my padwump and swallowed it. "I don't know what that says about us or them, but none of that means that Vyk or I want more than a fun fling."

"But he's your type. You said it yourself the very first day we were here."

I groaned. "You and your excellent memory can be really annoying sometimes, you know that?"

Before Ariana could answer, chattering in the doorway caught our attention. Britt, Jess, and Morgan walked in, and it seemed like they were all talking at the same time.

Ariana waved at them. "Over here!"

The women joined us, sliding into seats on the benches. I slid my overflowing plate of *padwump* to the center, so they could help me work through the overly ambitious stack of crispy strips.

Britta swept her gaze around our group, then it landed on me. "I guess it's okay that none of us are busy distracting Captain Gorman if you're here."

I thought back to Vyk knocking the man to the floor with a single punch and the captain lying on the black stone and groaning. "Maybe he's sleeping in, but I haven't seen him since yesterday."

Morgan nudged Britta in the side. "We walked him back to his quarters in the most roundabout way possible after the banquet, didn't we?"

Britta nodded as she snatched a slice of padwump off the top of the heap. "We did manage to traverse three of the four schools and go through almost every tower."

"It would be a miracle if he had any clue where his quarters are in reference to the rest of the academy." Morgan flipped her blonde hair off her shoulder. "He might not be sleeping in. He might be walking in circles."

Britta laughed as Jess shook her head. "Even if he finds his way through the academy, I put Torq on distraction duty."

"Torq?" Ariana wrinkled her nose. "You gave your boyfriend a shift?"

"He volunteered," Jess corrected. "He didn't like seeing me pretend to flirt with the captain, so he agreed to help us keep the guy busy and away from you."

Ariana let out a low whistle. "That Drexian must be crazy about you."

Jess smiled shyly. "He is, actually."

Morgan smiled brightly at her fellow cadet. "Why shouldn't he be? Jess is brilliant and beautiful, and she has amazing taste in friends."

Britta and Jess laughed and groaned while Ariana winked at me from across the table.

"Well, thank you," I said. "I really appreciate you all helping me, but I hope that Devon got the hint that I'm not into him."

"Because guys are great at taking hints," Britta muttered.

I knew she had a point, but I was hoping being knocked out cold had been the hint Devon needed to back off. As I considered telling my friends what had happened, Torq rushed into the room.

Jess instantly perked up, her eyes flaring wide as he came up behind her and gave her a kiss that was anything but shy. The Drexian had no problem displaying his affection in front of us, which made me like the guy even more.

"I thought you were on envoy duty," Jess said a bit breathlessly.

Torq pinned me with a sharp gaze. "I just came from dropping him off at the surgery."

The rest of the woman gaped at him. "What? Did he have another accident?"

Torq shook his head brusquely. "He says he was attacked, but he didn't see his attacker. He also claims that Fiona was with him when it happened."

All eyes swung toward me, and no one spoke for a few beats.

"I was with him," I finally admitted, my mind racing with the new information that Devon hadn't seen that it was Torq who'd hit him. That or he didn't remember. He had hit the floor pretty forcefully.

"Did you see who attacked him?" Torq asked.

I drew in a deep breath. "It was me. I'm the one who hit him."

Ariana sucked in a breath, and the other women looked at me as if I'd just sprouted horns.

Torq narrowed his gaze at me. "You hit him so hard that he was knocked unconscious?"

The Drexian did not believe me, but I didn't care. I couldn't let Vyk take the fall for defending me. He already had enough strikes on his record. He did not need another black mark on his reputation when he'd only been protecting me.

"Why?" Ariana asked in a soft voice. She knew my history with Devon, but she also knew how important it was to me that he turn in a positive report. Hitting him would be ensuring the opposite.

I decided to tell a partial truth. "He got aggressive. He wouldn't let me go. I had no choice but to get physical."

Ariana's expression became steely. "I wish I had been there to help you."

"Same," Britta said, her eyes hard and menacing. "Maybe then he wouldn't have gotten back up."

"It wasn't all that." I tried to laugh it off, even though I knew if I removed my long-sleeved shirt, they would see the finger marks on my arm. "I took care of it."

Torq held my gaze for another few seconds before standing. "I should go. I asked them to keep him sedated until they healed the bruises, but I should brief the Academy Master."

I stood as well. "I should go check on the captain."

"Not alone." Ariana popped up and the rest of my friends followed suit. "We'll go with you."

My throat constricted but I shook my head. "I'll be fine, especially if he's sedated." They grumbled but I insisted. "I promise."

I headed for the door before Torq had finished kissing Jess goodbye, and I broke into a run as soon as I was in the corridor. But I had no intention of going to see Devon.

I needed to find Vyk.

CHAPTER
FIFTY-FIVE

Vyk

My fingers shook as I gripped the tiny hold and swung my foot high to reach the next protrusion from the climbing wall. Sweat trickled down my bare back and chest as I heaved myself up higher and dragged in a breath. I balanced on one foot as I scanned above me for the next combination.

Since the holds on the walls were changed frequently, there was little chance of memorizing the best routes, as it was different with almost every climb. But that's what I wanted. I wanted to have to focus so hard on the climb that my brain could dwell on nothing else. The last thing I needed was my mind whirling with thoughts of the night before.

Pausing for a breath allowed the treacherous doubts to wiggle their way into my mind, and I grunted in frustration as the insidious intrusions became an intolerable barrage.

What did Fiona think of me? Did she regret saying yes? Did she still despise me? Did she want more, or did she wish to never lay eyes on me again?

I shook my head hard enough for my ears to ring then I thrust one arm high to reach for a hold that seemed beyond my grasp. My fingertips closed over it, and the flush of victory pulsed through me as I tensed every screaming muscle in my arm to pull myself up the rest of the way. My legs dangled for a moment before I straddled one wide to rest on a flat-topped hold. I swiped the back of my hand across my sweaty brow and huffed out a satisfied breath. There was nothing like pushing oneself to the brink of exhaustion to purge rational thoughts from your mind—or traitorous ones.

"Vyk!"

I scowled at myself. Now I was not only hearing my own voice berating me, but I was also hearing hers.

"Vyk! Come down here!"

Okay, that was not in my head. I peered down between my legs and spotted Fiona standing at the bottom of the wall. *Grekking* hell, what was she doing here?

The woman's hair was still tousled, and she had her hands braced on her hips. I could not see her expression clearly, but I sensed that she was not pleased. So much for climbing to escape my problems. Apparently, they had chased me down.

I eyed the distance to the mats before pushing off the wall and spinning around as I dropped. Fiona shrieked and jumped back before I landed in a crouch beside her.

I stood and gave my arms a shake then eyed the woman I'd seen in much less than the dark uniform she now wore. "I am down."

She opened her mouth as if to argue with that then released a heavy breath. "I had to tell you before anyone asked."

"Tell me what?" Was this about last night? I had thought we were in agreement about wanting to keep what had happened between us, but maybe we had both been naïve about how fast rumors spread in the academy.

"Dev—the captain is in the surgery. He doesn't remember who hit him yesterday, so the story is that I did it."

I balked at this. "No. I hit him. If there is blame to take, I will take it."

She rolled her eyes. "Why am I not surprised that you're being a stubborn hardass about this?"

"I am not being a hardass or stubborn, but I will not let you take the blame for something I did. I do not regret hitting him. He was hurting you. He deserved it."

"Agreed, but I can say I hit him, and everyone will be cool with that. If you hit him, it's another black mark on your record. You can't take many more strikes."

I was not sure what a black mark meant or what a strike was exactly, but I got the idea. Fiona was not wrong. Admitting to hitting the captain would certainly raise eyebrows and probably provoke an investigation, especially since he was supposed to be an honored guest, and the admiral had asked me to help ensure that he gave the human exchange program positive feedback. I had already taken the captain through the gauntlet, which resulted in an injury, and the admiral suspected ulterior motives on my part. This would only prove him right and make it easy for the envoy from Earth to claim that the Drexian Academy was inherently dangerous and the Drexians who ran it naturally violent.

Even so, I would not have a female take the blame for my actions. I would not have Fiona admit to something that I did.

I slapped my hands together and the last remnants of chalk sifted to the floor like snow. "Drexians do not hide from consequences. If there is blame to be laid, I want it."

Fiona threw up her arms and made an incomprehensible noise of frustration. "Why? What's the point? Just to prove that you're tough? Just so he knows you can kick his ass? Just so I know how strong you are? News flash, big guy, I already know. You pinned me last night. Or have you forgotten already?"

Heat roiled in my core as images of her wrists pressed to the small of her back flashed through my mind. The small of her back, her round ass tipped up, her legs spread as I split her. I bit back a moan as my cock thickened. "I could not forget that."

"Good." She hitched in a breath as she held my gaze, her own eyes flashing hot. "Since you left so quickly this morning, I thought maybe you wanted to pretend last night never happened. Maybe you want us to go back to the way things were before?"

I took long strides toward her, and she backed up until she'd hit the climbing wall. Fiona had to drop her head back to continue holding my gaze as I pressed my body to hers and pressed her to the wall. "There is no going back, Fiona. Not now. Not ever. You are mine. I thought we had established that last night when I fucked you until you screamed my name."

She drew in a quick breath as she bit her bottom lip. "I didn't scream your name."

I reached down and hoisted her legs up so that they straddled my waist. "No? I remember hearing my name on your lips."

Her breath caught in her throat as I rocked the hard bar of my cock against her. "I didn't scream it."

"Then what are we waiting for?" I growled, as I crushed my mouth to hers.

CHAPTER
FIFTY-SIX

Fiona

I reached overhead and grabbed two of the holds to take some of the weight off him. He flicked his gaze up, his comprehension instant as he took the opportunity to slide my pants over my hips and slip them all the way down my legs, tugging off my boots along with them.

When my pants puddled on the floor and I wore only the thinnest snippet of black lace panties, he released a shuddering sigh. "I am a Drexian warrior. I am an Inferno Force commander. I have survived battles, lived in space, and endured extreme conditions. Why can I not resist you?"

"Why do you want to resist me?"

A snarl writhed from his lips. "Desire makes you weak, vulnerable, easy prey."

I hitched my legs around his waist. "Then am I your prey, or are you mine?"

He cupped my chin in one hand and dragged his thumb across my lower lip. "You are mine. You are always mine."

I gave him a teasing grin as I put my hands on his shoulders, my fingers slipping on his slick flesh. "Then prove it, Commander."

With a tortured growl, he crushed his mouth to mine as his hands cupped my ass. I hooked my ankles behind his waist and rocked into him, moaning into his mouth when the hand on my ass slid so that his finger darted beneath the fabric of my panties.

I rocked my hips into his hand, craving the feel of him inside me. But he did not slip his finger inside me. He moved it back and forth until the tip found my clit and he circled the swollen nub with the same deft strokes that his tongue was using to caress mine. The heat that had been roiling in my core was now sending flames skittering across my skin as I arched into him.

Tearing his lips from mine, Vyk seared me with a molten gaze before sliding his finger from me and dropping down so that my legs hooked over his shoulders. I almost cried out from the loss of his touch, but he quickly palmed my ass, holding me high as he spread my legs and buried his face between them.

My hands still held onto the climbing holds above me, but it was only for balance since Vyk was holding almost all of my weight as I let my legs fall open. I sucked in a breath as he used his tongue to nudge my panties aside and parted me, and my fingers trembled on the holds when he found my clit again and began to flick his tongue over it.

I tipped my head back and closed my eyes as I let the pleasure wash over me. Why did I feel so free with the Drexian, when he was the one who had challenged me the most? How could I go from wanting to kick him in the nuts to spreading my legs for him without a second thought? And how did the strict, disciplined security chief make me forget every rule as he willfully broke them himself?

I opened my eyes and cut my gaze to the door. There was nothing to stop anyone from walking in and seeing the Drexian with his face between my legs or hearing the deep-throated moans he made as he worked his tongue over me. The academy might not be teeming with cadets, but it was far from deserted, and Vyk was doing nothing to stifle his own sounds of pleasure. My heart pounded as I imagined being caught, then my pulse spiked as I thought about being watched.

The idea of another Drexian watching Vyk eat me should have made my face burn with embarrassment, but it didn't. It only made my release chase me with more ferocity, the thought of others hearing us making me release my own breathy gasps.

I rocked my pussy into his mouth as pleasure built within my core, throwing back my head as my body detonated in a cascade of trembling and twitching, until my fingers were barely clinging to the holds on the climbing wall.

Vyk let loose a possessive growl, and the vibrations tickled my sensitive flesh and sent wave after wave of tremors through me as I tried to steady my ragged breath.

I dropped my hands to his shoulders, my nails gripping his skin as he kissed the inside of my thighs. "More, Vyk. I need more of you."

He took my legs, lifting them off his shoulders, sliding them back to his waist, and standing so that he loomed over me again. He yanked the front of his pants down, notching the broad crown of his cock at my entrance. "What do you need?"

I was panting now, desperate for him to fill me and hungry for the feel of him inside me. I bit back an irritated groan. "You know what I need."

He met my gaze, and his eyes were pools of black so hot and fiery that I forgot to breathe for a moment. "Tell me."

I braced my feet above his ass to take matters into my own hands, but Vyk gripped one hip to keep me from sinking down, shaking his head as if I'd been a naughty girl. I huffed out a breath that morphed into a needy groan when he slid his cock so it brushed over my clit. "I need you inside me." I raked a hand through his hair, baring my nails so I scraped his flesh and hoped to draw blood. "I need you to fuck me hard and make me forget why this is a bad idea."

He flinched as my nails dug into his scalp but gave me a wicked grin. "I am going to fill you so full and fuck you so hard that you realize that my cock is the only one you need." He used his grasp on my hip to drive me down as he thrust up, burying his length with a single, powerful stroke. "You should know that my bed is the only one you belong in, and I am the only one who gets to fuck you."

I stifled a scream as my body stretched to take him, but the sensations of pleasure followed quickly on the heels of pain, and I released a hungry sigh. "So *grekking* arrogant."

He husked out a dominant laugh as he moved me up and down. "It is not arrogant to know that you were made to fuck me." He glanced down and bit his bottom lip. "You stretch so perfectly around my cock and take every bit of me so well."

"That doesn't mean this isn't a bad idea," I managed to say.

He grabbed my hips with both hands and pounded me onto his cock. "Tell me again that this is a bad idea."

I lost the ability to think as his thumb reached around and feathered across my exposed clit, and I rolled my head back. "Vyk."

"That's right. Scream my name."

I bit my lip, but gasped when he slid his thumb away. "Vyk, please."

"Please what?" His voice was a low, ominous hum as he drove me down on his cock again and again. Then he slid his thumb across my clit again, sending shockwaves through me as my body imploded around his. My pussy clenched mercilessly around his cock, as I squeezed my eyes closed and flashes of light danced across the darkness of my lids.

I could hear his grunts as he pistoned into me and my screams as he finally held himself deep inside me and roared as he pulsed hot and furiously. I sagged onto him as I realized what I'd heard amidst the tangle of sounds, what I'd screamed as my release had slammed into me.

His name.

CHAPTER
FIFTY-SEVEN

Volten

I thumped my hand against the black hull of the fighter as the sun glinted off the glossy surface. There was no better time to walk through the shipyard than when the day was young, and the light was still breaking over the horizon. Since the cadets were gone and even some of the instructors had taken time off, the expanse of stone that held the academy's ships was deserted except for me.

A clang sounded at the far end of the shipyard, causing me to jerk to attention. At least, I had thought I was alone.

I tracked the sound, weaving around the hulking ships that remained silent and asleep. Who else would venture out this early, and who else would be meddling with my ships?

My pulse quickened as it occurred to me that it might be Ariana. Of anyone, she was the most likely suspect to be poking around the vessels, although she usually came with me to the shipyard and didn't sneak out without telling me. Especially since she'd told me she would be having breakfast with Fiona and then doing some paperwork.

Ariana did not lie. Not to me.

Another sound of metal hitting metal made me walk faster, as I homed in on the ship perched at the farthest corner. I rounded the pointed nose of a fighter and blinked at the vessel with its ramp down.

A transport ship? Who would be poking around a sturdy, but not combat-equipped, transport vessel? It was hardly the type of ship Ariana would fly, unless there was no other option.

I touched my waist, remembering that I didn't carry a blaster or blade around the academy, especially when I was only checking on the fleet. Why would I? Of course, I had learned the hard way that attacks could come at any time, even if I had been lulled into a sense of security at the academy. It had not been long ago that the school and my home world had been surprised by a Kronock attack.

"That was because we had a traitor in our midst," I said aloud. "That was before we improved our security protocols."

I stiffened as I approached the ramp of the ship, holding my breath as I walked quietly up the incline. I was being paranoid, I told myself. There was no way this was anything but another Flight instructor or even one of the few remaining cadets.

I headed for the cockpit, pausing in the doorway and expelling a breath when I saw the Drexian sitting in the pilot's seat. Then I realized that I didn't know the Drexian. "Who are you?"

He twisted his head at my question. "Prax."

I stared at him. That told me nothing.

"I brought the envoy from Earth," he continued, as if reading my mind.

My shoulders relaxed. "You have been here all this time? My apologies. I should have greeted you sooner. We are always glad to welcome a pilot to the Academy."

He shook his head and turned back to the console. "I did not stay after dropping off the envoy. I only returned in the night."

This startled me. Why would the pilot leave and return for such a short visit? The fuel needed for that many jumps would usually preclude such quick trips. "Was your return always planned to be so close to your arrival?"

He grunted, the sound showing his general displeasure. "It was not, but I do not make the decisions. I only fly where I am told to fly."

I understood that, but that did not answer my larger question. "Why were you sent back early?"

"That is not a question for me." He flicked his gaze to me and to the insignia on my uniform. "If you want to know why the human is cutting his trip short, you should ask him, Lieutenant."

Cutting his trip short? We had barely welcomed the man with a banquet, and now he was departing? I knew of the incident on the gauntlet, but I was aware of no other reason the human would have for leaving so quickly on the heels of his arrival. I did have a sinking feeling that it did not bode well for the human exchange program.

"You said you arrived in the night. When were you summoned?"

"Yesterday." He frowned as he scanned the readouts scrolling across the shiny screen of his console. "The human is lucky that I had not traveled all the way back to the nearest space station. I had stopped at an outpost to refuel and rest. Otherwise, he would have had to wait until the original departure date."

"He is lucky," I mumbled as my mind swirled with questions. Perhaps the most crucial one was, who else knew that the human was planning to leave so soon? Had the admiral been briefed? Someone must have known, otherwise how had the captain sent a message to the pilot? "I assume you were contacted by the Academy Master or the officer at Earth Planetary Forces who arranged the envoy's visit?"

He spun around again, his brow furrowing. "Actually, no. The human captain contacted me directly. He asked for a way to reach me before we arrived on Drex. He said that he hoped to achieve results quickly so he could return to Earth."

Achieve results? Hadn't he been at the academy to observe and assess? What kind of results did he mean? Unease tickled the back of my neck and even the nodes running along my spine prickled.

The Drexian pilot might be legit, and the human envoy might also have been on a genuine mission from Earth, but something felt off. As a pilot, I operated on plenty of gut instinct, and my gut was screaming at me that something was wrong.

"Do me one favor, Prax," I said as I took a step back.

He met my gaze and inclined his head. "Ask it."

"Do not depart until you have received authorization from me directly. No matter what anyone else might tell you. I am the senior Flight officer at the academy right now, and this ship-yard is under my command."

He gave me a curt nod. "Understood."

I spun on my heel and strode off the ship toward the looming black towers. It was time to get answers.

CHAPTER

FIFTY-EIGHT

Vyk

I held my shirt in one hand as I stepped into the corridor and glanced back at the climbing wall that was now empty. Fiona had slipped out first, and I had given her ample time to leave the School of Battle before I'd followed. It had not been long enough for my heart to stop pounding or the sweat to cool on my skin. Every time I started to steady my breath, I thought of Fiona and my heartbeat went into over-drive. At this rate, I would never cool down.

Not that I wished to rid myself of the heat that being with the woman provoked in me. I had never felt as alive as when I was with her. Not when I'd been in Inferno Force battles. Not when I'd interrogated enemy combatants. Not when I'd risked my life by going into Kronock space. Nothing made me feel as elec-trified as being with Fiona.

"You don't have the captain in there with you?"

I jerked at the voice from behind, pivoting to see Kann grinning as he approached. "The captain?"

"The human?" Kann raised a brow. "You didn't challenge him to the wall like you challenged him to the gauntlet, did you?"

I barked out a laugh with such unnatural force that he jumped and glanced uneasily at the door to the climbing wall.

"You didn't, did you?" Now his voice wasn't teasing.

"I did not." I evened my voice, sweeping an arm wide. "But you may check if you wish."

Kann shook his head and laughed. "I trust you."

I grunted and resumed walking down the corridor toward the main hall with Kann by my side. At least the Drexian did not suspect that I had anyone else with me on the wall. But who would ever guess that Fiona had been pressed against it only minutes earlier?

"I did not know you were a fan of the wall," Kann said to break the silence of our walk.

"There is nothing like the wall for focus." This was true, and it had been the reason I had been climbing. "It helps center my thoughts."

"I am still surprised that you were not a Blade."

"Irons and Blades are not always as different as we seem. Both require discipline and focus." I cut a glance to the Drexian. "I would have been proud to be a Blade."

He puffed out his chest as we walked under the stone arch with the curved blades carved into it, but the sight of his friend

Volten stopped him from saying more about our schools. "Volt!"

The flight instructor was taking long strides with his head down as he crossed the main hall, but he stopped when he heard Kann call out.

"You look like you are on a mission." Kann eyed his friend. "What has happened?"

"Nothing has happened." Volten scowled. "At least, not yet. It might be nothing, but it might also be something..."

Kann grabbed his friend by the sides of the arms. "You are not making sense."

Volten slid his gaze from Kann to me. "Did you know that the human envoy is leaving?"

My breath caught in my chest. "I did not." I thought of putting him in the surgery and a chill went through me. Was he leaving because of me? If so, there was no one to blame for the fallout but me, no matter what Fiona might think. I had acted rashly, and now the human exchange program would have to pay for my violence. "Do you know why?"

Volten shook his head. "The only reason I know anything is because I found the pilot prepping the transport in my ship-yard. He was summoned to return early, and it was done directly by Gorman."

"I thought he was here to make an assessment of how the humans are faring at the Academy." Kann sounded confused. "Has he already done that? It has only been a couple of days."

"He planned to stay longer, but he told his pilot that he hoped to achieve his results sooner." Volten scraped a hand through his hair. "My instincts tell me that true purpose of his visit here might not have been what he claimed."

I suspected the flight instructor was right. Gorman had come here for Fiona. That had been obvious when he'd grabbed her and refused to release her, but I could not say that without also revealing that I had knocked the man unconscious for the crime of touching Fiona. I had promised Fiona I would not tell, although keeping that secret might not be possible for much longer. Not if everything so many had done for the success of the human-Drexian exchange was at risk.

"Where is he now?" Kann asked.

I slipped on my shirt, not caring that I was still damp with sweat. "He is with the surgeon."

Volten and Kann both swung their heads to me, obviously startled by my answer and that I had knowledge they did not.

"At the moment, it does not matter why he is there," I said, although the moment when it did matter was barreling toward us.

Volten blew out a breath. "Okay, but we need to talk to him. We need to know why he decided to leave early and what this means for the future of humans at the academy."

I started forward, practically jogging up the broad stairs that curled up to the second level. The two instructors kept pace with me, and we strode in silence up the stairs, past the cadet dining hall, and down a side corridor to the surgery.

My pulse jangled at the thought of confronting the captain again, although he did not remember that it had been me to knock him out. I did not like the idea of hiding the truth. I wanted him to know it was me. I wanted him to know that he had deserved it. I wanted him to know that he had lost.

The door was open, and I was the first through it, sweeping my gaze across the spartan interior of the school's medical bay. Instead of spotting the human stretched out on one of the beds, the long room was empty. Only a tall, bearded Drexian stood at the far end peering at a tablet.

"The human," I barked. "Where is he?"

The surgeon lifted his head, studied me for a beat, then looked back down. "Gone."

Volten sucked in a breath. "Gone?"

"Discharged," the surgeon corrected himself without glancing up. "He came out of the sedation and was very eager to get back to work."

Work. I almost laughed out loud. I had a very strong suspicion that work was not foremost on the human's mind. But I was almost certain about what did consume him, and I needed to find her—fast.

CHAPTER
FIFTY-NINE

Fiona

My hair was still damp from the shower, but I hadn't bothered to dry it completely. I was already getting a late start to the day, not that I wanted to dwell on exactly why it was approaching midday, and I was only now heading to my office.

My pulse fluttered as I hurried through the dimly lit halls, and for once, I missed the cacophony of cadets that usually filled the school. It was easy to get lost in the crowd of burly Drexians, with their booming voices and thunderous stomping of boots. It was easy to pass unnoticed through the sea of dark uniforms, even if my blonde hair made me an anomaly among the dark-haired Drexians. It was still easy to be anonymous when the ancient school was brimming with activity.

Now that the cadets were on break, not so much.

That was why I power-walked from the female tower, taking steps two at a time even though my legs weren't nearly long enough. I needed to get back to work and regain some of the focus I'd lost since Devon had arrived.

Not that the captain was completely to blame. He hadn't been the one fucking me against the climbing wall. My cheeks warmed at the memory and flamed more furiously as I realized just how lucky we'd been not to get caught. My heart tripped at the very real truth that the possibility of getting caught had been part of what had made it so hot.

"You're acting like a Wing," I scolded myself as I strode under the School of Strategy's archway. "An Assassin should know better than to take a risk like that."

But that had been the thrill of it. It was something I knew I shouldn't do, something I would never normally do, something that was a huge gamble. And I hated to gamble when the odds were against me.

I flashed back to the card game with Vyk. "Clearly, the commander makes me break all my usual rules."

Despite having spent most of the night with him and now succumbing to him again this morning, I had no idea where things stood with Vyk—or where I wanted them to stand. I knew that he drove me crazy, but he also drove me *crazy*. He was the last guy I should want—a set-in-his-ways Drexian who had made no secret of his feelings about both women and humans—but he was the only one I couldn't seem to resist. Every fiber of my being knew that he was the opposite of everything I stood for, everything I'd worked so hard to achieve, everything I claimed to believe in, yet his deep voice sent shivers down my spine, his touch electrified my skin, and his presence made it impossible for me to breathe normally.

I'd gone into our deal thinking that I could take charge and set the rules, but that had quickly fallen apart. Vyk was not the type to be managed, and all my strategic plans had flown out the window as soon as he'd touched me.

I cursed under my breath as it struck me that he'd countered all my arguments with kisses that had snatched my breath from me. I'd tracked him down to insist that I take the blame for striking Devon, but he hadn't agreed to anything I'd said. He distracted me in the most thorough way, and only now did I realize that he had made no promises.

"The Drexian is maddening." I fisted my hands by my side.

He'd insisted that I was his while making no promises to me. Was he toying with me or had he changed his mind about humans? I didn't doubt that he wanted me, but was it anything more than a lust-fueled fling? I'd enjoyed my share of those, but for the first time, I didn't like the idea of ending things.

I was typically the one who slipped out in the middle of the night. I was the one who wanted to keep things casual. So why did I want to change the rules now? What kind of spell had the Drexian cast over me? Sure, he was hot and hung, but was that really enough to make me think about spending more than a few sweaty nights together? Was I actually allowing myself to consider what it would be like to *be* with him for longer than a matter of weeks? Did I want more?

The real question was, did I want more than he did?

I blew out a frustrated breath as I stomped through the door to my office, barely breaking stride to let the door glide open. My walk had done nothing to settle my thoughts or purge my brain of the swirling emotions making it impossible to focus on work. But I would have to concentrate, if I wanted to make any progress on the search for Ariana's sister, and my own preparations for the coming year of classes.

I was so caught up in my thoughts that I'd almost made it across the room and to my desk before I glanced up. Then I stopped short.

"Devon?" What was the captain doing sitting at my desk? I scanned his face, which showed only faint signs that he'd been knocked out by Vyk.

He stood, his expression inscrutable. Did he think I'd attacked him, or had Vyk already gotten to him and confessed?

"I am leaving." He didn't make a move toward me, so we remained on either side of my desk staring at each other.

His announcement did not surprise me, although my stomach clenched because I knew what it meant. "I think you got the wrong idea about the academy. I promise that it isn't a dangerous place."

He finally moved, stepping around the desk stiffly. "You are the one with the wrong idea about this place. If you stay here, you will not survive to return home."

Well, that was dramatic, even for someone who clearly held a grudge against the Drexians because of his unpleasant visit.

"I know things haven't gone like you probably expected they would, but—"

"This is not about me, although I now know that you won't be able to see the truth as long as you stay here surrounded by these..." his face contorted with rage for a moment, "usurpers."

"The Drexians are our allies," I reminded him.

"We do not need them," he said through gritted teeth. "Not anymore."

I had never known that Devon despised the Drexians so much, but it was obvious that he was beyond reason. "You never intended to give a fair report on the exchange, did you?"

He choked back a rough laugh that held no mirth. "None of that matters. Not when this academy won't be standing for much longer."

I went still. "What do you mean?"

He held out a hand. "I mean that I came here to take you back before the attack."

CHAPTER

SIXTY

Ariana

I stopped jogging when I reached the edge of the cliff, braced my hands on my knees, and bent over as I sucked in greedy breaths. The Drexians might have impressive holo-technology that could recreate the most elaborate environments, but I still preferred working out the old-fashioned way. I inhaled the salty air and watched the spray kick up from below as the waves pounded the high rock face.

This was where I came when I wanted to clear my mind. This was where I came if I wanted to run to the point of exhaustion and banish all thoughts of Sasha from my mind, even if it was only for a few minutes. It wasn't that I didn't want to think about my sister but worrying about her so much had started to make me feel crazy.

I knew that the Drexians and my friends were doing everything they could to find her but imagining her being held captive by the Kronock made it impossible for me to focus on anything else. At least Fiona's personal drama had distracted me for a bit, although I didn't like to see my friend in turmoil. And the thought of the captain grabbing her against her will made the blood pound in my ears.

I clenched my fists until the nails bit into my flesh. Maybe I should pay a visit to the captain and tell him what I thought of entitled men who presumed they could do what they wanted without repercussions. Even better? I could tell Volten what the human had done. He and the other Drexians would be more than happy to explain Drexian honor to the guy.

I smiled at this thought, getting more malicious pleasure from that idea than I should have. I was still considering it, when the device in my pocket trilled.

I always brought it with me when I ran outside the academy buildings, but I was surprised that it was going off. I rarely used it within the academy, and it had been a while since I'd received a message or vid call.

I pulled it from my pants pocket and glanced at the screen before answering. "Hey, Nina, it's been a while."

My cousin worked on the Island, one of the Drexian space stations designed to house tribute brides and their warrior husbands. We hadn't spoken much since I'd arrived at the academy—we were both busy with new jobs and new Drexian mates—but she knew all about Sasha and the plan to rescue her.

"No kidding." Nina's voice crackled as her images warbled on the screen. "I've been trying to reach you for days."

"Really?" That was odd. I'd received no transmissions or attempted calls. Then again, maybe that was the weird part.

"Really." She frowned. "I've been worried about you."

"You don't need to worry about me. I'm fine. We're still working on pinpointing the place where Sasha's being held, but I think we're clo—"

"Ariana," she cut me off, "how are the preparations going? Is the academy ready or can I expect you to come here until the danger has passed?"

I stared at her image for a beat. "What danger?"

She ran a hand through her dark hair and huffed out a breath. "Have you all received no transmissions?"

My heart, which had started to return to its normal patter, began to race again. "I don't know. Why? What's going on?"

"You know that we formed an alliance with the Taori, right? Well, they have been tracking the Sythian swarm, which is even more terrifying than the Kronock."

I'd heard some things about the horned warriors who were traversing multiple galaxies to hunt down a deadly swarm, but my understanding was that it was far from Drex.

"Apparently, the swarm splintered and part of it went off in another direction," Nina said, her voice dropping. "Drex and the Academy are now in its possible path."

My stomach clenched as I backed away from the edge of the cliff and started to half run, half stumble toward the academy. "I didn't know. No one here knows."

"I'm telling you, your communications are down."

My mind spun in a thousand directions as I started to run. "What about the envoy from Earth? Did he know about this?"

"You mean the guy who was sent there to warn you about it and assist with preparations and evacuations—?"

I didn't hear the rest of what she said because as I drew closer to the towering black stone walls of the academy, the connection was lost and my cousin's face vanished. It didn't matter. I knew what I needed to know, and I knew who was to blame.

"*Grekking* men," I said as I broke into a sprint.

CHAPTER
SIXTY-ONE

Fiona

All I could do was stare at Devon as his words sifted into my brain. I looked at his outstretched hand, but the idea of taking it was unthinkable. Had he said what I thought he had? I gave my head a quick shake, unwilling to believe that he was serious. He was exaggerating and trying to scare me into going with him. He could not be serious. But a small voice in the back of my brain warned me that he was very serious.

"What did you say?" My voice cracked as I took a step away from him.

"I'm here to get you out before the imminent attack. If you know what's good for you, Fi, you'll come with me."

"And if you know what's good for you, Captain, you'll never call me that again," I spat out, each word sharp.

Whatever veil had been keeping me from seeing Devon as he truly was had been ripped away, and I could finally see him for the weak, cowardly bully that he was. Now my biggest regret was that I hadn't actually been the one to knock him out.

He flinched but clenched his teeth until his jaw trembled. "You'd rather stay here with these jarheads than come back with me? What is it? Do you actually like it here? Do you think this crumbling castle isn't destined for a bulldozer?" Then his eyes flickered with malice. "You really are fucking one of them, aren't you? You lied to me before. Is that it? Did you spread your legs for one of those aliens like you did for me?"

Fury pounded through me, fueling my rage and making my body shake.

"Well, we both know that it won't last, right?" He smirked coldly. "You've only got one good night in you, isn't that right?"

"In your case, one night was too long." I spun around to stomp away, but he caught my arm and whirled me back to face him.

"You think you're going to run away from me again?" His voice was a snarl as he jerked me flush to him. "I don't think so. Not again."

I pushed away from him, but something sharp cut into my side. I glanced down to see the sharp blade of a dagger pointed into my waist.

"Once we get back to Earth, you're going to see that I did this to save you." He jerked me forward, the blade nicking me again.

I sucked in air and tried to tilt my middle farther from the blade, but he tugged me back and the blade went into my flesh again. "*Grekking* hell!"

"Stop talking like them," he ordered, as we lurched unevenly toward the open door.

"What's your plan, Devon?" I asked, steeling myself from the pain in my side. "You're going to drag me through the halls and hope that no one sees you? Then, what? We fly away and hope no one notices?"

He grunted, the exertion of pulling me alongside him obviously taxing him. "They'll be too busy to care about one missing human."

I dragged my feet to make it harder for him to move. "Why? What do you know?"

He let loose a dark laugh. "There's more than one threat out there, you know. The Drexians are so obsessed with their sworn enemy that they have no idea what's coming for them."

I glared at him. "If you want me to come with you, tell me what the..." I stopped myself from saying *grek* "—hell you're talking about."

He stopped and heaved in a breath. Now that I was close to him, I could see that he was pale, and his eyes were bloodshot. He might not appear bruised, but he was not at peak health.

"The Sythian swarm. It split into two swarms, and Drex is now in the path of one of them. Like I said, if you want to survive, you'll leave with me."

Fear iced my skin as I thought about all my friends at the academy, friends who would be in the path of the swarm. Then rage washed over me and replaced the cold terror with hot prickles of heat that crawled across my flesh like ants. "How long have you known?"

Shame flitted over his face, but he frowned and took another step. "It doesn't matter. If the Drexians are so tough, let them figure out how to beat the swarm."

"There aren't just Drexians at the Academy. Are you really going to sacrifice all the humans here because you're jealous of the Drexians?"

He didn't like that, growling as he jabbed the tip of the blade into my side again. "I'm saving you."

"I'm sure you'll get a fucking medal for that," I muttered.

"Once we get back home, you'll see that I was right. You'll forget all this Drexian brainwashing and see that we were good together. You'll see that we belong together."

That would never happen because I would kill him long before we reached Earth. But antagonizing him wasn't helping. It was actually getting me lots of stab marks in my side. I took a breath and released a dramatic sigh. "Maybe you're right. Maybe I do belong back on Earth with you. Maybe we can have more nights together, and I'll forget everything about this place."

He cut his gaze to me, his eyes hopeful but wary. "I am right. You'll see. It will be just as good as it was before. That night we had before you left should have been the first of many. Now it can be."

We'd reached the door, so I paused and forced myself to smile at him. "I'd like that."

Devon leaned in as if to kiss me, but just as I instinctively recoiled, a figure stepped from the shadows and into the doorway. The captain's eyes went wide as he turned and registered Vyk looming over him with a look of pure venom in his eyes.

I took the moment of distraction to step back, cock my arm, and punch the captain as hard as I could in the side of the head. The man dropped to the floor and the blade clattered from his grip.

Vyk's unreadable gaze slid to mine then to the man in a heap at our feet.

I shook out my hand and shrugged. "It was my turn."

CHAPTER
SIXTY-TWO

Vyk

I bent down and retrieved the dagger before the human could regain consciousness, scowling when I realized that it was one of the ancient battle blades that I had hanging on the walls of my office. How had I not noticed that one was missing?

That thought was quickly banished from my brain as I remembered what I had just overheard. The captain had mentioned a night together with Fiona. The night before she had left. That did not bother me, even though her claims that there was nothing between them were not totally accurate. There had been something.

"Was that true?" I rasped.

Fiona was still staring at the man she'd struck, but she gave me a bewildered look. "Was what true?"

"That you want more nights with him?" I could barely force the repugnant words from my mouth.

She made a face. "Seriously? You think I would want to spend another second with a guy who was holding me at knifepoint and put everyone at the academy at risk?" Folded her arms over her chest. "You really think I would spend the night with you, not to mention what happened on the climbing wall, and then be into this guy?"

I grunted. "I do not understand human females very well."

She laughed dryly and shook her head. "No kidding."

"I would not have let you go," I blurted. "I made that mistake once before, and I will not make it again with you. I would have fought for you."

Fiona lips quirked into a brief smile. "So, all that talk about me being yours wasn't just Drexian dirty talk?"

I balked at this. "You think I said something I did not mean?"

"Maybe I don't understand Drexians very well."

I closed the short distance between us, stepping over the captain who had started to move and groan. I gave the man a quick thump on the head with the heel of my boot, and Devon slumped back into silence. "I am happy to help you understand Drexians better."

"And I can tell you everything you need to know about women."

"I only need to know about you," I told her. "I meant every word I said. There is no one but you, Fiona. Not for me. There never has been. Not from the first moment I saw you."

Her jaw dropped. "But you despised me. You despised all human women. You made things miserable for us here."

I curled my arms around her waist and pulled her to me. "I have never despised you. If I despised anyone, it was myself. I believed falling for a female was a weakness. I had cared for a tribute bride once—at least, I believed I did—and I let her rejection break me. I promised myself I would never be so weak again."

"You don't have it in for humans?"

"If I did, would I have made a bet forcing myself to spend time with one?" I cocked my head at her. "Would I have attacked a guest of the academy? Would I have spread your—?"

"There you are!" Ariana practically skidded to a stop as she burst into the room. Her chest heaved, and her side-swept bangs flopped over her eyes. She pushed her hair aside, as she glanced from me to Fiona and then to the collapsed captain on the floor.

I instinctively stepped away from Fiona, although I instantly regretted it.

"I can explain," Fiona started, before Ariana flapped a hand at her.

"No need. I'm glad you took him out after what he's done."

I had thought that Fiona had meant that she could explain why I was embracing her, but maybe that was not news to her closest friend.

"You know?" Fiona asked. "How?"

Ariana put a hand to her waist and grimaced. "Nina told me."

"Nina?" My confusion deepened. What were the women talking about, and what did it have to do with the captain's obsession with Fiona?

Ariana flicked her gaze to me. "My cousin. She works on one of the tribute bride space stations. She's been trying to reach me, but academy communications have been down."

I scowled at this. It had been a couple of days since I'd gotten updated reports from High Command or my Inferno Force contacts, but I had been too preoccupied by the human envoy and my suspicions of him to be too focused on a lag in reporting. Now I scolded myself for this oversight.

"She isn't the only one who's been trying to reach us," Ariana continued. "I'm guessing there will be at least one ship arriving soon to give us the news they couldn't transmit."

Dread tickled the back of my neck. "What news?"

"A faction of the Sythian swarm has broken off and Drex is now within its potential path." Ariana straightened and glared at the man lying at our feet. "And he knew about it. He was supposed to warn us."

Fiona's expression was dark and deadly as she narrowed her gaze at the man she had once called colleague. "Instead, he wanted to see the Drexians and the Academy suffer. He wanted to take me with him, which is probably why he requested the assignment. He would save me, and I was supposed to fall into his arms with gratitude."

Ariana patted her friend on the arm. "We all have toxic exes. Not all of them try to eliminate an entire school, but this is not on you, Fi."

"It is not," I said, regaining my focus and sharpening my gaze on the traitor beneath me. "Why did you not tell me earlier?"

"I haven't known—"

"But you knew all this time we've been talking." I raked a hand through my hair.

"Sorry, I guess I got caught up in," she waved a hand at me then at herself, "us."

I liked thinking that we were an us, but there wasn't time to dwell on how much had changed since the card game. "Now that we know, we need to prepare for the onslaught."

Ariana nodded. "I ran into Britta and Morgan while I was searching for you, Fiona. Britta is working on restoring communications and Morgan went to brief the Academy Master."

I continued to be impressed by the humans, and the female flight instructor was no exception. I wished to continue my conversation with Fiona, but now was not the time. I had something I needed to do first.

I bent down and heaved the limp captain from the floor. "Our guest will no longer be leaving and saving his own skin."

Fiona looked at him with pure venom. "The dungeons?"

I gave a single nod.

"For the first time, I wish there were monsters down there," she said.

I met her gaze and gave her a small smile. "Then for the first time, we are in agreement."

CHAPTER
SIXTY-THREE

Fiona

Ariana kept pace with me as we hurried down the corridor. Part of me didn't know where we were going, but a bigger part of me didn't care.

Vyk had taken Devon to the dungeons, which meant that I no longer had to think about the guy, or my past, or worry that he could be lurking somewhere waiting to corner me. I hadn't realized how on edge I'd been since he'd arrived. My gut had told me from the beginning that I couldn't trust him, even though I'd tried to ignore it. I'd told myself that I was overreacting and that he was a decent guy, the same BS that women always fed ourselves when we knew better.

Devon was not a good guy. I might have made a mistake by sleeping with him once, but there was no way that I was going to let that haunt me. And there was no way I was going to

330

allow myself to feel guilty for misjudging a guy who'd done a damn good job of fooling everyone.

But not Vyk.

I grinned to myself as I remembered that Vyk had instantly disliked Devon. He hadn't trusted him, and he'd told me from the start. Turns out the security chief's battle instincts were right, although I suspected he disliked the captain for many reasons.

"Volt!" Relief filled Ariana's voice as we entered the main hall, and she spotted her fellow flight instructor and boyfriend.

He was escorting another Drexian pilot and wore a stern expression. It softened when he saw Ariana, though. He inclined his head toward the other pilot. "Captain Gorman will not be needing his transport pilot anymore."

"Not since he's currently residing in the dungeons," I told him.

Ariana glanced at me. "He was planning on taking Fi with him when he escaped and left the rest of us to face the Sythians on our own."

The pilot's mouth gaped, and his bronze skin paled a few shades. "I had no idea."

"We do not hold you responsible for the actions of your passenger," Volten said. "You will soon be able to redeem yourself by evacuating some of the academy residents."

The Drexian threw back his shoulders. "I would be honored to assist."

"Who's evacuating?" Ariana asked, peering over her shoulders as more instructors hurried past us.

The news of the imminent attack had clearly spread quickly, and the corridors that had been quiet since the cadets had abandoned them were now buzzing with footsteps and worried conversation.

"I am sure that the admiral will want to send his wife out of the path of danger," Volten said. "Then any females who—"

Ariana held up her hands to stop him. "I hope you aren't about to suggest that all the women jump ship?"

He furrowed his brow and swept his gaze around him. "We are not on a ship—"

"It's an expression," I said, before Ariana could snap back. "I think what your girl is trying to say is that we're not leaving."

Ariana nodded vigorously, and Volten pressed his lips together. Before the two could launch into what I could only imagine was going to be an epic lover's spat, a voice from above interrupted them.

"This female is also not leaving."

We all peered up to see the admiral's wife Noora descending the wide, central staircase with her Vexling attendant by her side. Reina's vertical, blue hair jiggled as she walked, and she wrung her spindly fingers in front of her.

Noora's dark hair was pulled up high in a tight bun, but instead of the flowing, gossamer gowns she usually favored, she was wearing form-fitting, buff-colored pants and a zip-up jacket. She looked more like a fighter pilot than a tribute bride. Reina still sported a vividly colored, starburst-print dress that reached her knees and left plenty of long, thin legs encased in hot pink tights.

"You are not evacuating?" Volten asked, as the pair reached the bottom of the stairs and walked toward us.

Noora smiled at him as if the academy was not in grave danger. "Not if Zoran stays, and you know as well as I do that a Drexian would never abandon his post."

Reina bobbed her head up and down. "We are part of the Drexian Academy, and we are staying."

Volten rubbed a hand across his forehead, and I suspected that he was stifling a groan. "Does the admiral know of your decision?"

Noora twitched one shoulder. "He was not surprised."

"I have heard that human females can be very stubborn," the pilot said, which garnered him pointed looks from all the women.

Volten quickly turned to the pilot. "If there is no need for evacuation, then we can use you in the coming battle."

The Drexian's chest puffed out even farther. "I welcome the chance to defend Drex and the academy."

"Do we have any idea how close this swarm is or its size?" I asked, feeling an overwhelming need to assess the situation. If the swarm hit Drex, it would take out the academy and all the occupants of the Drexian home world. I knew the planet had its own defenses and many warriors, but the potential loss of life made bile tease the back of my throat.

Noora tipped her head up. "You should ask Zoran. He is receiving all the information from High Command that was withheld from him. I am sure he would welcome input from skilled battle strategists." Then she scanned our group. "Is Commander Vyk not with you?"

"He escorted the human traitor to the dungeons," Ariana said with a grin. "Actually, dragged is a better word for it."

Reina's large eyes popped open wider. "Oh, dear. Did the captain have another accident?"

I wiggled my fingers, which were still a bit sore. "He had a well-deserved run-in with my fist."

Noora winked at me. "That must have been a nice break for Vyk's hand."

Volten jerked a thumb toward the exit to the shipyard and pinned Ariana with a look. "We should head to the fighter jets and make sure they're ready."

I gave Ariana a quick hug. "I'm going to meet with Zoran. Stay safe."

"Always." Ariana grinned at me, as she took Volten's outstretched hand.

I felt a pang of longing that Vyk wasn't near. I might not know exactly where I stood with him, but his presence made me feel secure and protected. It was a feeling I'd never known I would even tolerate, much less desire, but I did.

The pilots ran off in one direction, and I looked toward the stairs.

"Shall we?" The deep, rumbling voice from behind me sent a shiver down my back.

I didn't need to turn to know it was Vyk as warmth suffused my body and heated roiled in my core. I reached for his hand,

and it enveloped mine as he gave it a gentle squeeze. "Let's do it."

Noora and Reina gave me knowing smiles as they stepped aside for us to pass. Then the sirens began to wail.

CHAPTER

SIXTY-FOUR

Vyk

I did not release Fiona's hand as we raced up the stairs, but I did slow my pace to adjust for her smaller stride. Even so, we raced down the hallway and burst through the open door of Admiral Zoran's office.

Tivek barely glanced up as he bent over the broad desk next to Zoran. The admiral did not look up, although he addressed me before Fiona and I had crossed the long room.

"Tell me what you know, Commander."

"Not enough," I said. "The human successfully blocked our communications, but it is my fault that I was distracted and did not notice the gap in transmissions. He must have disabled my communication settings when he broke into my office, or he deleted warning messages."

"Or both," Fiona said in a low voice that dripped with rage.

"I should have connected the dots sooner and known that there was a swarm coming. I did read reports of the Kronock reporting colonies being devoured. I should have known."

Fiona squeezed my hand fiercely. "It is easy to think that now, but you had no way to know."

She might be right, but that did not make me feel better. I was the security chief. I should have seen the signs.

"You are not the only one who was too focused on the envoy's visit to note the change in communications." Zoran glanced up, flitted his gaze to my hand holding Fiona's, and then returned his attention to the tablet on his desk. "I suspect that was the captain's plan."

Fiona cleared her throat. "I am also to blame. I might have been the reason he requested the assignment and withheld important information."

Zoran grunted. "There is not one to blame but the human who betrayed our alliance." He curled a fist on the desk. "I assume he has been handled?"

"He is unconscious in our dungeons," I said, even though a part of me wished that he had regained consciousness when I had imprisoned him. I would have enjoyed an Inferno Force-style interrogation.

Zoran waved a hand in the air. "As you can hear, our long-range, proximity sirens have been triggered, but we have not pinpointed the location of the enemy."

"Does this swarm have stealth technology?" I asked, my heart stuttering at the thought.

"No, but from what I understand, the swarm is not a typical fleet of ships either. That could be making it hard for our sensors."

Tivek cleared his throat. "Incoming transmission from High Command, Admiral."

Zoran straightened as a life-sized, holographic figure flickered to life beside me.

I pivoted to look at the Drexian with dark, shaggy hair and a sash crossing his dark uniform. I knew High Commander Dorn, but not from his position on High Command. I knew him from his illustrious time as an Inferno Force Commander. I released Fiona's hand so I could thump a fist across my chest just like Zoran and Tivek.

Dorn acknowledged our salutes with one in return, even though as High Commander, he owed us no such honor. But Dorn was not your typical member of the High Command. Yes, he came from a prestigious clan, but he had always preferred life on a gritty Inferno Force battleship on the outskirts of the galaxy, and he had always respected the service and honor of his fellow Drexians.

"I regret that we must see each other this way," he began, "but I am grateful to finally reach you."

The admiral nodded. "We have just become aware of our jammed communications and of a traitor in our midst." He added quickly. "This time a human, not a Drexian."

Dorn frowned and scraped a hand down his scruffy cheeks. "The envoy from Earth?"

Zoran made a sound in the back of his throat that was his version of a yes.

Dorn rocked back. "Then I will not waste your time, Admiral. I have transmitted all the information we have on the Sythian swarm and the recent change in its composition and trajectory. We would have preferred you had this days ago, but the situation is not yet dire."

"Then why are our proximity sirens sounding?" Fiona whispered to me.

"You do not believe an attack is imminent?" Zoran asked even as the sirens echoed in the corridors.

"The last sighting of the swarm was still far from Drex," Dorn said. "There is time to prepare and fortify. We are sending reinforcements."

Zoran tipped his head in a small bow. "Thank you. I had hoped that another rescue would not be required so soon after the last."

"This could not be helped." Dorn squared his shoulders. "Our home planet and the Academy must be defended. I will contact you again shortly once you have had time to review the reports."

Then his transparent image shimmered for an instant and was gone.

Zoran's shoulders relaxed a fraction, but he pinned me with a hard gaze. "I need you to tell me why the proximity alarms are sounding, if the High Commander still believes the swarm is far away."

I gave him a sharp nod, spun on my heel, and then hesitated.

"I should stay here and help with any battle plans," Fiona said with a measure of regret in her voice.

She was right. She would be better used with the admiral, but I did not like the idea of leaving her.

"Take the Assassin," Admiral Zoran said, meeting my gaze with one that told me he understood more than I had suspected. "You may need her strategic skill more than I will."

Fiona released a breath, and I did not wait for the admiral to change his mind. I grabbed her hand and bolted from the room. Having her by my side gave me renewed strength, and I could not help thinking how much had changed since my first day at the academy, how much *I* had changed.

We dashed down the hall, I pressed my hand to the panel for my door and rushed inside with Fiona. Once I was behind my desk, I released her hand, activated my tablet, and started to scan the flood of transmissions that had been suppressed. At the same time, I pulled up at the readouts for the security systems and proximity alerts.

There was no doubt about it. Something had triggered the security net I had set up to detect incursions into Drexian space farther away from the planet. I flicked my hand up to cast a holographic recreation of the star chart into the air. As I squinted at the approximation of the space surrounding Drex, it was evident where the alarm had been triggered.

"But there is nothing there," I muttered as I stared at the empty space.

"That's impossible," Fiona said, as she gazed at the holographic image. "There has to be something out there, unless it retreated. Do swarms retreat?"

I could not answer her because I did not know. I knew precious little about this new enemy of ours. As I huffed out a frustrated breath, an alert sounded from my screen. I read the coordinates then remembered to breathe as I read them again. I was being hailed by someone beyond the planet but not beyond Drexian space.

I exchanged a glance with Fiona before I tapped my finger to accept the hail, bracing myself for whatever enemy might appear, although I could not imagine what a bloodthirsty Sythian who was bent of devouring everything in its path would look like, or how it would communicate

The creature that appeared on my screen had silvery horns curling around his ears, dark hair pulled up into a knot atop his head, bright-blue eyes that seemed to glow, and black markings on his skin that curled up his neck. He was no Sythian.

"I am Runn of the Taori."

CHAPTER
SIXTY-FIVE

Fiona

My heart stilled as the alien on the screen introduced himself. It wasn't like I was ignorant of other beings in the universe. I was on an alien planet, after all, and living among Drexians, who were decidedly not human. But this Taori was nothing like the Drexian warriors who could pass as larger, more muscular humans. No one would mistake the horned creature and his impossibly blue eyes as anything but otherworldly.

He leaned closer and a pendant hanging from his neck swung forward. "To whom am I speaking?"

Vyk shifted beside me. "I am Commander Vyk of the Drexian Empire, security chief for the Drexian Academy."

The alien who had called himself Ruun inclined his head. "I am a science officer for the sky clan of the Taori, which is why I am here."

"Where?" Vyk asked. "You do not appear on our tracking systems, although you did set off our sensors."

The Taori frowned. "We should not have set off your sensors."

"You have stealth capability?"

Ruun moved his head from side to side, as if accepting this reluctantly. "We can fly behind the veil."

The alien's speech was unusually formal for someone who looked like such a terrifying badass, but I was intrigued by him. I'd heard about the Kronock and their lizard-like appearance, but this was my first encounter with an alien with non-humanoid features.

Vyk braced his hands on his desk. "I assume you are here because of the swarm."

"I am. Your people assisted mine on Gerron. Now we are here to render aid to your planet and academy."

"Tell me about the Sythian swarm," Vyk said. "How do we defeat it?"

Ruun let out a strangled laugh. "The Sythian swarm is difficult to defeat because it is unpredictable and adaptable and will never stop."

I shot a look at Vyk. That did not sound good.

"They are not a typical enemy," the Taori continued. "They do not reason or employ strategy. They cannot be negotiated with or threatened. They only consume."

I swallowed hard. The Kronock had attacked Earth, but when our forces had fought back—supported by the Drexians—they had retreated. It sounded like the Sythians would not.

Vyk cursed under his breath. "Then how do we win? How do we survive?"

"You don't." Runn locked his gaze on Vyk. "The only way to survive the Sythian swarm is to avoid it. Even if you decimate their numbers, they will regenerate and continue to feed."

Vyk shook his head roughly. "There must be a way to destroy them. Every enemy has a weakness. No species is indestructible."

Ruun grunted. "They are not immortal or indestructible. They do die, and it is not difficult to kill one or even many, but there are so many of them and they move with such vicious speed that it is easy to be overwhelmed and overrun."

The thought of a swarm of feeding aliens descending on the academy made my stomach churn. The stone corridors had been intimidating at first, but now they were home, and the thought of them being overrun was horrifying.

"What about tricking them?" I asked.

Both aliens turned their attention to me, and Ruun cocked an eyebrow.

"I know that's what you did on Gerron." I gave the Taori a hint of a smile. "I read the reports and studied the strategy. You tricked them with holograms."

Ruun nodded slowly. "True. That was a plan developed by a Drexian and his human mate, if I am not mistaken."

I knew that it had been Nina, Ariana's cousin, who had been a part of the plan, but that bit of information didn't seem relevant to the moment. What was important was that they had successfully drawn the swarm away by a holographic sleight-of-hand. If a swarm's strength was its hive mind and lack of reason, it was also its weakness.

"What about doing something like that here?" I asked. "Could we use holographic technology to hide the planet so the swarm wouldn't stop? If they don't know we're here, they would have no reason to pause their hunt for things to devour."

Ruun sat back and absently stroked the tip of one horn. "Hide an entire planet?"

I spotted a long tail swishing behind him and tried not to stare. The Taori also had long, fur-tipped tails like lions?

Vyk emitted a low rumble. "Drexians do not run from battle."

I put my hands on my hips and pivoted toward him. "This isn't running. It's protecting your home world. Feel free to attack the swarm in space if you must, but we can't leave Drex and the academy like sitting ducks."

Vyk silently mouthed the words "sitting ducks" to himself as I turned back to Ruun.

"Why don't I talk to a few of the engineers here about setting up a holographic screen while you and our security chief coordinate efforts for an attack on the swarm *after* it passes us by?"

Ruun tipped his head to me. "You are not the first human female I have encountered who has been as fierce and clever as any Taori."

I wanted to ask him where he'd encountered human females, if he hadn't been on Gerron when Drexians made first contact with the Taori, but there was no time, not when we had a planet to hide.

Ruun slid his gaze to Vyk. "Is she your mate?"

"She is mine," Vyk growled without a moment's hesitation.

I glanced at him as a flush of pleasure made my heart trip in my chest.

He returned my gaze, his eyes flashing heat. "Yes?"

I bobbed my head without speaking as he curled an arm around my waist.

"I thought as much." Ruun chuckled. "You have the same bewitched look I have seen on several of my Taori brothers with human mates."

If that bothered Vyk, he didn't show it.

"After we evade and destroy the swarm, I look forward to introducing you to many of the bewitching humans here."

Ruun grinned. "I will hold you to that."

I didn't have time to wonder what the women at the academy would think of the Taori as I stepped from Vyk's grasp and backed toward the door. "Good luck coordinating the battle. I need to find some Irons."

CHAPTER

SIXTY-SIX

Jess

I bent over the parchment and inhaled the comforting scent of dust and crumbling leather. There was nothing as soothing as the smell of the Stacks, which was why I liked to come here even when classes weren't in session. That, and the fact that it was quiet and calm, things that were both in short supply when the academy was brimming with cadets.

The sound of the door scraping open made me look up from the ancient text, but it was the muffled wail of a siren that made me straighten. Why were the academy sirens going off? And how long had I been tucked away within the book-lined walls of the Stacks without hearing them?

Heavy footsteps smacked the floor and told me that it wasn't one of my female friends looking for me. I would recognize Torq's confident stride anywhere.

"Over here," I called, my voice echoing in the quiet.

His pace quickened, and he soon popped around a high book-shelf, his stern expression realizing when he spotted me. "I thought you might be here."

"What's going on?" I glanced at my papers, wondering if I should gather them or leave them behind.

"Not sure, but it can't be good." He held out a hand. "Come on."

I sighed and gave a final, longing look at the unrolled parch-ments before abandoning my table and taking his hand. Torq's grip was warm and solid as he led me through the labyrinth of shelves and tables until we'd reached the door, which he swiftly pulled open.

Outside the Stacks, the siren wail was louder, and I could feel tension crackling the air. Something was happening, although I couldn't imagine what.

"Where are we going?" I asked as we walked toward the center of the school and my pulse quickened along with my footsteps as I tried to keep up with Torq.

"To get answers."

At least there were no sounds of the academy being under attack—no explosions or blaster fire or fighters flying low overhead. "Are we sure this isn't a drill?"

"It's no drill."

I glanced up to track the familiar voice, as Fiona ran down the stairs from the second floor. "What is it?"

"Long story short, there may be part of a Sythian swarm headed for Drex."

"How did we not know about this?" Torq asked, his grip on my hand tightening.

Fiona's jaw quivered with barely suppressed fury. "Captain Gorman kept the intel from us."

"*Grekking* bastard," Torq muttered. "Where is he?"

"In the dungeons and knocked unconscious the last I heard."

From her tone of voice, I had a feeling she had something to do with him being knocked unconscious. I definitely hoped she did.

"Have you seen Britta?" Fiona asked me then swung her gaze to Torq. "Or any Iron?"

I shook my head. "Not since breakfast. Why?"

"Another long story, but I need someone who's good at tech to help me implement a crazy plan that just might save us from the Sythians."

"Britta is your girl," I said. "But I don't know where—"

"I'm whose girl?" Britta asked as she emerged from a nearby stairwell at a jog with Morgan right behind her.

Fiona blew out a breath. "Just the Iron I need. How would you like to show off your holographic design skills?"

Britta grabbed her high ponytail and tugged two ends of it to make it tighter. "Count me in."

Morgan glanced overhead. "Does this have anything to do with the sirens?"

"Long story short," I said, "we might be in danger from an alien swarm, but Fi has a crazy plan to stop them that needs some serious tech chops."

Morgan glanced at Britta. "Hence our brilliant Iron friend."

Britta nodded as if she heard this type of request every day. "I'm in. What do you need?"

"First, I need to know where we can go to work on some seriously intense and large-scale holo-technology." Fiona rocked back on her heels. "Then I need to know how we can recruit more Irons to help us."

"Easy." Britta shrugged and jerked a thumb over her shoulder toward the archway leading to the School of Engineering. "Irons like to tinker. All the best tech is in our school, and I'll bet most of the instructors are, too."

"Then let's go." Fiona started toward the high arch with the crossed hammers etched into the ebony stone.

"You sure you don't want to find out who these guys are first?" Morgan asked in a near whisper, as she stared at the door that led to the shipyard.

We all turned to see a group of massive, bare-chested creatures striding into the academy with swishing tails, silver-striped horns on their heads, and dark marks covering almost every inch of their exposed skin.

"*Grek* me," Britta said under her breath, as the aliens' boots pounded the floor.

Torq tensed beside me, and Kann emerged from the School of Battle to come stand between us and the aliens who slowed to a stop.

Morgan leaned close to me without taking her eyes off the imposing aliens. "This is the best-looking swarm I've ever seen."

Fiona

I PUT a hand on Kann's arm. "These are the Taori, our allies."

He glanced at me quickly then back at the group of warriors, but he did not relax his stance. Maybe a Blade wasn't the right Drexian to turn to when it came to diplomacy. To be fair, the Taori's tails had not stopped swishing behind them.

"She is correct," the alien at the front of the group spoke, his voice deep and rough. "We are the Immortal Army of the Taori, and we have come to battle the swarm with you."

Kann shifted, the stiffness in his shoulders unwinding. Now they were speaking in terms he would embrace—armies, allies, battles. I glanced at Torq, who had also stopped scowling.

"Welcome to the Drexian Academy," I said, even though it was far from my job to be the one to say it. I didn't have time to wait for all the introductions to be made. Not when I needed to get Britta and the Irons to work. "I'd love to stay and chat, but I need to put our plan to evade the swarm into action."

One of the Taori stepped forward. "Ruun told me of your plan. I am Zav, a science officer on our sky ship. I am here to offer my skills."

I waved him forward. "Then welcome aboard, Zav."

His brow wrinkled as he walked toward us. "But we are not on a sky ship."

"It's a figure of speech," Britta said, smiling at the alien with long hair braided on one side and numbers etched into his skin along with curling lines.

I didn't blame her for being entranced by him. I had never seen a science office who also looked like he could have jumped off the back of a Harley before, but Zav did with his scruffy cheeks, low-slung leather pants, and black cord necklace with a blade-shaped pendant dangling between his pecs. It was hard for me not to stare, and I was very much into Vyk.

"Why don't I escort you all to engineering?" Kann flicked a glance at Torq. "My Blade brother will take the Taori delegation to Admiral Zoran."

Torq thrust out his chest as he released Jess's hand and cleared his throat. "Follow me."

Morgan and Jess exchanged a look, but I pinned them with a stern look. "I won't be in engineering for long. There is still a need for us to devise an overall strategy." In case the holographic ruse didn't work, I thought, but did not say.

"I was on my way to Zoran's office," Morgan said. "I got a summons from Tivek."

I didn't have time to ask why the admiral's adjunct was summoning one of my Assassin cadets. There was too much going on to question something so minor, although it struck me for not the first time that the Drexian seemed to have more power than a typical adjunct. "Then I will see you both there."

The women hurried off, getting ahead of Torq and the Taori while I resumed walking toward the School of Engineering with Zav, Britta, and our Blade escort, Kann.

"Ruun said you wish to create a holographic diversion so massive that it hides the planet," the Taori science officer said as we passed beneath the archway and proceeded down the long corridor to the engineering building.

Britta swung her head to me, her eyes flaring. "You want to hide the entire planet?"

I hadn't been in the School of Engineering for more than a cursory tour when I'd first arrived, so I glanced at the stained-glass slats in the walls of the hallway that let in slivers of colored light that mottled that glossy, obsidian floor. Strange warbling noises emanated from deeper within the school, reminding me of a techno dance party that had been set to slow motion and making me wonder what kind of experiments were going on in the high-tech labs.

I focused on Britta, who seemed to be completely unaware or unaffected by the noises. "If the swarm cannot see Drex, they won't stop to devour all life on it. They are not a rational enemy that uses logic or even high-tech sensors to search for targets. They're a swarm of hungry monsters razing whatever they can see."

"If they can't see us..." Britta tapped a finger on her chin as she picked up her pace.

"Holographic technology has been used to trick the Sythian swarm before," I told her.

Zav nodded at me. "When the Taori made first contact with the Drexians on Gerron. A human and Drexian came up with a plan to fool the swarm using holographic trickery."

"It worked," I said. "I thought we could do the same thing again on a bigger scale."

Kann caught up to Britta and cast her a sidelong look. "Is it dangerous to use holo-technology on such a massive scale?"

She gave him a crooked grin. "No more dangerous than anything Blades do on a daily basis."

"But we are Blades," he argued, "and you are..."

His words drifted off as he jerked his gaze away and curled his hands into fists by his side. "We cannot risk our best minds on a project that could be deadly."

I matched his long strides as we reached the end of the corridor. "If we don't succeed in diverting the swarm, we could all be dead."

Britta stopped outside a metallic door, touching Kann on the arm before putting her hand to the side panel and waiting for the door to glide open. "This is just as safe as anything in the academy."

"That's what I am afraid of," Kann muttered darkly, as he watched her walk into the holo-lab.

"Do not worry." Zav gave the Blade a sharp bow. "I will ensure that your female colleague remains safe." Then he stepped into the dimly lit lab.

Kann crossed his arms over his chest and growled.

CHAPTER
SIXTY-SEVEN

Vyk

I shifted from one foot to the other, as I stood behind the admiral's desk and stared at the holographic star chart hovering in the air as it transmitted real-time data. Two Taori flanked me, and Tivek stood beside Zoran.

"We will soon know if the ruse is working," one of the Taori warriors said, his tail snapping back and forth behind us.

The planet, the school, and all the ships had gone silent until we were certain the swarm had passed. It was too dangerous to risk being detected, so all communications had been halted. My stomach twisted as I thought about all the Drexians on my home world counting on us to protect them. I knew that every Drexian would fight to the death to defend the planet, but if the ruse did not work, the swarm would be merciless.

I desperately wanted to leave the office and find Fiona. She had taken it upon herself to coordinate the plan that involved Irons and now Taori, but she had not returned since she had left my office much earlier. I knew from the Taori that she was in the School of Engineering, but that was the last I had heard. We only knew what information was able to be detected by sensors, which meant I had not heard from Fiona since she'd run off to find some Irons.

If I was not the academy's head of security, I would have been tempted to march into the Irons domain and retrieve her. But that sounded much too needy and completely unlike the stern, rigidly disciplined Drexian that everyone believed me to be, that I believed myself to be.

I scowled as I kept my gaze locked on the holographic dot that represented Drex, and smaller ones that stood in for each of the fighters patrolling the planet. If I was not the unyielding Inferno Force Commander who brooked no dissent and certainly did not miss the presence of a female—a human female—then who was I?

Was it possible for a seasoned warrior to change? Could a Drexian who had spent most of his life convincing himself that he needed nothing but honor and battle and duty soften? I had already confessed my true emotions to Fiona, but that was not the same as allowing every Drexian in the academy to know that we were together, especially when the cadets returned.

Would having a human mate undermine my authority? Would I be seen as weak because I cared for a female—a human female?

Then I expelled an angry huff of breath. I was just as dangerous and powerful as I had always been, maybe even more so because I had someone to protect that I would gladly kill for. Not to mention that Fiona was no less of a fierce warrior herself, and being with me had not changed her willfulness one bit. I choked back a dark laugh. It might have made her more stubborn and challenging, if that was possible.

"Commander?"

I jerked my attention to the admiral, and then realized that everyone was staring at me.

"You were making sounds," the Taori nearest me explained, one of his dark brows lifted in unmasked curiosity.

Admiral Zoran's head was angled, and I could have sworn that he was fighting the urge to laugh.

"Apologies, Admiral. I was thinking about...an Inferno Force battle."

"A funny one?"

I suppressed a groan. Had I been laughing? Before I could come up with a reasonable explanation for laughing as we awaited a possible swarm invasion, a cluster of blinking red dots appeared on the star chart.

"The swarm," one of the Taori said, venom practically oozing from the words.

The other Taori flinched. "It does not feel right to observe them. We should attack."

I banished all thoughts of anything but the swarm from my mind. "I understand your frustration, but protecting Drex and the Academy are more important than striking a blow against the Sythian swarm."

The Taori grunted, but they moved restlessly as we watched the flurry of red dots. The blue dots indicating our fighter jets and the Taori ships assembled in a defensive formation but did not approach the swarm, and I held my breath to see if Fiona's plan would work.

Minutes seemed to drag by as no one spoke, no one breathed, no one moved. Then as quickly as the swarm had appeared, they shifted course and moved away.

Admiral Zoran leaned forward and braced his hands on his desk. "The threat has passed."

"For now," one of the Taori said under his breath.

When the swarm vanished from the star chart, the Taori turned to Zoran. "We should return to our hunt. It is still our mission to destroy the swarm."

Zoran thumped a fist across his chest in salute to the two aliens. "I am grateful that you suspended your hunt to save our planet and academy."

"Your holographic technology continues to impress us," one of the Taori said. "Would you consider allowing one of our science officers to stay behind and learn more about it?"

Zoran tipped his head in a sharp nod. "It is the least we can do."

The Taori strode to the door, but they had to jump back as Fiona rushed inside and almost ran straight into them. She skidded to a stop and danced around them before making a beeline for me. When she reached me, she stopped and hesitated, forcing herself to look at the admiral and Tivek. "We did it. The plan to hide the planet using holo-technology worked."

I should have let the admiral respond, but I couldn't. I was too relieved to see Fiona and too grateful that she would be safe from a swarm attack. I closed the distance between us in two long strides, curling an arm around her back and pulling her flush to me.

Fiona looked up at me, her lips parting in surprise before I captured them in a hard kiss. When I pulled away, I spun us both around to face the admiral and his adjunct. "I have decided to take this woman as my mate."

Fiona swung her head to me. "*You've* decided? Don't I get a say in this?"

I held her gaze with mine. "You do not want to be my mate?"

"I didn't say that," she sputtered, "but you can't just announce it like that without asking me first."

"Then I am asking," I husked, jerking her even closer and lifting her slightly off the ground.

Fiona rolled her eyes. "Yes, but only because someone really needs to teach you how to handle women."

"You do not like the way I handle you? Then why do you moan—?"

"Aaagh," Fiona let out a strangled sound as she put her hands on both sides of my face and pulled my face to hers. "You'd better shut up and kiss me before I have another urge to kill you."

I forgot all about the admiral and his adjunct, as I followed Fiona's suggestion and kissed her until she no longer wanted to kill me.

CHAPTER
SIXTY-EIGHT

Fiona

"Are you going to raise?" I eyed Vyk across the long, wooden table in the staff dining room, only breaking eye contact to glance at the significant pile of credits between us.

It had been several days since we'd successfully averted a swarm attack and a card game had seemed the perfect way to blow off some steam. Several bottles of Noovian whiskey later, the rest of our friends had either bowed out or gotten bored of losing to Vyk

He slid his gaze from me to his cards, then to the pile. "If I do, you will be out."

I leaned back, glad that it was only the two of us remaining, just like it had been the first time we'd played against each other. "Just because I'm out of credits doesn't mean I can't bet."

"You still owe me from our last bet."

I gaped at him before realizing that he was right. I technically had only spent two nights in his room. "The climbing wall counts as one."

I was glad no one else was around to hear the throaty rumble of his laugh. "I did enjoy the climbing wall. I'll agree to that. Now, what do you have to wager that I do not already have?"

I blinked rapidly at this. "Just because we share a bed now doesn't mean you have everything."

"I believe it does."

I couldn't help smiling. The gruff Drexian had gotten much better at showing his feelings, almost to the point of it being awkward for everyone around us. He made no secret of his affection and his unquenchable desire. "That's sweet, but you're assuming that you'll win."

He moved his head back and forth. "I believe I will win."

"Still so cocky."

"Confident," he corrected.

I leaned forward. "Okay, well I'm confident that I can beat you, so let's talk wagers."

Vyk braced his forearms on the table, grinning at me like a wolf preparing to pounce. "Last time, I set the wager. This time, I will let you."

I thought for a moment. What did I want from the commander that I didn't already have? "Tell me that you love me." He opened his mouth to speak but I cut him off. "Tell me that you love me more than life itself and that you would do anything for me. Tell me that your life didn't begin until you met me, and that I'm the best thing that has ever happened to you. Admit that you fell in love with a human woman, and that you were wrong about us from the beginning. Tell me that you were wrong about me, and about all the humans at the academy." I held up a finger. "Oh, and tell me that you will spend the rest of your life making up for being such a colossal dick to me when we met."

His eyes were wide, but he nodded. "You have yourself a deal."

Satisfaction flushed my cheeks. As demonstrative as the Drexian was with his affection, he had still never told me he loved me. The warrior was still a Drexian of few words, and they were mostly growls. Not that I minded his growls.

I fanned out my cards, grinning at the high hand that could only be beaten by one or two other hands. "Well?"

Vyk studied my cards, his shoulders sinking as he laid his own hand on the table facedown. Then he raised his head and locked his gaze on me. "I love you, Fiona. I love you more than life itself and I would do anything for you."

I drew in a sharp breath, startled by his statement even though it was what I had wanted. I wasn't only surprised he'd remembered the words, I was stunned by how intently he was saying them. He wasn't just repeating them by rote. He meant them.

"My life did not begin until I met you." He pushed back the bench, and it scraped loudly across the stone floor as he stood. "You are without a doubt the best thing that has ever happened to me."

My heart pounded as he walked around the table and took my hands in his. "I have fallen in love with a human woman. I have fallen in love with you, Fiona."

He pulled me up so that I was standing, and I stepped over the bench so I could face him. My throat was tight as I looked up at him.

"I was wrong about humans, I was wrong about the human women at the academy, and I was especially wrong about you." He cupped my chin on one hand and leaned down so that our faces were so close I could feel his breath. "You are the most incredible, brilliant, talented, gorgeous female I have ever encountered in all my years and all my travels across the galaxy, and I love you more than I believed it was possible to love someone."

My breath was shallow as tears blurred my vision and my heart hammered relentlessly. I had not imagined that I would win or that he would say such sweet words to me—and mean them. But there was so much intensity and feeling in his words they were no longer the ones I'd given him. They were his own.

The walls I'd so carefully built from my own pain and loss crumbled to dust, and I saw in his eyes that his own barriers were gone. Neither of us were holding the other at arm's length so we would not be hurt, disappointed, abandoned. Neither of us were letting fear rule our hearts, but instead of feeling panic that I was so unprotected, I felt relief. Relief and joy.

I couldn't remember feeling such happiness since before my brother died, but even thinking of Jack now didn't bring the usual twist of pain in my heart. It made me smile, which I know he would have loved. He had loved making me smile and laugh, something I'd almost forgotten in my desperate attempt to shield my heart from being broken again. I managed to nod as I fought off tears, even though my throat was so tight it was impossible for me to speak.

"Oh," he added with a smile, "I will spend the rest of my life making up for being such a colossal dick to you when we first met." He brushed a kiss across my lips and then scooped me into his arms. "Starting now."

He started toward the door, but I glanced back at the table.

"What about my winnings?"

He laughed as he walked. "Who said you won?"

I curled my arms around his neck and leaned my head against his shoulder. "Oh, I won."

CHAPTER
SIXTY-NINE

Kann

I ran across the suspended bridge as it swayed over the deep, misty chasm, the rickety wooden slats cracking and wobbling beneath my feet. An arrow zipped past my ear and was so close it ruffled my hair.

"*Grek* me." I forced myself to keep my gaze forward as I raced toward the other side that was blanketed in fog, my heart hammering. There was no point in looking back and confirming what I already knew—the aliens were gaining on me.

This wasn't the first time I had faced off against the pygmy barbarians of the Lanthow, but today, they seemed faster than usual. Or I was slower. I gritted my teeth and lifted my knees higher, refusing to believe that they could catch me, even though the looming fog prevented me from seeing how much farther I needed to push myself before my feet were on solid ground again. Well, as solid as the ground got for Lanthow.

Another arrow skimmed my shoulder just as I squinted through the white haze to make out the edge of the chasm. I was almost there. I pumped my arms and bent low as the bridge shook from my relentless pace. Then I lengthened my stride, giving a final leap through the air to reach land as everything around me dissolved. The bridge fell away, the fog vanished, and I landed on nothing but the hard floor of the holo-chamber.

"What in the *grekking* hell?" I popped to my feet, wincing from the pain of my knees hitting something much harder than soil.

I strode to the exit, pressing the panel for the door to slide open, and stomped into the corridor. Two figures at the control panel jerked to standing. Well, one jerked and one merely glanced over at me.

"Were you in there?" Britta slapped her hands to her cheeks as I glared daggers at her and the Taori, who was cocking his head at me in either confusion to amusement, not that I cared at that point.

"Yes, I was in there," I snapped. "You did not check before you opened the operating panel?"

Britta's face flushed. "I was showing Zav the holo-chamber programming. I guess I got too excited and forgot to check."

I exhaled, calming myself as I watched Britta's pained expression. I knew the cadet well. She did not make mistakes. "It is fine. I am not hurt." Even though my knees stung from the impact, a Blade would never admit to such a minor injury.

LEGEND

ber," Zav said. "I understand that they are extremely lifelike,
although they should not be dangerous. Is that correct?"

"Correct," I admitted.

"As long as the safety protocols are engaged and functional,"
Britta said, with a nervous giggle.

Zav nodded. "I should go. As part of my posting here, I must
check in periodically with the Academy Master's adjunct."

"Tivek?" Britta tugged two sections of her high ponytail to
tighten it. "He's also really good at Drexian cards." When the
Taori raised an eyebrow, she shrugged and laughed again. "Not
that you'd ever need to play cards during a check-in."

"I hope not." The Taori stroked a hand down the length of one
horn as he walked away.

When he was out of ear shot, I pivoted back to Britta. "I've
gotten used to the Taori being a bit enigmatic, but what is up
with you?"

Britta released a tortured sigh. "I don't know. The alien makes
me nervous. I know I'm supposed to be acting as his liaison
while he's here, but every time I'm around him I feel like an
idiot."

I studied the female before grinning. She had a crush on the
Taori. I put an arm around her shoulders. "I can help you, you
know."

She gave me a side-eye glance. "Help me with what?"

"Help you seduce the Taori, of course."

367

Her eyes flared wide. "Seduce the...what? I didn't say...wait, you can?"

"If there is one thing I am exceedingly good at, aside from battle, it is seduction. If you want to entrance the warrior, I can tell you how to do it."

"But he's Taori and you're Drexian."

I grinned at her. "Males are males."

She studied me with suspicion. "Are you sure you know—?"

I cut off her protests by using a single finger under her chin to tip her gaze to meet mine. Then I stared deep into her eyes until I saw the all-too-familiar flash of heat. I leaned over so that my lips brushed her ear, and I felt her shudder. "Of course I am sure. Do you doubt me?" I pulled back to gaze into her eyes again as she nodded silently, but it was my breath that was quick and shallow. It was my voice that cracked when I finally spoke. "Good."

Suddenly, I had the strongest urge to crush my lips to hers and see if her soft lips tasted as sweet as they looked, but I stepped back and cleared my throat. Britta was a cadet, and we had become friends. Friends who did *not* kiss each other.

"So, you'll teach me?"

I blinked at her, tearing my gaze from her curvy mouth. "What? Oh, yes. I will teach you."

She smiled brightly as she started down the corridor, giving me a wave before turning away. "Thanks, Kann."

I waited until she had rounded the corner to lean a hand against the wall so I would not stumble. *Grek* me. What had just happened, and what had I promised?

EPILOGUE

The Drexian reached a hand through the bars and stroked his fingers down the side of Sasha's face, making heat stir in her core and her skin buzz with desire she had no business feeling. "I promise I will get you out, beautiful. I am looking forward to getting lucky."

Sasha jerked her head away from the Drexian's hand. "Don't hold your breath, buddy." She swung an arm wide. "We're in cells. Separate cells. And I hate to be the one to break your heart, but this place is impossible to escape. Believe me, I've tried."

The Inferno Force warrior grinned at her, white teeth flashing through the dark shadows. "Nothing is impossible, sweetheart."

She narrowed her gaze at him. He was hot, but his arrogance was starting to wear on her. "You're really going to have to stop calling me that."

He twitched one shoulder. "I do not mind calling you Sasha. It suits you, beautiful."

She almost laughed at him and the ridiculous situation. This was her rescuer? This cocky Drexian who seemed more interested in getting in her pants than getting her out of the prison was supposed to save her?

Sasha shook her head as she stepped away from the bars. "And what should I call you?"

"Deklyn from House Ashon." He gave her a small bow.

"So, Deklyn, how did you pick the short straw?"

He wrinkled his brow. "Short straw?"

"Being sent into Kronock territory to find a POW probably wasn't your first pick of assignments."

He squared his shoulders. "I volunteered. We all did. There is no greater honor than bringing home a fellow warrior."

Sasha had never considered herself the mushy type, but his words made her throat tighten. She'd convinced herself that she would never be found and would live out the rest of her days as a prisoner of the Kronock, so to have someone show up after all this time was almost overwhelming. She blinked quickly as the back of her eyelids burned. "You said you were one of the scouts sent to find me. That means there are others out there."

His gold eyes glittered at her. "There are, and since they're also Inferno Force, they'll find us. We just have to be ready when they do."

"What do you mean be ready?"

"I mean that we're going to break out of here and save my Inferno Force brothers some work."

Sasha wasn't able to stifle the laugh that burst from her lips, although she wasn't happy by how maniacal it sounded echoing off the stone around them. She wasn't the crazy one, after all. He was.

"You think we're going to break out of a Kronock prison?"

He nodded, unfazed by her laughter and obvious disbelief. "That's the plan."

"Don't you think that if it was possible to break out, I'd have already done it?"

Deklyn scratched the dark scruff covering his cheeks. "Are you trained in criminal techniques like picking locks and disabling alarms systems?"

She stared at him. He looked more like a cage fighter than a safe cracker. "No, are you?"

"Actually, I am. One of my Inferno Force brothers is married to a former cat burglar, I think you call them on Earth. She taught me the basics."

Sasha shook her head. This was getting stranger and stranger. "You're going to break us out using skills taught to you by a cat burglar?"

He stretched his arms over his head, and Sasha could not stop herself from gaping at his rippling stomach muscles. "That was my plan, unless you have a better one." He flashed her another sultry smile and brushed his long hair from his face.

Sasha managed not to roll her eyes, but not by much. Why did this guy have to be one-hundred-percent her type?

"I don't have a better plan," she finally conceded.

"Then we'll go with mine." Deklyn ambled to the bench soldered into the wall and stretched out along the length of it.

Sasha waited for a few seconds before she realized that he'd closed his eyes. "You're napping? What happened to our break-out plan?"

The Drexian opened one eye. "We are still breaking out, but we must wait for the right time."

Sasha spun on one heel and started to pace her cell again. "The right time? You might want to make sure it's before the Kronock take you to be tortured."

His breath hitched. "Have they tortured you?"

Even though he was on her side, the menacing rasp of his voice sent a shiver down her spine. "No, but there were others in here who were tortured." She glanced at the now empty cells. "They're gone."

Deklyn closed his eyes again. "Do not worry about me, beautiful. They will not break me, and they will not put one more scaly finger on you." His voice was a velvety growl. "That I promise you."

Despite Sasha's lingering shock at the Drexian's arrival and his outrageous claims, she believed him. More importantly, she did not trust herself for a second with the guy whose voice had just made her both shudder and sigh.

~

Thank you for reading Legend! For more hot and hunky Drexian warriors, don't miss Obsession, book 4 in the Warriors of the Drexian Academy.

Order Obsession!

This book has been edited and proofed, but typos are like little gremlins that like to sneak in when we're not looking. If you spot a typo, please report it to: tana@tanastone.com
Thank you!!

ALSO BY TANA STONE

Warriors of the Drexian Academy:

LEGACY

LOYALTY

LEGEND

OBSESSION

SECRECY

REVENGE

Inferno Force of the Drexian Warriors:

IGNITE (also available on AUDIO)

SCORCH (also available on AUDIO)

BURN (also available on AUDIO)

BLAZE (also available on AUDIO)

FLAME (also available on AUDIO)

COMBUST (also available on AUDIO)

The Tribute Brides of the Drexian Warriors Series:

TAMED (also available in AUDIO)

SEIZED (also available in AUDIO)

EXPOSED (also available in AUDIO)

RANSOMED (also available in AUDIO)

FORBIDDEN (also available in AUDIO)

BOUND (also available in AUDIO)

JINGLED (A Holiday Novella) (also in AUDIO)

CRAVED (also available in AUDIO)

STOLEN (also available in AUDIO)

SCARRED (also available in AUDIO)

The Barbarians of the Sand Planet Series:

BOUNTY (also available in AUDIO)

CAPTIVE (also available in AUDIO)

TORMENT (also available on AUDIO)

TRIBUTE (also available as AUDIO)

SAVAGE (also available in AUDIO)

CLAIM (also available on AUDIO)

CHERISH: A Holiday Baby Short (also available on AUDIO)

PRIZE (also available on AUDIO)

SECRET

RESCUE (appearing first in PETS IN SPACE #8)

ALIEN & MONSTER ONE-SHOTS:

ROGUE (also available in AUDIO)

VIXIN: STRANDED WITH AN ALIEN

SLIPPERY WHEN YETI

CHRISTMAS WITH AN ALIEN

YOOL

DAD BOD ORC

Raider Warlords of the Vandar Series:

POSSESSED (also available in AUDIO)

PLUNDERED (also available in AUDIO)

PILLAGED (also available in AUDIO)

PURSUED (also available in AUDIO)

PUNISHED (also available on AUDIO)

PROVOKED (also available in AUDIO)

PRODIGAL (also available in AUDIO)

PRISONER

PROTECTOR

PRINCE

THE SKY CLAN OF THE TAORI:

SUBMIT (also available in AUDIO)

STALK (also available on AUDIO)

SEDUCE (also available on AUDIO)

SUBDUE

STORM

All the TANA STONE books available as audiobooks!

INFERNO FORCE OF THE DREXIAN WARRIORS:

IGNITE on AUDIBLE

SCORCH on AUDIBLE

BURN on AUDIBLE

BLAZE on AUDIBLE

FLAME on AUDIBLE

RAIDER WARLORDS OF THE VANDAR:

POSSESSED on AUDIBLE

PLUNDERED on AUDIBLE

PILLAGED on AUDIBLE

PURSUED on AUDIBLE

PUNISHED on AUDIBLE

PROVOKED on AUDIBLE

BARBARIANS OF THE SAND PLANET

BOUNTY on AUDIBLE

CAPTIVE on AUDIBLE

TORMENT on AUDIBLE

TRIBUTE on AUDIBLE

SAVAGE on AUDIBLE

CLAIM on AUDIBLE

CHERISH on AUDIBLE

TRIBUTE BRIDES OF THE DREXIAN WARRIORS

TAMED on AUDIBLE

SEIZED on AUDIBLE

EXPOSED on AUDIBLE

RANSOMED on AUDIBLE

FORBIDDEN on AUDIBLE

BOUND on AUDIBLE

JINGLED on AUDIBLE

CRAVED on AUDIBLE

STOLEN on AUDIBLE

SCARRED on AUDIBLE

SKY CLAN OF THE TAORI

SUBMIT on AUDIBLE

STALK on AUDIBLE

SEDUCE on AUDIBLE

About the Author

Tana Stone is a USA Today bestselling sci-fi romance author who loves sexy aliens and independent heroines. Her favorite superhero is Thor (with Aquaman a close second because, well, Jason Momoa), her favorite dessert is key lime pie (okay, fine, *all* pie), and she loves Star Wars and Star Trek equally. She still laments the loss of *Firefly*.

She has one husband, two teenagers, and two neurotic cats. She sometimes wishes she could teleport to a holographic space station like the one in her tribute brides series (or maybe vacation at the oasis with the sand planet barbarians). :-)

She loves hearing from readers! Email her any questions or comments at tana@tanastone.com.

Want to hang out with Tana in her private Facebook group? Join on all the fun at: https://www.facebook.com/groups/tanastonestributes/

Copyright © 2024 by Broadmoor Books

Cover Design by Natasha Snow

Editing by Tanya Saari

Cover image by WANDER AGUIAR PHOTOGRAPHY LLC

All rights reserved.

No part of this book may be reproduced in any form or by any electronic or mechanical means, including information storage and retrieval systems, without written permission from the author, except for the use of brief quotations in a book review.

This is a work of fiction. Names, characters, places, and incidents are the products of the author's imagination or are used fictitiously and are not to be construed as real. Any resemblance to actual events, locales, organizations, or persons, living or dead, is entirely coincidental.